DOUBLE JEOPARDY

In Havenchester Detective Sergeant Julie Cooper has been working undercover to crack a major drugs ring, resulting in the drugs baron being safely jailed. But when she becomes the victim of a drive-by shooting that leaves her seriously injured and her aunt dead, Julie hires private detective Alec Tanner to help her find the killers. Julie and Tanner's investigation leads to a vicious gangland boss, plotting to avenge himself on his cheating girl-friend. Together, as they endeavour to uncover the truth, Julie and Tanner find time beginning to run out for them to prevent further murders — including their own . . .

MARTIN STRATFORD

DOUBLE JEOPARDY

Complete and Unabridged

ULVERSCROFT
Leicester

First published in Great Britain in 2010 by
Robert Hale Limited
London

First Large Print Edition
published 2011
by arrangement with
Robert Hale Limited
London

British Library CIP Data

Stratford, Martin.
Double jeopardy.
1. Organized crime- -Fiction.
2. Drive-by shootings- -Fiction.
3. Private investigators- -Fiction.
4. Detective and mystery stories.
5. Large type books.
I. Title
823.9'2–dc22

ISBN 978–1–44480–524–6

Published by
F. A. Thorpe (Publishing)
Anstey, Leicestershire
Set by Words & Graphics Ltd.
Anstey, Leicestershire
Printed and bound in Great Britain by
T. J. International Ltd., Padstow, Cornwall

This book is printed on acid-free paper

For my wife Pat
Thank you for all your support,
encouragement, belief and proof-reading.
With all my love.

1

The man who had engineered the two murders stood in the shadows fifteen feet back from the mouth of the alley. He wore an old raincoat with the collar turned up and a hat pulled down low over his eyes. This was partly to hide his face, but also to keep out the icy wind that blew between the buildings. He was holding a pair of night-vision binoculars to his eyes and stood patiently watching and waiting. In one pocket of his coat was a mobile phone, stolen that morning, and in the other a bottle of whisky. In the unlikely event of anyone using the alley at 10.30 on a Wednesday evening, he could swiftly swap the binoculars for the bottle and would slump down against the wall. The chances were that whoever came along would walk by quickly without giving him a second glance.

The alley opened out on to a small square in the entertainment section of the City of Havenchester, situated on the north-west coast of England. The square had a grassed over centre, a sprinkling of seats and five trees. It was crossed by three paths and was popular in the daytime with office and shop workers alike as a pleasant sun trap for eating lunch away from the noise and fumes of the traffic that flowed sluggishly through the city centre. In the centre of the grass was a statue of the Duke of Wellington — after whom the square was named — sitting stoically on his horse and no doubt wondering why God had invented pigeons. A mixture of offices and shops lined the square, with a small independent cinema lurking in one corner. The alley divided two blocks of Edwardian houses that had been converted into offices and were dark and unused at that time of night. Directly across the square from the alley was a restaurant that served good, unpretentious food and drink and had an accordingly discerning regular clientele. It was called Little Italy, a fact proclaimed by a modest illuminated sign over the front window.

From the watcher's position in the alley, it was possible to see in through the wide front window of the restaurant, unadorned apart from a single menu placed at eye level on the right-hand side by the door. With the binoculars, it was almost possible to lip read the two women who sat at the last table to the left of the window. He was not concerned about what they were saying; he only wanted to ensure that it would be the last conversation that they ever had. The elder of the two women beckoned to the waitress and the man tensed for a moment, but they were only ordering coffee and he relaxed again, leaning his shoulder against the damp dark wall.

In the restaurant, Julie Cooper took a sip of her unsweetened black coffee, swept her long black hair back over her shoulder and smiled with great affection at her companion.

'At least we'll be able to do this more often again, now that it's all over.'

'Yes, I've missed our dinners together, and our shopping expeditions.' Joyce Kemp, Julie's aunt and godmother, raised her coffee cup and chinked it against her niece's. 'Here's to more good meals.'

'And to more shopping.'

'Even better.' Joyce was Julie's mother's younger sister and when the elder sister had died shortly after giving birth to Julie, she had been both companion and surrogate mother to the child when Julie's father was away. They were now each other's only remaining close relatives. Joyce had smooth, pale-blonde hair cut in a page boy style, twinkling blue eyes and a heart-shaped face. She was small boned and looked fragile, but had an inner spirit and resilience that made her a capable and formidable businesswoman.

Julie reached one hand across the table and squeezed the other woman's hand.

'It's been so good to talk to you, Aunt Jo. I think that's what I've missed most over the past eighteen months, not having someone I could trust and confide in when I needed to.'

Joyce nodded. Her niece was a detective sergeant in the Metropolitan Police having been fast tracked into the CID from university and promoted after spending over a year undercover, infiltrating one of London's biggest drug distribution networks, and a further six months following a series of arrests working on the court cases. Operation Snowball, which indicated that someone in the Met had a sense of humour, had ended two days before at the Old Bailey with the conviction of Theodore Jarrow, the head of the organization. Joyce had not questioned Julie too closely about that time and could only imagine what an enormous strain on her twenty-five-year-old niece it must have been. Although Julie's name and picture had been kept out of the papers, Joyce had gleaned enough from the story and the things that Julie had said to gain some impression of the stress of living a fictitious existence on a daily basis, knowing that a wrong word or a single

4

slip could mean exposure and probably a painful death. At least that was all behind her now.

Whilst growing up, Julie had often spent time at her aunt's flat, or on holiday with her, and the close bond that had been created had developed their relationship into that of close friends as well as relatives, particularly as Julie grew older. Even as an adult, Julie had still enjoyed visits to her aunt and one of the worst elements of her work undercover had been that she was unable to continue that contact, both in order to maintain her cover and to avoid bringing her aunt into danger. She now had a month's leave and was determined to make up for the past year and a half of stress and uncertainty.

'I need to spend a few days on business next week, apart from that I can have the rest of your leave off with you — if you want me to.'

'That will be great.' Julie smiled at the older woman. 'I just want to relax. Take the boat out, go diving, chill out.'

Both women were expert sailors and scuba divers and Joyce owned a motor boat that she kept moored at a marina a few miles up the coast. The coast immediately north of Havenchester was lined with coves and caves as well as a number of small islands that provided plenty of interest for skilled sailors and divers.

'It sounds wonderful.' Joyce returned her smile. 'It would have been even better later in the year, but we've dived at this time of year before.'

'Yes; I'm afraid I couldn't arrange for the legal system to organize its timetable in a way that was better suited for a holiday.'

'We could go abroad somewhere.'

'No.' Julie shook her head firmly. 'I've been living a lie for eighteen months; I want to spend the next four weeks as myself in a place that's familiar. I suppose I need to touch base with my real life again — if that doesn't sound odd.'

'Of course not, darling. We'll do exactly as you want.' Joyce squeezed her hand. 'But are you sure you want to spend your time with an old broad like me — haven't you got a nice hunk you can turn to for a romantic interlude?'

Julie grinned and squeezed back.

'Old broad be damned — your mental age is lower than mine sometimes. And as for romance, the sort of men I've been mixing with lately aren't the type I'd want a relationship with — most of them only want women for one thing.' For a moment her mind slipped back into the fictitious life she

6

had been living and she shivered suddenly.

'Sometimes I think I'd rather have a normal straightforward job, like yours.'

'Even the antique business has its criminal side, you know. Stolen goods, faked masterpieces, there's plenty of opportunity for the enterprising crook.'

'OK, I accept your life is as eventful as mine.' Julie finished her coffee.

'I wouldn't go so far as to say that. Let's go back to the flat — we have a long day's shopping ahead of us tomorrow.' Joyce signalled to the waiter, not realizing that she was also signalling the start of something else.

In the alley, the man was speaking into the mobile phone.

'They are about to leave — get ready.' He watched the two women put on their coats and walk towards the door. For the first time he felt real tension as the time for action was approaching. He waited for Joyce to open the door. The sound of the bell echoed faintly across the square to the alley.

'Now.'

The motor bike came out of a side road that led into a narrow lane which ran by the side of the cinema. The two women had turned left out of the restaurant and were walking past the darkened shops next door. They walked side by side, continuing to map

7

out their plans for the weeks ahead, heads slightly bowed against the wind, taking no notice of the motor bike coming towards them, gleaming black and gold in the street lights. The bike was not speeding, the two black-clad and black-helmeted figures riding on it not drawing attention to themselves.

As the bike approached closer to Julie and Joyce, the pillion rider unzipped the front of his jacket and pulled out a silenced pistol. Joyce was on the outside of the pavement, nearest to the road and Julie had turned towards her aunt, responding to something she had said. She heard the first shot as an anonymous plop. Joyce staggered and gave a low moan. There were two more shots that sent Joyce reeling backwards across the pavement as Julie looked at her, her own body frozen for a moment in horror and shock. Relief at the end of a long and dangerous operation had left Julie unprepared and had slowed her reflexes. Time seemed suspended for a moment as the bike drew level and the next bullet entered Julie's chest, spinning her round. The next plop merged with a blazing pain in her forehead and everything went black. Julie didn't hear the final shot that hit her again in the chest as she fell back limply and heavily against the grille covering a shop window, the back of her head smacking against the silvery metal. The pillion passenger was twisting round and had fired the last shot behind him. He faced forward again, replaced the gun inside his jacket and the bike moved on steadily, turned down into the road at the next corner of the square and was lost to sight.

In the alley, the man nodded in brief satisfaction to himself, noticing with mild surprise that his mouth felt dry from the tension. He turned and walked without haste back down the dark passageway away from the square. The alley doglegged and then it merged with another quiet street. He dumped the whisky bottle in a litter bin and walked on towards the car-park where he had left his Transit van. There were a few other pedestrians about, but nobody paid the slightest attention to him, just another person protecting their face against the chill wind and drizzling rain.

Back in the square, Julie and Joyce lay motionless on the pavement. Julie was slumped against the shop window, blood oozing through the front of her coat from the two holes in her chest and more blood trickling down her face from the wound in her forehead. Joyce lay on her back, arms outstretched, eyes open and staring sightlessly up into the night sky.

★　★　★

The man from the alley collected his Transit van from the multistorey car-park where it was just another anonymous vehicle amongst all the rest. As he drove down the ramp, he could hear sirens faintly in the distance and coming nearer. He wondered idly whether they were going to Wellington Square. He drove sedately through the city, careful not to attract attention. Traffic was busy enough to maintain the van's anonymity to the many CCTV cameras stationed strategically throughout the city but not enough to cause him any major delays. The city had recently mimicked London and introduced congestion charging, but that didn't apply in the evening so he hadn't left a record in that system. Not that it would have mattered; he had purchased the van legitimately the day before from another part of the country and using false documents that had been kept aside for some time, ready for any emergency should it arise. After twenty minutes, he was in the outskirts of the city, suburban housing mixed with local shops and some open countryside. Shortly afterwards he turned off on to a narrower, unlit road that delved deep into the wooded countryside that lay to the north. He was pleased to note in a strangely detached way that he felt perfectly calm now and was whistling softly to himself.

An hour after the shooting, he had left Havenchester well behind and was driving through the enveloping blackness of unlit country roads. Only an occasional headlight coming towards him from the opposite direction and providing brief moments of additional illumination broke the illusion that he was alone in the night. He was nearly at his destination and glanced briefly at his watch. He'd made good time and only hoped that the buggers were there ahead of him and hadn't got lost. He had everything planned out exactly, but you couldn't always rely on other people.

He turned off the road just ahead of the lights of a small village and, after a few minutes, arrived at the entrance to a disused airfield. His headlights illuminated a pair of broken wire-mesh gates which hung open, only half secured to posts that could have been templates for the tower at Pisa. His headlights carved the way through the dark, the van bumping up and down as he followed the old potholed road, now liberally spotted with grass and weeds and even the occasional bush, towards the main hangar. He drove inside and let out a small sigh of relief as the headlights revealed the motor bike and the two figures standing beside it. They had removed their helmets, which hung on the handle bars on each side of the bike like a pair of monstrous ear-rings. He pulled up and switched off the engine, leaving the headlights on so that they could see what they were doing. He wouldn't be there long enough to flatten the battery.

'Hi.' One of the bikers gave him a brief wave. 'Worked like a charm, didn't it?'

'It did indeed.' He got out of the van, bringing with him a briefcase from underneath the passenger seat. It had been a small, calculated risk to leave the case in the van in the car-park, but he hadn't wanted to carry it around with him whilst supervising the hit. At night a man with a briefcase was more memorable — and more likely to be a target for muggers — than one carrying nothing. He put the case on the bonnet of the van and the locks clicked sharply in the night air. In his peripheral vision he saw the two bikers moving towards him in anticipation. 'And you have earned yourselves a bonus.' His tone was conversational as he lifted the silenced gun that was the only thing in the case, turned swiftly and shot the nearest biker through the head. The second man reacted far too slowly. As his companion was toppling bonelessly to the ground, he tried to open his jacket to get at his gun, but was dead before his hand reached the zip.

The man from the alley walked over to the two bikers. There was no need to check their pulses, both had a neat red-rimmed hole in the middle of their forehead and both stared up at the gloom of the hangar roof with frozen shock in their open eyes. Allowing himself a moment's satisfaction, he returned to the van, put the gun back in the case, closed it and replaced it in the vehicle. Then he walked round to the back and opened the rear doors. There were two rolls of canvas and some rope inside. Each biker was carefully wrapped up and secured inside a shroud of canvas and the two parcels put inside the van. He then lowered a wide plank from the back of the van and rolled the bike up inside, securing it with two more lengths of rope. He satisfied himself that the bike wouldn't sway around, took the helmets off the handlebars and tossed them down beside the bodies of their owners. He then pushed the plank back into the van and closed and locked the doors. The man was sweating slightly, but he knew it was only through exertion, not worry. The whole of phase two had gone remarkably smoothly.

Only phase three remained. There was an old mine two miles away that he had reconnoitred that morning. The entrance to it had been secured with a rusty old padlock that he had already removed on his first visit and replaced with a new one that he had purchased himself from a superstore. Fifty yards in from the mine entrance was a short side passage full of rubble and other junk. An ideal place to dispose of his load and then he was finished for the night. All in all it had been a very satisfactory evening. You couldn't beat careful planning, and he felt particular satisfaction that he had been able to work out the plan and put it into operation in such a short time-scale.

Whistling softly, he got back into the van and drove away.

★   ★   ★

'How is she?'

Detective Chief Superintendent Leo Jason, a tall beefy man with a ruddy complexion and an unruly thatch of now thinning tawny hair that, coupled with his first name had given him the inevitable nickname of The Lion, did not like hospitals. His wife had died the previous year after a long battle with cancer and the smell and taste of the wards seemed to have filled his life for so long that he could hardly stand being in one. Even a private

14

hospital that had many of the attributes of a hotel couldn't dispel the feeling. He was a man who liked to be in control and having to hand that control over to doctors and nurses — no matter how capable he knew them to be — added irritation to the dislike. The fact that he couldn't smoke didn't help, either.

The doctor, a calm, attractive woman in her mid-forties and a very capable clinician, didn't sense the extent of the superintendent's feelings, but she felt the unease that many had when they visited a hospital and she smiled comfortingly as she answered him.

'Physically, she is making a good recovery. Considering that it is less than a month since she was shot and considering the extent of her injuries and the shock to her body, her physical recovery is amazing. Of course, she was in excellent physical condition.' She paused and glanced at Jason, as if to make the point that the same could hardly be said for him. 'Mentally . . . ' She pursed her lips and shook her head. 'To be honest, I am far more worried about her mental state. She blames herself for her aunt's death and that will take her a long time to get over — if she ever can.'

'We'll be offering her counselling, of course. There are some excellent doctors who work regularly with police officers.'

The doctor nodded doubtfully.

'I'm not sure she will be particularly receptive, but we'll have to try.'

'May I see her?'

'Of course.' The doctor glanced at him. 'She has already been fully debriefed — she insisted upon it, even though I felt she was too weak at that time.'

Jason raised a reassuring hand.

'Don't worry; I know about that — I've read the report in detail. I'm not here to undertake anything official. I'm her boss; this is mainly a social visit to see how she is doing. Last time I saw her, she was unconscious with three bullet wounds.' He didn't add that it wasn't just pressure of work that had kept him away since then, although he had made sure of being kept apprised of Julie's progress all the time. He had been all too aware of the outcome the last time he had been to see someone in hospital and he needed to be sure that she would recover before making a visit. He reflected ruefully that perhaps Julie was not the only one who needed counselling.

The doctor smiled again.

'I'm sure she'll be pleased to see you.'

Jason wasn't, but he nodded his thanks and was shown into the neat single room, bright and light with windows overlooking a garden area. Julie Cooper sat up in bed, a bandage

16

across her forehead. Her face was pale and her expression held little of the spark and animation that Jason, who had been in charge of Operation Snowball, knew should be there. She wore a baggy white T-shirt with a Rolling Stones tongue logo on it. A book lay open face down on the bed and she lay back on puffed-up pillows staring across the room at the blank screen of the TV that hung suspended from the ceiling like a geometric bat.

'Hello Julie.' He spoke gently, moving a chair closer to the bed and sitting down.

Julie moved her head and dipped it briefly in acknowledgement.

'Good morning, sir.' Her voice was stronger than he'd expected, but flat and empty of emotion. He thought briefly that he would rather she was hostile, blaming him for involving her in the operation that had had such a devastating aftershock for her, than showing nothing at all.

'Your doctor says you are recovering well.'

'Yes, I could be out of here by the end of next week.' She spoke like an automation, repeating what the doctors had told her. 'I took two bullets in the chest and both missed anything vital by a fraction. The first bullet saved my life: it spun me round so that the head shot went across my forehead rather than into it. They say I was very lucky.' She didn't sound as though she believed them.

'You were,' Jason decided to be brisk and businesslike to try to dent Julie's veneer of self-contempt. 'Although being young and fit helped as well.'

Julie didn't respond. She shifted slightly so that she could talk to Jason without moving her head too much and winced at the sudden sharp reminder of the broken ribs that had deflected one of the bullets.

'It doesn't change the fact that my job effectively killed my aunt.' The fingers of her right hand plucked at the edge of her sheet in a nervous gesture that was totally out of character. Jason felt the growing tentacles of despair — it looked as though the doctor was right and he was probably going to lose one of his best young officers.

'That's rubbish, and you know it. We didn't expect any retaliation once you'd given your evidence. Police officers have been attacked in the past to silence them before they can report or give evidence, but it is very rare for them to be attacked afterwards purely as revenge. There's no percentage in it and most professional crooks won't do anything unless it nets them a profit.' He glared at her, hoping to spark some sort of response.

Julie's mouth twisted into a humourless

smile. She knew exactly what he was trying to do.

'No, it breaks all the rules, doesn't it? It's a shame it isn't really a game and we can't just line up all the characters again afterwards and start afresh.' She paused and for the first time showed a little real interest in the conversation. 'Has Jarrow admitted that he ordered the hit?'

'No.' Jason pulled a face. 'The bastard admits that he isn't sorry it happened, but claims he knew nothing about it.'

Julie nodded. No surprises there then. It certainly didn't mean that Jarrow wasn't behind the killing. Being in prison is not a deterrent to ordering a murder — or any other criminal action — if you have the right contacts and Jarrow was as well connected as anyone in his area of business, with plenty of money to grease any necessary wheels. Not to mention plenty of time to make the arrangements.

'And the shooters?'

'No trace, I'm afraid. They were tracked on CCTV whilst they were in the city centre, but after that they moved off the radar. There's still a dedicated team working on it in Havenchester, and the Yard is providing back up. We've been watching for any known villains who might have been involved trying

19

to leave the country, but nothing's turned up yet. We've followed up a few sightings, but they were false alarms. If they'd any sense, they would have ditched the bike pretty quickly, and anything that's found abandoned that might be the one has been carefully checked out, but no joy so far. There's a lot of woodland and forest in that part of the world to search, not to mention several lakes.' He didn't mention needles and haystacks, but the thought was clearly there.

That didn't surprise her either. She nodded slowly.

'I'll need to continue my leave once I get out of hospital. I have to go back up to Havenchester for a while.'

Jason frowned.

'I hope you're not thinking of taking the law into your own hands?' He tried to sound disproving, although he privately felt that digging around up there might help Julie to get some of the hurt and self-recrimination out of her system. He made a mental note to speak to someone on the Havenchester force and get her a little unofficial support.

'My aunt is dead.' The minute trace of interest seemed to have died again. She took a deep breath. 'She had a flat and a business up there and I'm her next of kin. There's a lot I need to do.'

Jason nodded. If he had noticed that she hadn't answered his question, he didn't show it.

'Of course.' He nodded. 'We'll arrange some protection for you.'

'I wouldn't bother, sir — they won't try again.' Her eyes met his and reflected deep pools of pain. 'Jarrow has already sent me to hell. If he wants revenge he's got it. Why would he want to put me out of my misery?'

2

Julie got out of the taxi that she had taken from the station and the driver opened the boot and removed her two suitcases and travelling bag. She paid the driver and added a generous tip — chivalry should be rewarded. For a moment, she stood on the pavement and looked up at the block of luxury flats overlooking the river where her aunt had lived. Tall and slightly curved, the main impression was one of a vast glass yacht, its sail enveloping the wind. The views were, indeed, spectacular, as she well knew. Julie tried to analyse how she felt, depressed at the thought that her aunt would no longer be there when she arrived, but with an underlying comfort at returning to a place of which she had so many good memories, both of childhood and adulthood. It was two o'clock in the afternoon, the sun shone fitfully from a grey, cloudy sky and an occasional spot of rain floated in on the chilly wind. Julie shivered slightly, turned up the collar of her coat, lifted her cases and walked across to the entrance to the flats. Automatic doors slid open smoothly, the warmth of the foyer a welcoming haven from the wind.

A uniformed commissionaire sat at a desk to the right of a row of lifts. The entrance way was clean and bright, a fitting tribute to the level of service charges paid by the residents. The commissionaire lowered the newspaper he had been reading, smiled and nodded to her.

'Good afternoon, miss, it's good to see you back.'

'Thank you, Norman.' The commissionaire was an ex-soldier who had stood — and sat — guard over the desk since Aunt Joyce had moved in to the luxury apartments ten years before. Normally, Julie would have stopped and chatted for a while unless she was in a hurry, but today she just wanted to get upstairs to the sanctuary of the flat. 'Mr Kingsley is due at three o'clock. Send him up as soon as he comes, please.'

'Certainly, miss.'

The lift arrived and took Julie and her luggage swiftly up to the ninth floor — two floors below the penthouse, but if not in the lap of luxury, at least well over its knees. Julie reached her aunt's door — hers now — took the key from her shoulder bag and let herself in. She knew that Simon Kingsley had arranged for the flat to be cleaned and the beds changed ready for her. The smell of fresh furniture polish hung in the air as testimony to the presence of the cleaner.

Julie walked through the square hall into the large open lounge with its wide picture window, balcony and spectacular views across the river. She went across to the windows and stood for a moment looking out across the north of the city. The sun chose that moment to find a small slit in the clouds and the river gleamed as she watched it, rippling gently, like a thick, silvery brown snake. A barge drifted past and rounded the bend in the river towards Nelson Bridge.

Julie stepped back from the window and took her cases through into her bedroom. It was the one that she usually used, the middle sized of the three bedrooms. She was not yet ready to use her aunt's room as her own. She lifted the cases on to the bed ready to unpack, took off her coat and hung it up in the long fitted wardrobe with the mirrored sliding doors that made the room seem larger and brighter. The furniture was modern and functional, matching Julie's own taste.

Julie decided not to unpack immediately and instead started walking slowly through the flat, looking about her as she entered each room, pausing in anticipation. She did not quite know why at first and then she realized that she was waiting for her aunt to appear with her warm smile of welcome and her soft friendly voice. Squeezing her eyes shut against the tears that suddenly welled up, Julie went through to the kitchen and started to get coffee ready for Simon Kingsley's arrival. Although the pain of her loss had not lessened, she found over time that she could hold it enclosed for a while until she let down her guard and a memory flashed into her mind to tear through the fabric of the flimsy protection she had built up and cause the pain and tears to flood out again as strongly as ever.

She found that busying herself with simple mundane tasks helped and she spent far longer than was necessary preparing cups and saucers and sorting through the larder — which Kingsley had also arranged to be stocked — for biscuits.

Kingsley was prompt, ringing the bell at three o'clock exactly. Julie took his coat and led him through into the lounge. The solicitor placed his scuffed brown briefcase down beside a deep red leather armchair and lowered himself into it. Julie fetched the drinks and biscuits on a tray from the kitchen.

'Ah, chocolate digestives, you remembered.' He beamed with pleasure as if her small feat of memory was the most remarkable thing that had happened to him all day.

'Aunt Jo always said she had to get a packet in specially for you.'

'Indeed.'

Kingsley was a tall, thin, very intelligent, if occasionally rather pedantic, man in his mid-fifties with a rumpled, kindly face, topped by an unruly thatch of still thick grey hair. He had on a well-worn dark-grey three-piece suit, pale-blue shirt and grey and blue striped tie. His black Oxford shoes gleamed. At first glance, some assumed that he was rather fuddy-duddy, but they soon realized the keen mind that lay behind the mild blue eyes.

Kingsley leant forward, selected a biscuit, took a bite and surveyed his client anxiously for a few moments through gold-rimmed spectacles. He had known Joyce Kemp for many years, as a family friend as well as her solicitor and had met Julie on several occasions. He thought she looked drawn and tired, which was hardly surprising, considering what she had been through. Sitting opposite him on the settee, she nursed her coffee cup on her lap, her legs together in an almost schoolgirl pose.

'How are you?' he asked.

Whether it was his position as her solicitor,

or whether it was his links of friendship to her aunt, Julie felt she could be more open with him than she had been with the psychologist she had seen a few days earlier and who had tried in vain to get through her barrier of grief.

'Physically, I've amazed the doctors. Everything seems to have healed up pretty well. There's a scar on my forehead still, but that's starting to fade. People will soon stop thinking I'm Harry Potter's elder sister.' She pulled a face. 'Mentally, of course, as I'm responsible for killing Aunt Jo, it's a rather different matter.'

'You aren't responsible at all.' As a long time friend, Kingsley permitted himself the luxury of speaking rather sharply. 'The people who are responsible are the bastards who fired the shots and whoever paid them to do it.'

Julie sat silently for a moment. Then she gave a brief nod of acknowledgement.

'Not bad,' she said. 'In fact you're better at it than some of the doctors. Not any more convincing, I'm afraid, but better.' She paused and looked at him. Kingsley almost winced at the depth of torment in her eyes. 'I'm sorry, you are sweet to be concerned, but this is something I've got to try to deal with in my own way and in order to do that, I need to accept it in my own way, too. So let's just deal with business please.'

Even as she spoke, she knew that one small thing had changed. As she had been growing stronger and healing, she had found that there was another emotion as well as the grief building up inside her. It had begun in a small way, but had gradually grown to equal status — the rage (anger was too mild a word) that demanded retribution. But that was something she had no intention of sharing with her solicitor — not at the moment, anyway.

Kingsley deliberated on having another go, but decided (correctly) that it would be useless.

'Very well, you are, after all, the client.'

He lifted his case on to his knees and opened it, taking out a slim file.

'It's actually quite simple. Your aunt owned this flat and a number of very valuable investments. She also owned a half-share in the three antique shops that she ran with Laura Tilling. You inherit this flat, its contents, her car and the savings. Mrs Tilling inherits the half-share in the shops.'

'And how much are the savings?'

'They are considerable. The shops are very successful and have made her a lot of money. Even after death duties, you could live here quite comfortably without having to work again.'

Julie nodded slowly.

'Aren't I the lucky one?' she said in a detached, flat voice.

★ ★ ★

The River Haven bisected the city in a series of twisting curves, narrowing as it moved into the surrounding countryside before disappearing underground in a roughly north-easterly direction.

The main shopping area, including a vast new covered mall, was situated in the centre of the city on the north bank of the river. Citizens of Havenchester spoke of going north in the same sense as Londoners spoke of going up west. Apart from the new mall, most of the shops were in original Regency or Georgian buildings which were rightly protected by the city's planning laws and so an aerial view of the area showed tall buildings to the south and generally much shorter ones to the north, as if the city had been given a rather lopsided Mohican haircut. Spreading out from the central hub of shops lining the river itself, rather like the rays of a sun half dipping over the horizon, were a number of narrower streets, some merely cobbled, which had survived the centuries and housed many of the more exclusive shops and businesses.

JL Antiques was situated in one such small street in the centre of the city. The street consisted of several very exclusive shops that served the needs of the very rich and those who aspired to be. On one side was a gentleman's bespoke tailor whose family had been clothing the rich and famous since the late eighteenth century. On the other was a jeweller, the contents of whose windows sparkled under carefully positioned artificial light. On the day after Simon Kingsley's visit, Julie walked from her apartment block to the shop. It took nearly an hour, but she felt the need for the exercise after having been confined to her bed and hospital for a number of weeks. She wore jeans and a padded jacket and felt warm from the exercise despite the cold wind. There was a steady stream of pedestrians filing past the shop windows, although most seemed to be browsing rather than seriously considering a purchase. Having glanced at the prices in the jeweller's window, Julie couldn't say she blamed them.

There were bow windows on either side of the antique shop's doorway. One window contained five Victorian paintings displayed on easels that perched on steps of wine red velvet. Each painting displayed portraits of various no doubt eminent persons of their age, apparently in various stages of dyspepsia. The other window contained two modest displays, one of delicately painted porcelain figures and the other of silverware.

A bell rang with an appropriately subdued toll in the depths of the shop as Julie opened the door and went inside. There were two well-dressed assistants, one male and one female, both dealing deferentially with clients — a shop like this wouldn't dare admit to having a customer. The shop appeared well stocked without being cluttered, with a series of smart display cases for the smaller items and larger pieces placed strategically around the floor. A number of paintings hung around the walls, all of them cleverly lit to show them to maximum advantage. An attractive woman with short-cut brown hair and wearing a simple black trouser suit and white blouse came forward quickly from the back of the shop as she saw Julie come in.

'Julie, how wonderful to see you.' She took Julie's hands in her own, kissed her on the cheek and stepped back. 'How are you?' Her good-natured, slightly plump face radiated an equal mixture of bonhomie and concern.

'Not too bad, thanks, Laura,' Julie smiled at her aunt's business partner and closest friend. 'How are you and Archie?'

'We're fine. He's here today.' Laura Tilling's husband was the senior partner in a firm of accountants that managed the books of the three JL Antique shops, amongst many others. 'Come through.'

Julie followed Laura through a curved archway to the rear of the shop where there was a large office with two side doors, both closed. Seated at a desk on the left-hand side and peering with close attention at a computer screen was a well-built man with short dark hair and an amiable, rather angular face. He looked up as the two women came in, smiling and rising from his chair as he saw Julie.

'Julie, it's good to see you again.'

'Hello, Archie. Still doing your sums, I see.'

'No rest for the wicked.' Tilling gave her a boyish grin and kissed her cheek. 'Sit down.' He offered her the swivel chair next to the second desk and Laura pulled another chair round from the corner of the room to use herself.

'I'm sorry we weren't able to stay long after the funeral,' Laura said, 'I felt we were rather abandoning you.'

Julie shook her head. Her aunt's funeral had been held the week before in a cemetery just outside the city. At Julie's own request only a few chosen close friends had come and she had returned to London herself immediately afterwards.

'I'm just grateful to you for coming; it was a bit of a last minute rush. I'd only been out of hospital a couple of days, so I wasn't feeling much like socializing. I just felt I needed to get that first bit of closure out of the way so I could move on. I'm sorry if some of her other friends and business associates would have liked to have been there, but I didn't feel able to cope with that. I suppose it was selfish of me.'

'Not at all. After what you had been through, everybody totally understood. I thought perhaps we could arrange a memorial service later in the year, when you're feeling up to it.'

Julie felt a rush of affection for the other woman.

'That would be good. Give me a chance to settle things a bit and we'll talk about it.'

'Of course, there's no hurry.' Laura leant forward in her chair. 'How are things really?' She looked at Julie with concern and in the presence of two friendly people, Julie felt her strength begin to crumble a little and the need for support start creeping through. She took a deep breath and pushed the feelings to the back of her mind.

'Going through the things at the flat is pretty stressful,' she admitted. 'I started yesterday evening and I've been at it all morning. I keep finding things that remind me of something Aunt Jo and I did together and I have to stop for a minute, so it's rather slow work. I needed a break from that and I wanted to come and see you and thank you properly for the flowers, so I walked over after lunch. I thought I could pick up any personal stuff from her office as well, if that's OK?'

'Of course. Come though and have a look now.'

Laura opened the left-hand door and ushered Julie through into her aunt's office.

The office was quite small but neatly appointed with a quality carpet and wallpaper and a Queen Anne desk. A computer stood on another table to one side of the desk and there were two comfortable chairs. Julie opened one of the desk drawers and looked across at Laura.

'You'd better go through it with me, if you have time. I don't want to take any stuff that you need for the business by mistake.'

Laura nodded.

'The main thing relating to the business is her address book and I've already taken that because I needed to refer to it and contact people. Let me know if you're likely to want any addresses from it. Joyce didn't do much in the shop itself, as you know. She spent most of her time travelling round to look for stock and talk to clients. She was so well liked and had such a wide range of contacts. And she had such a good eye — she seemed to know almost instinctively if a piece was genuine or a copy.' Laura shook her head sadly. 'She is such a loss, both as a friend and for her contribution to the business. She was so good with people as well as spotting a good piece.'

Julie nodded, trying to focus her mind and keep back the memories that were itching at her brain.

At the top in the first drawer was a red-covered diary. She lifted it out and it fell open at a page in early February. There was an entry in her aunt's neat writing: '7.30 dinner with J at Little Italy.' Julie felt the tears well up again and closed her eyes to hold them back. Laura came over and saw the entry. She gave her a hug.

'I know, why don't you come to dinner this evening? I bet you haven't seen anyone apart from Simon since you got here.'

Julie hesitated. She knew that what she needed more than anything else was company, although she felt very little like making conversation. For a moment she was going to refuse, giving in to the reluctance to make an effort. She looked at Laura's expectant face and suddenly found herself changing her mind.

'Thanks, I'd love to.'

'Good, that's settled. Let's say seven o'clock. We can have a drink first. You know where we are?'

'Yes.' Although she had never been to the Tillings' house herself, her aunt had told her about it. 'I've got the address, and I know the area.'

'That's fine. Look, let me leave you to go through the desk at your own speed and get out everything you want to take. Then I'll have a quick look through it before you go. As you're walking, if there's a lot to carry, I'll take it home and you can pick it up this evening.'

★ ★ ★

Laura and Archie Tilling lived in the Brambly Wood area of the city. Not quite as upmarket as Stansfield, where the millionaires gathered, the area nevertheless attracted the rich and prosperous and was considered one of the most fashionable places to live. Some of the houses backed on to a tributary of the river which left the main flow to meander for

36

nearly half a mile in a loose crescent shape past houses and through Brambly Common before rejoining its parent again. The Tillings' house was a large, five-bedroom modern detached residence with a long garden that sloped down to the river. It had been extensively renovated about twenty years before and Laura and Archie had been living there for just over five years, having purchased it at a relatively bargain price from the previous owner who was emigrating and wanted a quick sale.

Julie reached the house promptly at seven. She drove up the sweeping gravel drive in her aunt's pride and joy — a dark maroon MG that she had often said matched her perfectly — mature and sporty, with a surprising turn of speed. Julie parked by the front door, got out and rang the bell. She stood for a moment admiring the front garden, which looked neat and well groomed in the lights from the street and the house.

Laura opened the door, wiping her hands on the apron she wore to protect a well-made burnt-orange dress, and gave Julie a big smile and a hug.

'I'm so glad you came, I was afraid you'd ring up and cancel.'

'To be honest, I nearly did.'

Laura took her inside and hung her coat on

a hallstand that looked like a small tree next to the downstairs cloakroom. The hall was large and felt bright and spacious with a few items of tasteful furniture. The parquet floor gleamed and looked fit for a small dance. Doors led off from the hall on either side of a wide staircase.

Julie handed over the bottle of white wine she had brought with her. 'I know Archie is a connoisseur, but the man in the shop assured me it's good quality.'

'Thank you. Come through. That's the study,' — Laura indicated the first door on the right leading to the front room — 'and that's the dining room on the other side. We'll give you a tour later, if you like.'

Laura led the way across the gleaming floor. Julie had decided to try to feel better by dressing up for the occasion and her three-inch heels felt liable to sink into the polish on the floor with every step. Laura took her through to the big living room at the rear of the house. It held a comfortable three piece white leather suite, an impressive home entertainment system, including a plasma TV that wouldn't have been out of place in a small screen cinema, an antique bureau and two display cabinets of porcelain figures. French windows looked out across a long, neat garden, the illumination of a three-quarter moon showing a wide, long lawn bordered by trees and bushes glowing silver in the moonlight.

Archie stood up from one of the armchairs, kissed Julie on the cheek in welcome, thanked her for the wine and offered her a drink. Laura excused herself for a moment to deal with a minor crisis in the kitchen. Julie knew from Joyce that Laura was an excellent cook and prepared the meals herself whenever she could.

'You have a lovely house,' Julie said, sinking into one of the armchairs, which seemed to mould itself to her body.

'Thank you. We were lucky to get it. The shops had just started really taking off and we decided we wanted to move more upmarket. We'd only been looking for a couple of weeks when this became available and we snapped it up straight away.'

'How did Joyce and Laura meet?' Julie asked. 'She never told me that much about the business.'

'They were both working as technical advisers for an auction house. Joyce worked there part time and also had a small antique shop in an arcade in the city. She sold mainly small pieces — porcelain, silverware, that sort of thing and made a reasonable living. Laura specialized in painting and they got talking at work and became friends. Laura and I were already an item — although I was on a very lowly rung of the accountancy ladder in those days. The girls talked about merging their skills and buying a bigger shop. I put together a business plan for them and we managed to sell it to the bank. After a couple of years, it was going so well that we opened the London shop, and two years ago one in New York. There's always a market for European antiques in America and once you get a reputation for reliable supply and quality, you can't go far wrong.'

'Don't tell me he's boring you with our business history.' Laura heard the last few words as she came back from the kitchen.

'Julie asked me about it, I swear,' Archie protested.

'Perfectly true,' Julie admitted, relaxing into the comfortable atmosphere. It was good to talk about her aunt with those who really knew her well.

'Why don't you take Julie into the dining room? Dinner will be ready in a minute or two.'

The dining room was at the front of the house and was dominated by a magnificent mahogany dining table and chairs. Gleaming plates, lit by a chandelier, vied with each other to dazzle the beholder. Julie soaked in the atmosphere of the room as Archie poured wine and Laura wheeled in a heated trolley.

'We don't always dine in such splendour,' Archie assured their guest with a smile. 'This is purely in your honour.'

The meal was excellent. The three courses melted in the mouth and for a short time Julie felt able to set her grief to one side. After a perfect lemon soufflé, they had coffee back in the lounge. Conscious of the need to drive home, Julie refused more wine and the rest of the evening passed off very quickly. Stories about Joyce inevitably came into the conversation to remind her of her loss like worrying a painful tooth. Laura had a fund of tales of their time in the auction room — particularly occasions when clients considerably over-estimated the worth of their items until brought sharply down to earth.

For the first time since the shootings, Julie felt as though she could relax. The sense of empty ache was still there, but at least the food and good company dulled it a little. When she left and got into the MG to drive away though, the pain came back with a vengeance and she knew with even greater certainty that before long she needed to take action and take it quickly.

It was time to start fighting back.

★ ★ ★

At ten o'clock the following evening, Julie Cooper parked her car in a quiet residential area of the city, turned off the engine and sat for a moment. She had never visited the area before but knew it was famous, or infamous, for its night-time activities. Julie had no real professional knowledge about Havenchester and that was a gap in her education that she desperately needed to fill if she was going to do anything about her aunt's murder. She knew that a rich source of information about the criminal underbelly of any urban area was often the local prostitutes, particularly those who had been around the block (often literally) for a few years. Even if they had no direct contact with the local higher up criminal elements, they would hear things whilst going about their business and would know who to be particularly nice to and the places and people to avoid. She was going to try to tap into that source of information.

It wasn't perhaps the greatest plan of all time, in fact Baldrick would probably have rejected it, but she had to start somewhere and it was better than doing nothing. If the killing had been contracted to someone local they were almost certainly connected to organized crime in Havenchester and most such organization's leaders had a thumb — if not other parts of their anatomy — in the sex trade pie.

Julie had decided that if she was going to get one of the street girls to talk she needed to blend in and appear to be no more than another working girl. After her time under-cover, she was very comfortable playing a role and felt no more than the usual stirring of anticipation as she locked her car and walked back to the end of the street.

She was wearing a short black skirt, a tight white blouse with a low neck made even more revealing by a number of undone buttons, and a pair of high-heeled shoes. A short mac barely reached to the bottom of her skirt and would provide little protection against the chill night air.

The road that she came to was a little wider and busier than the one where she had parked. A couple of cars drifted past, the drivers trying to appear casual as they peered around, and she drew into the shadows of a convenient hedge. The last thing she wanted was to have to deal with an interested punter.

When the road was temporarily clear, Julie crossed over. She was in a street of terraced houses, wheelie bins standing outside like so many short grey sentries awaiting morning collection. It might have been any ordinary domestic street apart from the two or three girls strolling along the pavement on the other side of the road. Julie glanced across but they looked too young for her purpose.

She walked towards a junction some fifty yards away where she could see a woman in a short, tight dress and pink fur jacket standing on the corner. Beyond her, further night-time walkers were in evidence. It looked as though she would have plenty of choice.

Julie crossed the junction and approached the standing woman who was staring towards her, her narrow face pinched and pale. The woman appeared to be in her thirties, which could mean she was anything from early twenties upwards, but she certainly had the appearance of having been around long enough to fit Julie's criteria.

The pale blue eyes in the lean face narrowed as Julie approached.

'This is my spot, bugger off.'

Julie raised her hands placatingly.

'It's OK; I'm not trying to muscle in on your pitch.'

'What do you want then?'

The eyes narrowed even further as the woman studied Julie more carefully. Puzzlement slipped into her gaze and the thin lips tightened.

'You're not from round here.'

Julie shook her head and launched into her prepared story.

'I've just moved up from London. I need to earn some cash and I need to talk to someone, find out a bit about the local scene.' Julie dug her hands into the pockets of her coat and shivered. 'I'm actually after an inside job, I don't like the cold.' She tried a companionable 'I'm-just-another-working-girl-trying-to-earn-a-crust' smile. 'Can you give me the names of any clubs where I might find something?'

The other woman said nothing, her expression still suspicious.

'Could we go somewhere and talk?' Julie pressed her.

The woman shook her head.

'I can't afford to lose the time.'

'What if I pay for an hour of your time?' Julie suggested.

The woman's hostility thawed a little as the conversation became more familiar.

'Girl on girl is extra,' she said.

'Nothing like that, really,' Julie assured her. 'I just want to find out about the local scene, the places that are OK and the ones to avoid. Can we just get a cup of coffee somewhere?'

As the woman hesitated she looked over Julie's shoulder. Her eyes widened in fear and she moved back from Julie without speaking.

'What's going on here? I don't pay you to stand around chatting.'

Julie turned round. The speaker was a lean, balding man with a scarred olive complexion wearing a well-cut fawn suit. He eyed Julie up and down with a slow appraisal, an appreciative smile cutting across his face. Julie looked past the newcomer. He had stepped out from the passenger side of a car that had pulled up at the kerb nearby. And the driver's door was opening.

Julie cursed to herself. She was really off form. Normally when undercover she was totally aware of her immediate environment and any changes to it. Not being so could often lead to very unpleasant consequences.

'So what have we here?' A gold tooth gleamed briefly at the edge of his mouth.

Her plan was clearly going down the tubes at a record speed, but Julie tried to salvage the situation.

'I'm looking for work in a club. I was just asking for directions.'

The man shook his head in mock reproof.

'You don't want to be working indoors, darlin'. It's much healthier in the open air.'

The car driver had reached the pavement. Like his boss, he was also bald, but he was not smiling and he was built on a mountainous scale.

Great, Julie thought, I run into a pimp and his enforcer first crack out of the box.

'I'm not interested,' Julie started to turn away.

'Not an option.' The pimp's smile widened. 'Come with us and we'll give you some on the job training.' He nodded at the driver.

Julie hesitated. She knew that she could probably disable both men, but it would involve moves that few street girls would be able to use and the last thing she wanted was to draw attention to herself. At least, no more than she had already.

As mountain man reached out to grab her arm, Julie pulled from her coat pocket the bottle of cheap perfume she had used to add scent to her role. She squirted the enforcer full in the face. He bellowed and slapped his hands to his eyes.

Julie dodged a lunge from the pimp, dropping the bottle in the process, pushed past the hooker, who was gaping at her open-mouthed, and ran back the way she had come. She couldn't move as fast as she would have liked. High heels were not the most ideal footwear in a chase and twisting her ankle was not a desirable option. She had an idea that once the big man's eyes had stopped smarting he would be keen to get his own back.

It was vital that she got to her car with a sufficient head start to be able to drive away before the pimp caught up with her, and that was becoming increasingly unlikely. She could hear his pumping breath as he gained on her and risked a quick glance back over her shoulder. Panic nearly set in. Another few yards and he would have her.

Julie grabbed the handle of the nearest wheelie bin and turned in a half circle, pulling it round behind her. It was heavy and the effort felt like it was forcing her arms from her shoulders, but the bin swung round and toppled over into her pursuer's path.

The pimp tried desperately to jump over the sudden obstruction but the edge of the bin caught him on the shins and he hit the pavement with a thudding slap and a loud curse. Julie darted across the road and down the street where she had parked her car.

She pulled her keys from her shoulder bag, unlocked the door and pulled it open. She slid into the seat, jammed the key into the ignition, started the engine, put the car into gear and slammed and locked the door in one continual fluid motion. Fortunately she was parked far enough away from the car in front to pull out without manoeuvring and her last sight of the pimp was his glaring face in her rear-view mirror as she roared away.

Julie turned left at the first opportunity, then right and left again, pulling into the side of the road only when she was sure that not even the fastest sprinter could catch up with her. She sat clutching the steering wheel tightly, her breath coming in shuddering gasps as reaction set in and tears started to trickle down her cheeks.

What an abysmal cock up. She shook her head in frustration and self-anger. She was a mess. It had been a mad idea in the first place and she'd gone at it with no real preparation, driven by the need to do something, the need to overcome a feeling of being surrounded by high brick walls, isolated and powerless. All she had achieved was to make herself feel even worse. At least the pimp and his minder weren't likely to spread the story about being defeated by a woman — it wouldn't do a lot for their street cred.

Julie took some deep breaths and dabbed at her eyes. Had she subconsciously put herself into danger as some sort of self punishment for the deep responsibility that she felt for her aunt's death? She wasn't usually given to such psychological self-analysis. Maybe she was just uncaring about her own safety?

Getting herself beaten up, or worse, wasn't going to achieve anything. Julie put the car into gear again and moved off. She was as determined as ever to get to the bottom of the shooting, but that night's fiasco had made her equally determined about something else as well.

She couldn't do it alone. She needed help.

3

Alec Tanner had no way of knowing on that bright, chilly Monday morning in March that his life was about to change forever. He sat at his desk, an expression of calm contemplation on his craggy face with its thoughtful, humorous brown eyes beneath a thatch of shaggy brown hair. He ran a pencil meditatively along the edge of his broken nose and shifted his slightly under six-foot body into a more comfortable position.

Tanner was the owner of a detective agency, the staffing compliment of which consisted of Ella Lang, who ran the office and did some office-based enquiry work when required, the extremely capable Ted Manning, who shared the main investigatory work with Tanner, and Danny Worenski, who claimed, accurately, that he knew more about computers than the people who made them and could hack into anything anywhere. Danny did a lot of the agency bread and butter work as he had an accounting background and undertook financial and other credit checks on both individuals and organizations. They made, Tanner reflected, a good team. A fourth member of the firm had left just after Christmas having got homesick for his London roots. For the moment, they were managing without taking on anyone else.

The agency was based in a converted Victorian terrace in West Coven Road on the edge of the financial district of Havenchester. All the three-storey former houses along the road had been converted into offices. His building held a secretarial agency on the ground floor, the detective agency on the first floor, a firm of architects above that and the top floor had been divided in two housing an importing business and a photographer. It was an eclectic mix that seemed to work and none of the businesses interfered with or had much to do with each other.

Tanner had arrived in the office later than usual that morning following a late night that had concluded satisfactorily for a client who wanted proof that one of his employees was selling information to a rival company. Tanner had obtained the necessary photographic evidence, but had not got home until the small hours.

Ella Lang came into the office with a mug of coffee and the post. She had a round, pretty, cheerful face surrounded by a mass of curly chestnut hair. Big golden hooped ear-rings swung rhythmically as she moved. As usual, her tight skirt was more north than south and there was a three-inch gap between her belt and tight, curving top that displayed an interesting view of firm, light-coffee coloured flesh. She grinned at her boss.

'I've made an appointment for you at eleven — a Miss Julie Cooper. She rang about half an hour ago and asked to see you particularly. I told her Ted was a far better detective, but for some reason she insisted on seeing you.'

'Obviously she only wants to deal with the highest echelons of the firm,' Tanner told her, ignoring her rolling-eyed response. 'Show her in when she arrives.'

Having indulged in their usual amicable repartee, Ella went back out to continue running the office and Tanner decided it was time to tackle his post. He reached for his letter opener in the shape of a small oriental sword, musing idly that as an aficionado of detective stories he should have been worried that he'd be found one evening sprawled across his desk with the knife in his back.

Julie arrived punctually and was shown in by Ella. She shook hands with Tanner, her handshake cool and firm, and he motioned her to one of the two client chairs in front of his desk. She had gone for a confident business look, wearing a well-cut and slightly severe dark-blue suit with a knee-length skirt under an open black leather coat.

Tanner felt an immediate attraction. It was not just physical — although he imagined he could practically see the sparks crackling between them — but as their hands touched he had an almost tangible feeling of warmth towards her. For a moment something in her eyes seemed to echo his feelings and he knew that she had felt the same reaction. Then some sort of emotional shutter swung down and the moment passed, although its after effects seemed to hang in the air between them. Tanner sat back down behind his desk and with a little effort got his professional persona into gear.

Julie sat and smoothed her skirt as she looked round the office, noting the large partners desk and the leather swivel chair behind it, the three grey filing cabinets (partly for effect as Ella had most of their records computerized), the two comfortable client chairs and the low coffee table between them. She glanced at the tall yucca plant that loomed like a triffid next to the window with its view of the offices opposite and a brief glimpse of the river beyond. The visual tour of the office gave her time to get her feelings under control and, when she looked back at

Tanner, her expression was calm and controlled, all emotion firmly locked away.

Ella came in with a cup of coffee that she placed on the table. For a moment her eyes met Tanner's and she raised one eyebrow with a questioning look of amusement before going back out again. Sometimes, Tanner thought, Ella knew him too well.

'How can I help you, Miss Cooper?'

'Do you recognize my name?' Her voice was smooth and silky with a slight huskiness thrown in for good measure. Tanner considered popping outside briefly for a cold shower.

His brow crinkled briefly.

'There was a shooting a few weeks ago . . . ' he began.

She nodded. 'I was one of the victims.' She took a deep breath and described the events of that night.

'Jarrow claims he had nothing to do with it,' she said at the end. 'That is, of course, crap — but I can't do much about him. What I can do is track down the men who did the shooting and whoever instructed them.'

'Where do I come in?'

'Although Jarrow operated from London, he had contacts all over the country. Whoever did the shooting knew this city; I am convinced they were local. I spoke to the city police this morning — DCI Mariner, who is in charge of the investigation into the shooting. I told him I wanted to do a bit of investigating myself and, although he wasn't happy, he said he'd allow it provided I reported back to him immediately if I found out anything. He suggested I spoke to you when I said I wanted someone to help me. I also rang my aunt's solicitor, Simon Kingsley, after I'd spoken to Mariner and he said he used your firm regularly and would recommend you. That was good enough for me so here I am.'

Tanner nodded. Mariner's father and Tanner's uncle had been close friends in the force. Tanner and Mariner had always got on well and he took care not to tread on official toes too often and to bring Mariner into those cases where he felt it appropriate. This arrangement had proven to be mutually beneficial and Mariner tended to cut the agency some slack when he could.

'What exactly do you want me to do?'

'I don't know this city very well. I used to come and stay with my aunt, but I need someone who knows the underbelly, the dirty places and the nasty people.'

The recommendations had perhaps lost a little of their gloss, Tanner reflected ruefully. They seemed to suggest that he was the man with a detailed knowledge of the grimy side of life.

'DCI Mariner admitted to me that the police investigation has run out of steam,' she went on. 'The shooters have disappeared into thin air and no one is talking. I want to hire you to work with me. I want you to take me round to meet some people who might have been involved and stir them up a bit, see what happens.'

'On the basis that if you poke the wasps' nest enough, the queen will come out?'

He had a feeling that in earlier times she might have smiled.

'Something like that.'

'Of course, we're likely to be pretty severely stung before that happens.'

Any trace of amusement vanished.

'I'm happy to risk that, if you are.'

Tanner thought for a moment. He took a large scale map of the city centre from his desk drawer, went round to the other side of the desk and spread the map out on the coffee table. He sat down in the other client chair and indicated the map.

'Tell me exactly what happened and where, as much as you can remember it.'

Julie leaned forward to study the map, her hair swaying down in a gleaming black curtain, her teeth worrying her lower lip as she focused on difficult memories. Finally, she extended a neatly manicured finger to indicate the side of Wellington Square where the restaurant was situated.

'I don't remember much,' she said. 'We came out of the restaurant and started walking to our left. We walked side by side, Aunt Jo nearest the road. We were talking, catching up because we hadn't seen each other properly for eighteen months, not paying much attention to what was going on around us. I don't remember noticing anyone else walking in the square. The bike is a vague memory, coming towards us, not speeding, with two black, helmeted figures. I barely looked up at it until Aunt Jo groaned and started to fall. My reactions were far too slow — not that I could have done much. I just felt shock then immediately fear, a blow in my chest, then pain and darkness.'

Tanner nodded.

'They didn't ride round the square to get to you?'

'I'm pretty sure they didn't — I didn't see them when we came out of the restaurant. I think I'd have noticed them if they had ridden round from the other side of the square.'

'So they probably came out of the road leading into the corner of the square that you were walking towards.' As he leant further forward to study the map, Tanner was aware of her subtle perfume and had to resist the urge to reach out to her. Maybe a cold shower would be a good idea.

'Yes. The police found no one who saw them hanging around at the corner, though, nor in the road itself.'

Tanner focused back on what she had said and thought for a moment.

'There could have been a third person spotting for them.' He put his finger on the map. 'I think there's a narrow lane here behind the cinema. If the bike was out of sight round there, they would have been out of general view but they wouldn't have seen you come out of the restaurant. Yet they moved into action as soon as you came out. If a spotter was watching the restaurant, they could have seen you about to leave and tipped off the bikers.'

Julie nodded.

'You could well be right — but I didn't see anyone.'

'What happened after the shooting?'

'I was out of it. According to the police report, a motor bike with two people on it was seen pulling into Target Road just after the shooting. That means they went down the first road at the other end of the square. The man who found us confirms that — he was coming from a road that led into the other side of the square and saw no bike. CCTV caught what was probably them for a short while, but couldn't trace where they went.'

'Was there anything else useful in the police report?'

'One bike fitting the description was stolen from a car-park the day before. That's one reason I think it was a local job.'

'Who was the owner?'

'He works for the council. The bike was stolen from the Town Hall car-park. The owner reported the bike missing the same evening. He was at a council meeting on the night of the shooting — plenty of witnesses. He's in the clear.'

'OK.' Tanner thought for a moment. 'Can I suggest something a little more subtle to start with than immediately poking the wasps' nest?'

Again, the humour showed in her eyes for the briefest flash before being snuffed out by the iron control imposed by the weight of her grief.

'If you like.'

'I'd like to consult with a colleague. Come with me, if you like.'

They went out into the reception area. Ella looked up from her computer screen.

'Is Ted free?' Tanner asked.

'Yes, he hasn't any appointments this morning.'

Tanner led Julie across to a door to the left of Ella's desk, knocked and they went in.

Theodore Ambrose Manning was sitting at his desk looking through a group of photographs spread out in front of him. As well as being street wise and very useful in a rough-house, he had a very keen brain for spotting something that was out of context. A little over six feet tall and broad shouldered, he favoured sharp suits and blindingly jazzy ties. That day's effort featured Donald Duck.

Manning was third generation British of West Indian origin and even supported the English cricket team — which Tanner felt showed a spirit of integration often above and beyond the call of duty. He was a loyal and committed friend and Tanner was always grateful that Manning was on his side.

He introduced Julie and Manning stood up and shook her hand, giving her a smile.

'What can I do for you?'

Tanner explained the situation.

'Two people, probably, but not definitely, male. They work together, aren't worried about killing a cop and they possibly went to ground for a while in early February. They may or may not have resurfaced yet.' Manning summarized. 'Somebody must have heard or seen them before in connection with something nasty going down. That sort of person doesn't just spring up from nowhere. They're bound to have some sort of previous incidents to their name, even if this was their first killing.'

He thought for a moment.

'They may not be local, of course, but that seems a reasonable assumption to start with.'

'So what will you do?' Julie asked.

He gave Julie his most charming grin; the one he boasted made women go weak in the knees — and elsewhere.

'I'll ask around.'

'The police have been asking for weeks,' Julie pointed out.

Ted Manning's smile broadened.

'People answer me,' he said.

How long will it take you?' Tanner asked.

Manning rubbed a finger over his chin.

'I can leave this for now.' His broad hand indicated the photographs on his desk. 'I'll do some telephoning this afternoon and fix up a few meetings for later. I'll need to do the rounds of certain clubs and bars and some of the people I need to talk to don't come out to play until the wee small hours. Give me until this time tomorrow.'

'So can we be doing anything else while we're waiting?' Julie asked, when they returned to Tanner's office.

It was a good question. Tanner realized that he did not want her to leave. Although they had only met for the first time an hour before, he knew he wanted to see as much of his new client as possible. Even though she would be back again the next day, he was eager to get to know her better straight away; twenty-four hours was far too long to wait. Tanner was sure that deep down she was feeling the same way. He hoped so, anyway.

'Is there anything you'd like me to tell you about how organized crime is structured in the city?' he asked. 'After all, you've hired me for my professional expertise in that area. We can't really plan our strategy in any detail until Ted gives us some names tomorrow.'

'You're pretty confident he'll come up with something.'

'I'm absolutely positive. If Ted says he'll do something by a certain time, you just have to set your watch and wait.'

'Sounds like a good man to have around.'

'He is.' Tanner glanced at his watch. 'Talking of setting your watch, would you like some lunch? I can send out for some sandwiches or, if you'd rather, there's a pub nearby that does a good line in snacks.' He paused, aware that he was starting to sound desperate. 'Or do you need to be somewhere else?'

'No, I don't have to rush away and a sandwich in the office sounds fine. Thank you.' She gave him a polite smile and again the hint of something warmer seemed to be lurking in her eyes.

When Tanner asked Ella to pop out and get some sandwiches she gave him a knowing grin and a raised eyebrow that he chose to ignore with dignity. Her grin got even wider.

Having organized lunch, Tanner returned to his office, sat down in the other client chair and decided to risk a personal question.

'Your aunt was your only relative?' Good old Tanner, he thought, subtle as a bulldozer.

Julie nodded.

'My mother died when I was born.' She stretched out her shapely legs and settled into her chair. Far from objecting to the question, she found herself content to talk about herself and her past. Perhaps because she felt comfortable with the pre-murder memories and perhaps she also felt oddly comfortable with Alec Tanner. 'My father was Kenton Cooper, the archaeologist. We had some great times together — half the time he acted like an older brother rather than a father.' The gentle smile returned. 'He used to take me with him on some of his trips abroad, except when I was at school. That was where he did act like my father — insisting that I got the best out of my education. Because he was abroad a lot, I boarded at school during the week and spent weekends either with my father or, if he was out of the country, with Aunt Joyce. During school holidays I would either go out to wherever he was, or stay with Aunt Joyce — there wasn't anyone else. When I got older, I learnt a lot of things at the archaeological digs that you don't learn from books or schools — particularly how to look after myself. We were in Thailand for a while and I used to go off exploring on my own. A monk, who was a friend of my father, taught me Ki Thi, which is their local form of self defence and builds up confidence. He became my friend, too and I've been back to see him a few times, even after my father died. That was in my second year at university. When I graduated, I joined the police. I had originally planned to follow in my father's footsteps and, if he had lived, I probably would have done, but after he died, I decided I needed to do something different. I didn't see myself as Lara Croft.'

Julie continued her story, almost as if

Tanner wasn't there and she was simply rerunning the film of her life to herself.

'I had always been close to my aunt; we used to do a lot of sailing, swimming and diving together around the coast. My father's death brought us even closer. She was the fixed point in the universe that I could always come back to. Now she's gone, it's like I've been set adrift. I'm not sure what I want with my life any more, so trying to get to the bottom of the shooting is giving me something to focus on.' She broke off abruptly. 'Sorry, I haven't been that open even with the tame psychiatrist they sent to see me. You are a good listener.'

She looked at him curiously for a moment and seemed about to say something else when a knock on the office door broke the thread.

Ella came in with the food and placed it on the table together with some fresh fruit and a couple of cartons of fruit juice. She had also brought in china plates and proper glasses for the juice. Treating a client to lunch was a special occasion and Ella liked to do things in style. Tanner thanked her and she gave him a most unsecretarial wink before leaving.

Julie opened her pack of sandwiches, took a bite from one and put it on a plate.

'Now it's your turn. What twists and turns of life have brought you here?' She poured juice for both of them. Tanner felt strongly that she was genuinely interested, not just making conversation as they ate.

'I've always lived in this city. My parents died in a car crash when I was in my early teens and I was brought up after that by my uncle — who was in the police then. When he retired, he opened this agency. I tried my hand at teaching, but it didn't work out, so I packed in my red marker pen and joined him as his partner in the agency. When my uncle died two years ago, I took it over.' He put on a TV quiz contestant voice. 'My hobbies are swimming and scuba diving and I go to the gym, without making a religion out of it. I also read detective stories — it's much easier in books. I've also done a bit of sailing — so we have quite a bit in common.'

She didn't rise to that.

'Are you married?'

'For a couple of years. It didn't work out and hit the rocks with a about the same force — and similar result — as the *Titanic*. We parted by mutual and reasonably amicable consent. She's remarried and lives in Scotland. They've got a couple of kids now. One or two attempts at relationships since then have fizzled out without much effort on either side and I am currently unattached and uncommitted to anyone or anything apart from this agency.' He paused. 'How about you?' He tried to sound uninterested. Julie told him later that he'd failed miserably.

Julie shook her head. 'One fairly long term boyfriend and a few shorter interludes, but nothing that led to anything. The last couple of years in the undercover operation haven't been conducive to a stable relationship.'

Tanner nodded.

'So, what's your view on the hit?' Julie asked, taking them back to the business in hand.

'It was probably arranged through one of the main crime organizations in the city. It could have been an independent, but that's unlikely.'

'Why?' She leant forward and poured some more juice. Tanner got another waft of her perfume but kept himself calm. No howling and salivating, he thought proudly, very professional.

'Firstly, the city is sewn up pretty tightly by the established mobs — they'd want their cut. Jarrow would know that and he wouldn't want to rock the boat — particularly if he's a sitting duck in prison. And secondly the independents tend to work solo — it's not the sort of career where you want a partner who could let you down. Organizations are different — they give more security.'

'If it was an independent, it will be virtually impossible to trace them.'

Tanner nodded.

'So let's assume they work for one of the mobs in the city. There aren't that many with that sort of clout. If that doesn't pan out, we can try the impossible later.'

'So now all we need is for Mr Manning to come up with the names.'

She got up as she spoke and Tanner helped her on with her coat. He felt again the twisting feeling in the pit of his stomach — he didn't want to see her go. He felt like a schoolboy having his first crush. It was ridiculous, but he didn't care.

'Would you like to go out to dinner this evening?' Tanner managed not to blurt it out too abruptly.

She frowned for a moment and he could see the hesitation in her eyes. They were standing by the office door, Tanner's hand on the handle, not wanting to open it. He knew he was getting vibes from her that were more than just perfume.

Julie could feel a mix of emotions stirring within her. Since her aunt's death, she had channelled her anger and guilt into a single-minded purpose that created a barrier against all other emotions. Now she felt that barrier, if not collapsing, certainly shaking a little, which was unsettling and almost frightening.

'Sandwiches for lunch, then dinner, do you treat all your clients that well?' Her soft voice held a lilt of mockery, and of something deeper she was finding it difficult to control.

'You're lucky; we have a special offer this week. Two free meals for every ten hours of contracted work.'

Her eyes studied him quizzically.

'You think we're going to spend that much time together?'

'More, I hope.' He was staring into her deep hazel eyes, willing her to give him a positive response.

For a moment, he thought she was going to say yes, then the humour and interest seemed to drain away.

'No, I don't think so, thank you. Maybe another time.' She was almost formally polite.

Tanner found that the door was open and she was walking away past Ella's desk.

'I'll be here at noon tomorrow, thank you for your help.'

The outer office door snapped shut. Tanner stood leaning against his office door jamb for a moment. Ella caught his eye, seemed about to say something and changed her mind. Yes, Tanner reflected, she knows me too well. He stepped slowly back into his office and closed the door.

4

Julie arrived as arranged at twelve o'clock the next day. Tanner took her padded jacket and hung it up as she settled herself into the same client chair as before. She was less formally dressed, in tight blue jeans, matching jacket and a white T-shirt. Ella brought in coffee and sandwiches and, as she left, Ted Manning came in. He dropped into the vacant chair and picked up a sandwich. In contrast to Tanner's open-necked shirt and casual attire, Manning wore a well-tailored suit with a pale-green shirt and a tie with Homer Simpson on it eating a hamburger.

'Boy, am I good,' Manning beamed at them.

'I know you are, O Great One,' Tanner said drily. 'So what have you managed to find out?'

'Well, the expense account took a bit of a beating, but it was pretty productive.' He took a swig of juice and decided they had been kept in suspense long enough.

'To cut a long evening and late night very short, there seem to be three pairs of likely local candidates. Harry Jarvis and Sam

Hesky, who specialize in beatings but could well have extended their repertoire; Angie and Findon Wilson, a brother and sister act; and Jethro Harper and Kevin Winston.'

'Any more details?' Tanner asked, knowing there would be.

Manning finished chewing his last bit of sandwich.

'Harry Jarvis and Sam Hesky are a couple of right charmers who would duff up their grannies for a couple of quid. They work for Vernon Bridger.'

'Who's Vernon Bridger?' Julie asked.

'A very nasty piece of low life,' Tanner told her. 'He has a number of unsavoury businesses that operate just on the fringes of the law but his main line of work involves selling sex and drugs — preferably both together. He's clever, though; the police have never been able to pin anything concrete on him. He runs a couple of girlie clubs and strip joints that get raided periodically, but he's been careful, or lucky, and nothing major has been found — even though there's undoubtedly prostitution and more going on at both of them. I had the pleasure of getting a thirteen-year-old girl out of one of the clubs on one occasion. I was able to get her out before anything nasty happened, but that meant Bridger could claim that he didn't know how old she was and, when he found out, he was going to send her home. He has a very capable pet solicitor.'

'The other reason he's mainly got away with things,' Ted Manning added, 'is because witnesses conveniently lose their memory or disappear.'

'Sounds a distinct possibility he's someone Jarrow would have had contact with,' Julie said.

Tanner nodded.

'If you want a nasty job done, Bridger is your man.' He looked across at his colleague. 'Do Jarvis and Hesky have a record?'

'Various juvenile arrests, car theft, robbery, that sort of thing, then they moved on to serious assault and robbery and any other nasty jobs Bridger wants doing. They have been with Bridger's crowd for quite a while. I also understand that they weren't seen in their usual haunts for a while last month, although they're back now. They were possibly lying low until the heat died down.'

'Or sitting somewhere sunny spending their bonus for a job well done.' Julie's voice throbbed with anger.

'Yes, they're definitely worth looking into.' Tanner looked at Manning again. 'What about the other candidates?'

'The Wilsons are more freelance than the

other two pairs. They'll turn their hand to anything they're hired for. Protection racket heavies, debt collectors, witness silencing, you name it. She's more vicious than he is — he holds them down whilst she sticks the knife in — often literally. They don't just work this city, so again Jarrow could have had contact with them.'

'And the last two?'

'Jethro Harper and Kevin Winston work for Harry Milton. They've been with him for about nine months — probably on his work experience scheme. The shooting is the sort of thing he might give someone like that as a test. Milton is even nastier than Bridger. He's more upmarket and he mixes with legitimate business, but that doesn't mean he's not involved in the dirty stuff, just that he uses gold knuckle-dusters. He owns a number of upmarket clubs, gambling as well as some more unsavoury things. In some ways he's worse to tangle with than Bridger because he's got the money to buy people. You never know who he might have in his pocket.'

'What charming people you know,' Julie smiled to take the heat out of the words.

'It keeps life interesting.' Manning smiled back.

'Do we have any photos?' Tanner asked.

'I had a word with Mariner and he said that he'd assume DS Cooper was asking and send round some mug shots — they should be here soon.'

'Haven't any of these people been looked at as part of the main police investigation?' Tanner asked. 'We need to check that with Mariner.'

'I mentioned that to him,' Manning replied. 'Mariner has been looking at local lads, but he had nothing that points specifically at any of these characters. Without any concrete evidence, he had no justification for any detailed police enquiries to focus on them. He has no objections to us doing so, though.'

'It does feel quite liberating to be free to follow our instincts,' Julie commented. 'I could get used to it.'

'I hope we're not teaching you bad habits,' Ted Manning remarked, as he reached for the final sandwich.

'Client's choice — who do you want to look into first?' Tanner asked.

'How about Bridger?' she suggested.

'Make sure you've got your bullet-proof underwear on,' Manning advised.

'I never travel without it.'

★　★　★

Alec Tanner knew that Vernon Bridger conducted most of his business from a pub called the Rocking Horse in the north-west side of the city, an area of run-down multi-storey flats where not all the rats lived in the sewers. The Rocking Horse was in one of the better parts of that area — people only urinated in the street after dark. Tanner left his car a few streets away and they walked from there. If they upset Bridger, he didn't want to come back to four flat tyres, or worse.

The mug shots had arrived before they left and they had studied them before setting out in case Jarvis and Hesky were lounging in the public bar waiting to be interviewed. Not surprisingly, they weren't.

The pub was gloomy inside with small mottled-glass windows and furnishings of well-scuffed dark wood. The atmosphere was stale from old smoke.

The mid-afternoon drinkers were being entertained by a selection from the battered juke box that stood in one corner. A singer Tanner couldn't identify was screeching some lyrics he couldn't understand. Behind the bar a man with arms like piston rods was serving and wiping glasses and the bar top with the same grubby cloth. There was a selection of bar food — either crisps or nuts, neither of which looked very appetizing.

Tanner knew that Bridger kept the pub deliberately dingy so as to discourage the casual punter and he thought that Julie looked as out of place as a diamond in a sewer. They crossed the dusty floor to the bar — at least they seemed to have cleaned up any blood — and Tanner caught the barman's attention.

'Mr Bridger in?'

'Who wants him?' He carried on wiping the bar. He wasn't exactly welcoming them with open arms, Tanner thought.

'Alec Tanner — tell him it's only a social visit.'

The barman emitted an unhygienic-sounding sniff and gave his new customers a good staring. They stood patiently waiting, staring back. Eventually he declared the staring competition a draw.

'Wait there.'

He lifted the hatch at the side of the bar, walked round to the left and knocked on a door at the rear. He went in; they continued to wait. A few minutes later the barman returned and indicated with a jerk of his head that they should follow him. Beyond the first door was a short passageway and then another door. Standing in the passage by the second door was the clone of the barman. Between them, Tanner thought, they probably had an IQ of around 6 on a good day, but that didn't mean that he was eager to challenge them to a fight. The second man frisked Tanner for hidden weapons, then turned to Julie. She opened her shoulder bag for him and then pulled her coat and jacket open. It was clear from her tight clothes that there was nothing concealed elsewhere. The bruiser thought about a body search, caught Julie's eye and decided it wasn't necessary. He nodded, opened the door and they passed on into the inner sanctum.

Vernon Bridger's office was a considerable improvement on the public face of the pub. It was well furnished, with a couple of paintings on the walls and a deep pile carpet. Bridger himself sat behind a wide desk. The immediate impression was of a square head with a short thick neck resting on a rectangular body. His face was red and imposing, with dark features, black curly hair and thick eyebrows. Julie thought that he looked a bit like a clean-shaven and plumper version of Groucho Marx except there was no cigar and very little humour. He wore a very expensive dark-blue suit that looked a size too small, with a white handkerchief peeking from the breast pocket of the jacket. His thick fingers flashed with heavy gold rings.

'What do you want?' he demanded,

suggesting he had little chance of winning a Mr Charm contest.

'I wanted to pick up some more tips from you about providing customer satisfaction.'

On both previous occasions when Tanner had crossed metaphorical swords with Bridger he had got what he wanted and Bridger had stayed out of jail. Tanner considered that to be honours even, but he knew he was unlikely to be on Bridger's Christmas card list.

Bridger eyed his visitor with increasing distaste.

'Who's the broad?'

Tanner looked at Julie.

'There you are, I told you he's a smooth talker.' He turned back to Bridger. 'This lady is Detective Sergeant Julie Cooper.' He paused. Bridger didn't gasp in amazement, stagger back, or look sheepish. In fact his expression didn't change at all. Tanner knew that didn't mean a thing. If Bridger had arranged the shooting, he would have known who Julie was already and had plenty of time to practise his best poker face.

'I thought you said this isn't official.'

'I'm on holiday,' Julie told him, looking round the room with the expressionless face that all police officers can adopt on appropriate occasions, giving the impression that they take special classes to perfect the look.

'She's visited all sorts of exotic locations,' Tanner said, 'but I told her that she hasn't seen anything until she's seen inside this pub.'

'Just cut the crap and tell me what you want.'

Tanner thought of suggesting that Bridger had seen too many American gangster movies, but decided to let it slide. He didn't seem to be getting particularly irritated, just bored.

'Jarvis and Hesky,' Tanner said.

At least that got a response. Bridger narrowed his eyes at Tanner, at least, as far as his podgy face could narrow, his eyebrows meeting like copulating caterpillars.

'Who?'

Tanner sighed. Bridger needed to take better acting lessons.

'Harry Jarvis and Sam Hesky,' he said. 'They work for you and we strongly suspect that they are responsible for the attempted murder of this lady and the murder of her aunt.' 'Strongly' was perhaps overdoing it a bit, but Tanner wanted Bridger to think that they knew more than they did — which, he reflected, wouldn't have been difficult.

Bridger blinked and sat back in his chair. Tanner got the impression that he did look a little surprised, but perhaps his acting lessons had been better than he thought.

'What's that got to do with me?'

'They are your employees,' Tanner pointed out.

Bridger flapped a dismissive hand.

'If someone hired them for a killing, they did it through you,' Tanner persisted.

'You're talking rubbish. Jarvis and Hesky do work for me from time to time, just running odd jobs, but I don't own them. They're big boys; they don't have to do what I tell them, and they don't work exclusively for me.'

'That's not what we heard. How can I get in touch with them?'

Bridger shrugged. 'How should I know? I'm not their mother. Maybe they've gone to London or to Glasgow. As I said, I'm not the only one who employs them.'

'I think you're lying,' Tanner said. 'I don't think they wipe their bums without permission from you.' Poke the wasps' nest, he thought, as per instructions.

'I don't give a monkey's arse what you think. Get out of here.' He was starting to get angry.

Yes, Tanner nodded to himself, definitely too many American gangster movies.

'By all means.' Tanner turned towards the door. 'We just wanted to let you know that we still think the hit was arranged through you, and we intend to prove it. We are very good at digging up skeletons. It'll save you a lot of aggravation if you tell us where Jarvis and Hesky are.'

'Piss off.' His face was getting even redder than usual. 'I'm not worried by threats from you two. And if you bother my employees, I won't be responsible for the consequences. They don't like people interfering in their affairs — and nor do I.'

'That's a shame, because that's exactly what we intend to do.'

As an exit line, it wasn't particularly snappy, but it added a further shade of red to Bridger's face, so Tanner was reasonably satisfied.

'And how do we think that went?' Julie asked, as they walked back to the car.

'We'll know if we get a reaction,' Tanner said. He paused. 'How about going for that meal this evening?' He saw her hesitate again and pushed on quickly, 'All in the line of business. We can discuss the next stage of our campaign. I know a very nice pub a few miles outside the city; it's got great views.'

She gave in and nodded.

'Strictly business,' she said firmly.

'Strictly business,' Tanner agreed.

'I'll need to go home and change.'

'I'll pick you up at seven.'

* * *

The pub was situated to the north of the city. It stood on the edge of a tributary of the Haven and the food and the view were all that Tanner had promised. The gardens were illuminated by clever but subdued lighting and they had a window table, looking out across the magical scene towards the river. It was a significant contrast to the premises they had visited that afternoon.

The food was simple and well cooked and they relaxed into each other's company. They talked about their past lives, compared boating and diving stories and Julie went into more detail about her experiences on the archaeological digs with her father. There were times when she dropped her guard and seemed almost happy, but then something she said would remind her of her aunt and the sadness returned. At the end of the evening, as Tanner helped her on with her coat, she thanked him gravely for the meal and he felt his own anger bubbling up towards the people who had taken away the carefree fun person he was sure lay behind her grief. He silently renewed his commitment to help her track them down.

They left the pub just after 10.30 and drove back to Julie's flat, stopping on the way at a twenty-four-hour superstore so that Julie could buy a jar of marmalade as she had run out that morning and forgotten to get any earlier in the day.

Tanner drove into the same public car-park opposite the apartment block that he had used earlier and found a vacant slot. There were a few empty spaces and a single light in the far corner. The night was cloudy with no visible moon and the steady drizzle that had been around all evening and had started to build itself up into something more substantial, had eased off for a while. There was no one about. Tanner assumed that the car-park was largely used overnight by local residents and most would be home indoors in the dry and warm by that time. They got out and had just walked round the car when the rear doors of a red Transit van parked six or seven spaces away swung open and four men got out. They were all large; they all carried baseball bats and they all wore rubber masks. Julie and Tanner were about to be attacked by four clones of President George W. Bush.

The attackers spread out into a semi-circle and moved towards them. Tanner glanced round. Behind them were cars and a solid wall; there was no obvious exit strategy. The car-park was hemmed in on three sides by windowless building walls and the presidents were between them and the only exit. Their options seemed severely limited.

Still, Tanner thought, there are two advantages to being outnumbered when you are being attacked. The first is that it makes your attackers cocky, and the second is that they can tend to get in each others' way. Both of these factors could work to his and Julie's benefit.

Tanner turned to face the man on the end nearest to him, making himself look scared which wasn't necessarily that difficult. Tanner backed away two steps and the president moved after him, his two nearest pals hanging back to give him space whilst the fourth went for Julie. Tanner hoped that Julie's Thai self-defence was as good as she had said — he couldn't do anything immediately to help her. Tanner suddenly changed direction, moving forward rather than back and got a vital split second of surprise and indecision from his attacker. Tanner ducked inside the man's swing and hit him hard in the solar plexus. He gave a funny sort of whistling grunt and fell away, leaving Tanner holding his bat. Tanner kicked him in the head as he went down — nobody said he had to play fair, and he was worried about Julie.

As he turned to face the other three men, Tanner found that he needn't have worried.

He saw the one who had gone after Julie subside to the ground having been struck with commendable force on the side of the head by a marmalade jar swung at the end of a plastic carrier bag. Not quite as effective as a club Tanner mused, but certainly more original.

The two remaining presidents found themselves in the unsettling position of having both the numerical odds and also the weaponry odds evened. Julie looked at though she could wield her confiscated baseball bat at least as effectively as the jar of marmalade. Tanner took advantage of the momentary hesitation and started moving towards one of the attackers as Julie backed slowly away from the other. Tanner's target moved back himself, which meant that Tanner was able to switch direction again and clout Julie's president on the back of the skull with a satisfying thud. He went down and lay motionless in a puddle.

The last man, finding the odds suddenly two to one against, turned and ran. They let him go.

Tanner turned to look at Julie.

'You OK?'

She nodded.

'Fond of marmalade in Thailand, are they?' he asked.

Julie nearly managed a smile.

'I'm going to have to buy another new jar; I think I must have broken that one.'

'Some people have no consideration.' Tanner managed to refrain from commenting that the guy had come to a sticky end. He was very proud of his self-control.

'That was sneaky.' Julie nodded towards the motionless form of Tanner's second victim.

'It's not just the ungodly who can fight dirty.'

Tanner rang the police on his mobile, requesting their attendance as well as an ambulance. Julie went round and removed the facemasks. None of the attackers looked familiar, nor did they show much sign of wanting to wake up so they had a quiet five minutes before the first police car arrived, closely followed by the ambulance.

Two minutes later, two CID officers turned up, one of whom was a detective sergeant Tanner knew by sight. Fortunately, he recognized one of the attackers as a thug with a long record, which helped to rubbish any defence they might have put up as being four innocent bruisers on their way to participate in a fetish baseball match when they were suddenly set upon by an unarmed man and woman.

Julie and Tanner's statements were taken verbally whilst the attackers, who had all regained varying degrees of consciousness, were inspected by the ambulance crew. Two were declared fit to be transported to the police station whilst the other (Tanner's second victim) was taken to hospital with mild concussion. The detective sergeant — vastly amused by the idea of marmalade being used as a defensive weapon — sent his colleague off in the ambulance with the third prisoner and the other two were put in the police car and taken away. All three ex-presidents maintained a sullen silence throughout this process.

Tanner and Julie undertook to call in to the police station the following morning to sign written versions of their statements and were then allowed to go back up to Julie's flat. The detective sergeant insisted on going with them to see them safely into the flat, just in case anyone else was laying in wait. No further attackers materialized, but they were both rather glad of the extra support. Despite what might be inferred from the antics of fictional private eyes, being attacked by four armed men was not a normal part of Tanner's daily routine.

★   ★   ★

Once the detective sergeant had gone, Julie motioned Tanner through into the lounge. She walked stiffly and felt as if she was on auto-pilot as reaction to the evening's excitement began to set in. Tanner felt a little shaky himself and was poised to demonstrate his prefect house training by volunteering to make them some coffee whilst Julie sat down and tried to relax.

'I miss her so much.' Julie slipped off her coat and laid it across a chair. 'And then those bastards . . . ' Her voice caught and she started shaking. She cupped her hands over her eyes and turned away. 'I'm sorry, I . . . '

'That's OK.' Tanner moved across, turned her gently towards him and held her in his arms, stroking her back and saying some of the meaningless things that tend to be spoken on such occasions. How, Tanner reflected bitterly, can it possibly be all right?

After the first moment, when she seemed about to pull away, Julie melted forward and clung on to Tanner, her body soft against his, her arms round him holding him tightly, her face buried in his shoulder. They stood like that for some time. At first, Tanner was just holding her, giving her the comfort of another human body to cling on to. Then she hugged him a little closer and he returned the hug.

They were never sure afterwards who started to take advantage of whom first. Suddenly they were kissing, a tentative brush of the lips first, then something more. The attraction they had been feeling towards each other since they first met, coupled with Julie's need for release and reaction to the attack built up to an explosion of emotion that they doubted if they could have controlled even if they'd wanted to. It made everything else irrelevant. They barely managed to get the clothes off each other without leaving them in shreds on the floor and they made love with such mutual ferocity and greed that it was almost as if Julie needed to beat her grief from her body.

Afterwards, they lay naked on the sofa in each other's arms in a dazed mutual ecstasy.

Julie moved slightly and lifted herself up on to one elbow to look into Tanner's face, her hair sweeping down across his cheek and bare chest.

'My God,' she said, 'I needed that.'

Tanner started to laugh.

Julie was suddenly grinning at him, her face lighting up in a way that he had always known that it could. She snuggled in even closer beside him. Some part of the twisted mass of grief and rage and hate that she had been carrying inside her for weeks had finally dissolved away.

'It is a well-known scientific fact that after being affected by a traumatic death people need to affirm life.' Tanner told her.

Julie considered that solemnly for a moment.

'And I thought I just needed a good shag.' Her eyes gleamed impishly. 'I didn't realize scientific experiments could be so much fun.'

'You do need exactly the right apparatus.'

She giggled.

'Of course, you realize this means that you are getting involved with a needy emotional cripple?' She was watching his face seriously.

Tanner moved his head and kissed her gently.

'I have fallen in love with a beautiful, clever, foxy lady and I have never felt happier in my life.'

'That sounds good to me.' She paused. 'Foxy?'

'It's a compliment,' he assured her. 'It may be a little sexist, but it's definitely a compliment.'

'That's all right then. It's the motive that counts.'

'Did I also mention the brilliant sex?'

'That could have been a one-off fluke,' she pointed out, the sparkle returning to her eyes.

Tanner grinned at her.

'There's only one way to find out.'

They decided after a period of prolonged scientific research that it had definitely not been a fluke.

5

It is a curious fact that it was a combination of Reggie Gray's weak bladder and poor sense of direction that provided the key which unlocked a trail of fear and death.

Reggie Gray was not in himself a very prepossessing person. A small, rat-like figure with a narrow face, shifty eyes and a pointed nose, he had lived off crime all of his life. He was a bully and a coward, a nasty if not uncommon mixture that led to his having been employed by a number of more intelligent people as a combination of messenger and enforcer. He was particularly effective in passing on unpleasant messages to those who were less violently inclined than he was. His specialist weapons were the knuckle-duster and the razor, both of which he could use very effectively, particularly if the victim was caught off guard, from behind, or was being held down. His current employer was Harry Milton, who called himself a business-man but was called a great many other things by both the police and others who came into contact with him.

On this particular evening, at the same

time that Tanner and Julie were dining together, Gray was driving back towards Havenchester from an errand in Birmingham that had concerned a deal involving the distribution of certain illegal substances in which his current employer had significant financial involvement. The person he had been sent to see had made the painful mistake of skimming rather more than his allotted percentage from the transactions in which he had been involved. Gray had left his victim regretting his greed with a face that was unlikely to be completely repaired.

The cold and heavy rain was a combination that aggravated Gray's difficulties. There had been an accident just north of Birmingham involving a heavy lorry that had caused a delay and two-mile tailback, which had eased neither Gray's temper nor his bladder. He had left the motorway a few junctions further south than usual in order to avoid the chaos and, although he was still travelling generally north, he had managed to get himself lost amongst some of the villages which are dotted about around the outskirts of Havenchester, much of which was still determinedly rural, despite the apparent wish of both local and central government to build houses wherever they could.

He found himself following a winding road

with a perimeter of tall, looming trees and becoming increasingly more desperate for somewhere he could both relieve and refresh himself. The road curved to the right and, as he rounded the bend, he saw that there was a light ahead. He slowed down and peered through the rain-spattered windscreen. The light came from a small pub that stood back from the road. As if by a sign, the rain started to ease and it had stopped altogether as he drove down the side of the pub to the car-park at the rear. Out of force of habit, he drove to the unlit back of the car-park and switched off his engine. Wasting no time, he ran across the puddle-covered gravel surface and entered the warmth of the pub with relief.

The pub was not packed, although there was still a reasonable number of people and a loud hum of noise. Apart from a couple of disinterested glances from people by the door, no one had paid him any attention as he went in. Gray dealt with his most pressing concern first and then made his way to the bar to order a pint of beer. He placed his order with the barmaid, paid, took a welcome sip and, leaning his back against the bar, turned to survey the pub and its clientele as he absorbed its warmth and atmosphere. There were tables dotted around and a number of dark nooks in angles of the walls, although not all were occupied. A noisy darts match was underway on the opposite side of the bar and a young man nearby was pumping money into a slot machine with intense concentration. The machine was giving out a lot of bright lights but not much in the way of cash. Gray pulled a face. Despite having most of the vices, gambling was surprisingly not one of them and he rather despised those who he saw as pouring their money away. He carried on with his survey of the pub's occupants.

He almost missed seeing them. A couple were sitting at a small table in a dark corner away from the main bar area, their heads close together as they engaged in what was clearly an animated and intimate conversation. Gray's glance swept past them, then registered what he had seen and moved back again. He paused with his glass to his lips, staring in stupefied amazement. He had never seen the man before in his life, but the woman he knew very well indeed. She had long, honey-coloured hair, a pretty face and, even though he could see little of it from that angle, he knew that she had a curving, well-proportioned body. Her name was Beverly Wallace and the only man she should have been in intimate conversation with was

Harry Milton. As Gray watched, the man reached out and took Beverly's hand, leaned over and kissed her on the lips. It was a long, self-absorbed kiss and dispelled any doubt that the relationship between them was passionate.

For a few moments, Gray was not sure what to do. Constructive thought — unless it involved razors or heavy, blunt instruments — was not his strong suit. Beverly Wallace and her companion did not seem to have spotted him and he realized that it would be best if they were kept in ignorance of his presence. He turned his back to them and moved further round the bar to where he was shielded from the direct view of the corner table by other customers. Gray took his mobile phone from his pocket and, under the guise of making a call, manoeuvred himself into a position from which he could take photographs of Beverly and her companion. That provided the evidence in case Milton didn't believe him. Gray finished his drink in three quick swallows, put his glass down on a convenient side table and made his way back to the door, careful not to look in Beverly Wallace's direction. Outside, he buttoned his short car coat and stepped out into the night. There was still some dampness in the air, but the worst of the rain seemed to be over for now.

Gray paused and looked round, searching for the familiar car. He saw it, parked to the left and in the shadow of a side wall. He checked the number plate just to make sure. Yes, it was definitely Beverly's car. What the hell was she playing at? Well, it was actually pretty obvious what she was playing at, Gray grinned wolfishly as he thought of that, but two-timing Harry Milton was a good way to find yourself in a ditch with a bullet in the head — if he was feeling generous. A cheating girlfriend would face something much more prolonged. She must be mad. Gray's smile broadened. If he was lucky, he might get a chance to participate in the punishment. He felt a stirring of anticipation as he thought of that.

Moving towards his car, Gray considered his options. He could follow Beverly's boyfriend and find out where he lived. Or, he could get back to Milton's house so that they would be waiting there to accuse her when she arrived home. He decided on the latter course. He had noticed a signpost at a T-junction just beyond the pub, so once he got his bearings he should easily be able to beat Beverly home; she had seemed in no hurry to leave. He would get back to Milton's house as quickly as possible. It would be fun to be there when she walked in unsuspectingly to face Milton's anger and he was sure she would soon tell them who the man was and where he could be found.

Gray got into his car and drove slowly out of the pub car-park. There was no sign of anyone else leaving. He should have plenty of time. He turned right on to the road and drove up towards the T-junction. Stansfield, an area of prosperous houses and even more prosperous owners situated on the outskirts of the city, was one of the places signposted to the right. With a nod of satisfaction, Gray turned that way.

The new road was unlit past the junction. Once again, tall trees bordered the road and soon the only light was from his headlights carving into the darkness. After a couple of miles, there was no sign of further habitation and no more signposts. There had been a couple of what appeared to be minor roads leading off from his road and Gray began to panic that he had missed his turning. The road was narrow and winding and had several deep puddles that threw water against the side of his car as he drove on, speeding up gradually as his anxiety built until he was travelling far too fast for the wet and muddy conditions.

Without warning, it started to rain heavily

again. Gray cursed as his windshield became suddenly obscured and the road dipped steeply downhill. He switched on the wipers in time to see the black and white zigzag warning of a curve looming up in his lights. He panicked and braked sharply, sending the car into a spin. The car skidded off the road between two trees and careered down a grassy slope before smashing headfirst into an old oak that had withstood the ravages of the centuries and had no intention of giving way to a cheap motor car.

Gray was jerked forward with the impact, his head smacked against the edge of the windscreen with a nasty thud and he slumped back in his seat, unconscious, blood trickling down the side of his face. The car lights had gone out when the car hit the tree, the engine died and silence and darkness returned. When the next car went past on the road five minutes later, the few signs that there were of the accident were hidden by the darkness and the rain.

★   ★   ★

Beverly Wallace drove up to the tall, wrought-iron gates and stopped. After a few moments the camera set into the brickwork of the right-hand post recorded her identity and the gates swung open. Beverly drove up to the front of the large 1930s house in Stansfield and pressed a switch under the dashboard. The doors to the double garage swung up and she drove in. She got out of the car, walked back outside and took a small remote control from her shoulder bag to close it again. She glanced at her watch. Eleven o'clock. Not too bad. Her stomach tightened at the thought of what she had to do that night, but she pushed the spurt of fear to the back of her mind. She must not do anything to raise any suspicions.

She let herself into the house and was just unbuttoning her coat when Harry Milton came out of his study into the large square hall. He stopped and looked at her, a smile on his face.

'Hello, Beverly — have a good evening?' He was a tall, well-built man with a narrow face and broad, square shoulders. He kept himself in good physical condition and the solid body was well muscled. When you saw him for the first time, he seemed amiable, even jovial, but if you looked into his eyes, there was a cold, calculating indifference that was anything but reassuring. He wore an expensive three-piece dark-blue suit with a thin white stripe, a pale-blue shirt and matching tie. He was always immaculately and expensively dressed, nearly always in a suit and tie, even when the weather was hot. He walked across to her and ran one hand up inside her coat as he drew her towards him.

'Yes, thank you,' she smiled, and managed to return the passion in the kiss that he gave her, as his big hand caressed her breast, squeezing it a little too hard and causing her to breathe in sharply.

'How is your sister?'

Milton liked to keep control of his employees and to constantly remind them that he could manipulate their lives. He was also pleased if, like Beverly, they had some spirit and an inclination to defiance; it meant that he felt even more power when they obeyed him. He allowed Beverly the freedom to go out but he always wanted to know where she was. A few months before she had started going to dance classes twice a week. Milton liked to move in rich social circles and had the money to indulge himself. He attended a number of social functions with other businessmen, some more scrupulous than he was and a few others less so. Beverly usually attended such functions with him and it added a touch of class when she could dance well, in addition to looking stunning in the expensive dresses he brought for her.

Beverly was also allowed to visit her sister

on a regular basis. Milton did not know that her evenings out often had little to do with learning new steps — not for dancing purposes, anyway — and that she had only seen her sister twice in the last three months.

'She's fine, thanks.' Beverly knew that Milton couldn't care less how her sister was. She gave a not wholly fictitious yawn. 'God, I'm bushed tonight; I think I'll turn in — unless you need me?'

Milton was obsessive about cleanliness, if he did want her she would have time to take the shower that would be needed to wash away more than just sweat and dirt.

'I may pop along later, but I've got some business to finish now.' He smiled, squeezed her breast again and turned back to the study.

The 'business' was probably waiting for Reggie Gray to report in. Beverly knew that he had gone out on an errand that afternoon. She hid a shiver and walked up the wide staircase to her first-floor bedroom. A number of Milton's employees and acquaintances frightened her, but Gray gave her the creeps as well. Comparing Gray to Milton was like being scared of a snake compared to being scared of a lion. At least the lion had some outward appearance of being soft and cuddly, even if you knew he wasn't really.

Beverly had been Milton's lover for over

two years, since he had spotted her working as a hostess in one of his clubs. They had separate bedrooms because he often kept late hours and he made a pretence of not wanting to disturb her. The truth was that he liked to keep her on her toes and on occasion would come in after she was asleep and expect her full attention. He didn't single her out for that sort of treatment, he kept all of his staff alert and ready to respond to his needs, whether related to business or pleasure. She knew that he saw her as just another of his employees, there to serve his needs and respond to his demands and to be removed when she became ineffective or troublesome, or he grew bored with her. After more than two years, she was aware that her position had lasted longer than many before her. That made what she was about to do a lot easier, if not less nerve-racking.

She got to her room and closed and locked the door. The bedroom was dominated by the large double bed that stood to the right of the door below a mirrored ceiling.

Beverly draped her coat over the end of the bed, crossed to the windows and drew the curtains. She undressed, went into the ensuite bathroom and took a shower. The hot water relaxed her a little and she quickly washed and dried herself. Putting on her dressing-gown, she walked back into the main bedroom. It irritated her that she had to behave as if there was something wrong about her secret affair, when she knew that it was her relationship with Milton that was grubby and demeaning. Still, after today there would be no more grabbing illicit pleasure in smelly hotel rooms and the back of a car, like cheating adulterers or fumbling teenagers. She hugged herself and felt a thrill of pleased anticipation coupled with the ache of fear at what Milton would do if he caught them afterwards — or caught her leaving.

Walking over to the wardrobe, she slid back one of the doors, took down two large suitcases from the top shelf, put them on the bed and unzipped the lids. Quickly and carefully, listening out for the sound of anyone coming upstairs, she packed the cases with clothes and other essentials and the few personal possessions that she valued. A loose floorboard at the back of the wardrobe was lifted and the money and jewellery she had accumulated over the past two years was added to the cases. After checking the wardrobes and the rest of the room to make sure that she hadn't forgotten anything, Beverly closed the bulging cases and put them back into the wardrobe. They were heavy, but she wouldn't have to carry them very far. She put them on the wardrobe floor, hidden as much as possible towards the back behind some long dresses and coats. Milton never looked in her wardrobe, so they should be safe enough there. She left on the top shelf a third case, not quite as large as the others and with a strap that meant she could carry it on her shoulder. That would not be needed until later.

Selecting jeans, a thick polo-neck jumper and some soft-soled trainers, Beverly put them to one side. That was all she could do for now. Her heart beating much faster than the recent activity warranted, she unlocked the door, turned off the light, removed her dressing-gown and got into bed. She lay dozing, the mixture of excitement and fear building inside her and making her toss and turn. She woke from a light doze just after midnight as voices came up the stairs and she felt herself tense as she prayed that Milton would not pay her a visit. He wasn't the most over-sensitive of men, but he was bound to sense the tension inside her if he came to her that night. She relaxed as the familiar voice passed her door and she heard him enter his bedroom. From what she could hear of the conversation, it sounded as though Gray had failed to show up and they couldn't raise him on his mobile. Milton was clearly not best pleased. After a few minutes, she drifted off to sleep again.

It was two o'clock when the soft alarm in her wristwatch awakened Beverly. She got out of bed quickly and dressed as quietly as possible, alert to any noise from the corridor outside. She crept to her door and eased it open. The house was silent and in darkness. Apart from herself and Milton, there were four other regular occupants of the house: Jack Pace, Milton's bodyguard and general enforcer, and Horace Soames, Milton's secretary and accountant, both slept on the same corridor as she did. There were two live-in domestic staff, Janice Gardner, the cook, and Jane Weston, a young woman who was loosely described as a maid but whose job description covered far more than hoovering and dusting and who had formed an attachment with Pace. Gardner and Weston slept in another wing of the house except when Weston was being entertained by Pace, but the other three would be roused if there was any unexpected noise.

Beverly had a small torch in her hand, but did not use it as she moved softly across the landing and felt for the banister rail. A window at the end of the corridor provided a little filtered light from the street outside, enough for her to make her way to the head of the stairs. She went carefully down the stairs, walking at the edge so that they would not creak. At the bottom, she paused again and listened carefully. There was no sound. She walked round to the cupboard under the stairs. Opening the door, she used her torch for the first time as she keyed in the password that switched off the alarm system. The system beeped twice as it turned off and Beverly froze, waiting to see if anyone had been woken by the brief noise. It was a good five minutes before the continued silence gave her the courage to continue.

If anything, it was even more of a strain to go back upstairs once more to her room, knowing she was getting closer to Milton again. There was no convincing explanation that she could think of if he found her wandering around the house in the dark, fully dressed and carrying a torch. Beverly took a few deep breaths at the top of the stairs to steady herself. Once back in her room, she took the cases from the cupboard, put on her coat and put the torch in her shoulder bag. With the empty case slung across her back and carrying the two suitcases, she left her room and carefully locked the door behind her. The longer it took them in the morning to realize that she had gone, the better. She made her way back down the stairs, once again glad that she would not have to carry her cases very far. It might have been more prudent to restrict herself to one main case and the one across her back, but she was determined to take away as much as possible from the last two years — at least in a material sense.

Outside the door to Milton's study, she put down the cases and took from her shoulder bag the duplicate key she had managed to get cut a few weeks before. She had taken Milton's own spare key from his desk and he had almost caught her when she returned it. The thought of what he would have done to her had he realized the truth gave her a moment of blind panic. Beverly took some more deep breaths, eased the key into the lock and turned it carefully. Even the faint click as the lock turned sounded like a crack of thunder in the silent house. This time she did not wait, from now on she needed to move as quickly as was prudently possible. Beverly opened the door, picked up her cases and went inside. It was tiresome having to move the cases with her each time, but if someone did wake up and come downstairs, she would stand still less chance of escaping detection if the cases were standing in the hall.

Putting her cases down just inside the door, Beverly locked the study door from the inside before she switched on her torch again and crossed to the large desk that dominated one side of the room. The room was wood panelled and had heavy leather armchairs and book-lined walls. Some books had been bought for decoration, but Milton had a good collection of volumes on both art and military strategy that he often perused. A number of original oil paintings were hung around the walls. Thick curtains covered the windows, but Beverly did not dare switch on a light in case it shone into the hall from under the door. The room smelt of Milton's strong cigars and gave the impression that his spirit was still in the room, watching her. Although that was just a piece of fancy, Beverly could have done without it slipping into her subconscious at that point. The only sound was the ticking of the ornate Louis XIV-style clock that stood in the centre of the imposing mantelpiece.

On the floor to the left of the desk stood a low table containing a globe. Beverly placed the torch on the edge of the desk and used both hands to move the table to one side. Beneath where the table had stood, a cleverly cut piece of carpet hid a small trapdoor and the door of a safe. It had taken Beverly some time to discover the combination, and she felt her heart thumping as she used it now, crouched by the side of the desk and peering down at the steel door below her. She turned the handle and lifted the door. It swung up and back, without sounding any alarms. Feeling a little happier now that she was so near to getting away, Beverly reached down and began to pack the contents of the safe into her spare case. It was mainly wads of money in pounds, Euros and dollars but there was also some diamonds, some packets of drugs and a small wooden box. Everything went into the case. She zipped the case shut, closed the safe and got to her feet again. Her hands were damp with sweat and she was shaking. She nearly tipped the globe off the table when she replaced it, and that made her sweat even more.

It was even more of a physical effort with the full case across her back and the two suitcases, but she got from the relocked study door to the front door and undid the bolts and the chain that secured it. As she opened the door and felt the cold early morning air cooling her hot forehead, she half expected to hear the alarms go off, but nothing happened. In the distance a police siren could be heard, proving that crime never slept. The thought made her smile wryly to herself as she pulled the front door closed. The snick of the front door lock seemed like a signal, heralding the point from which there was no turning back; all she could do now was to move forward and hope that her plans would work out.

The front drive seemed to go on forever. Beverly wished that she could have used her car, but opening the garage would have been an extra risk. Even if the noise didn't wake anyone, the car's absence was bound to be spotted early in the morning. This way should gain them an extra few hours, and that could be vital. She was trying to walk softly so as not to make too much noise on the gravel, but that in itself was difficult with the weight she was carrying. At least it had stopped raining heavily and there was enough light from the street ahead for her to avoid any obstacles.

At the gate, she put down the cases and stretched her aching arms above her head. She used her key on the gate, opened it, took her cases through and locked it again. The hinges creaked slightly and somewhere a cat called out as if in response. Fortunately, the camera was linked to the alarm system at night so there would be no immediate photographic evidence. The long wide road was deserted, the spaced street lamps giving it a silvery gleam. Beverly crossed quickly to the tall dark skeletal trees that rose from the woodland of the common on the other side of the road. She started walking to the left along a narrow asphalt path, split and crumbling with weeds. About twenty yards along on the right was a narrow muddy lane between the trees and she took that, the soles of her trainers slipping slightly on the damp ground. Her breath was coming in short gasps and there was a stitch in her side, a combination of her tension and the weight she was carrying. She should definitely have packed fewer clothes! The path was now no more than a muddy track and the light from the main road grew dimmer as she walked along, peering ahead to avoid the deeper puddles. Her designer trainers would be getting filthy. Still, she had plenty of money to buy a new pair.

Fifty yards down the lane, backed in where there was a flat grassy space between the trees, a car stood waiting in darkness, its bonnet pointing back the way she had come. There was just enough light in the gloom to make out Beverly's shape and, as she drew near, the driver's door opened and a figure came out and took the cases. Light from the car spilled out across the lane.

They kissed quickly and the driver hugged her.

'You're late, I was getting worried.'

'I was slower than I thought, I didn't want to make a noise.' She helped him to load her cases into the boot of the car as she talked. Relief flooded though her. She didn't have to carry the cases any further and she had got away with it: she was clear of the house without raising the alarm. 'I'm glad I don't have to earn my living as a burglar.' She turned towards him and hugged and kissed him again, feeling the relief turning to desire.

Her companion laughed and pushed her away gently.

'We'd better leave that for later. We don't want to hang around.'

They got into the car and, as the engine started into life, the headlights brought the trees into sharp outline. They drove back up the lane and turned right towards the motorway, away from Milton's house and on the first leg of what they hoped was the road to freedom.

6

When the front door-bell rang at 9.30 Julie and Tanner were sitting in the kitchen enjoying the warmth of the sun beaming through at them from a clear sky. They had just finished a leisurely breakfast, having first carried out a further check after waking up to make certain that what had happened the night before really hadn't been a fluke. They had both showered and Tanner thought that Julie looked delectable in a dark-blue silk kimono-style dressing-gown with a dramatic orange and red dragon pattern. Her hair was tied back loosely and her face looked fresh and very young without any make-up.

'Could you answer it, please, whilst I make myself more presentable?' She got up from the kitchen table, demonstrating that there was nothing but Julie under the kimono.

'My pleasure.' Tanner got up, kissed her, and walked through to the hallway as she went into her bedroom.

Tanner peered through the spy hole to make sure the visitors didn't intend a follow up to the violent activities of the previous evening. When he saw the rather crumpled face on the other side of the door, with its thatch of untidy, straw-coloured hair, he relaxed and opened the door.

'Good morning, Ancient.'

Detective Chief Inspector Richard Mariner grunted a greeting and walked past into the flat.

'Morning, Alec.' Mariner was wearing his usual creased blue suit and wrinkled raincoat and carried a battered briefcase.

'Come through to the lounge,' Tanner said. 'Julie will be out in a minute.'

'Right.' Mariner lowered his lanky form into a chair and placed his case at his feet. He affected a world weary and slightly bored expression that had often led people to assume — incorrectly and to their cost — that he was not particularly alert or clever. In fact, he was both, and was one of the most respected police officers in the Havenchester force.

'Making yourself at home, I see.' He raised an enquiring eyebrow.

'You know that we offer a full service.'

'I hope you aren't — ' He broke off as Julie came in, wearing jeans and a white sweater.

'Good morning Julie.'

'Good morning, sir.'

He stared at her closely for a moment, looked across at Tanner and then back at her.

'You look a lot better than when you first came to see me.'

'I've started to live a bit again. Would you like some coffee?'

'Yes please.'

'Carry on talking — I can hear you in the kitchen.'

'I've come to get your signatures on your written statements, to save you a trip to the station. I've also come to ask you not to start a war on my patch.'

'War?' Tanner tried to look offended. 'We are intent on spreading sweetness and light.'

Mariner didn't look convinced.

'Those goons last night didn't look very sweet after you two had finished with them.'

'Did they say who sent them?'

'No.' The chief inspector shook his head disgustedly. 'They're just local cannon-fodder. They've all refused to make a statement on the advice of their lawyer. There is one interesting thing, though: the man who came to give them legal representation has amongst his other clients one Vincent Bridger.'

Julie came though from the kitchen with three mugs of coffee on a tray.

'I said poking the nest would help,' she remarked.

'How about the van they used?' Tanner asked.

Mariner shook his head. 'Stolen earlier in the evening — just a dead-end.'

'It would be much easier if they used their own registered vehicles, wouldn't it? Crooks have no consideration.'

'Hmm.' He glanced across to the far side of the room where there was a small desk with a computer and other equipment. 'Is that an all in one printer?' He asked.

'Yes.' Julie looked puzzled.

Mariner nodded.

'Very useful, being able to make photo-copies.' He opened his case. 'Here are your statements, if you'd read and sign them.' He paused. 'Well I never,' he said in a dead-pan voice, 'I've put an office file in my case as well by mistake. It is confidential and for official use only, but I'm sure you wouldn't dream of looking in my case, would you?'

'Certainly not.' Julie put the tray down carefully.

'Could I use your bathroom?'

'Of course. The door to the left of the hall.'

'Thank you.'

Once Mariner had left the room, Tanner opened the case and took out the thin file. It contained biographies, addresses and con-tacts for the six potential shooters that Ted

118

Manning had identified. Julie had already switched on the printer and by the time Mariner returned, making some unnecessary noise about it, the file and its papers were back in the case and Julie and Tanner were studiously reading through their statements.

'Well?' Mariner asked.

'It all seems to be in order,' Tanner said, signing. Julie had already signed hers.

'Thank you.' Mariner placed the statements in his case. 'Of course, there's no proof that Bridger instigated the attack on you last night, and I doubt if we'd ever be able to prove it.'

Tanner nodded. 'We wouldn't expect it.'

'So can I ask — unofficially of course — what you intend to do next?'

'The fact that Bridger didn't like the idea of us poking around and asking questions about Jarvis and Hesky suggests that they might be worth looking into,' Julie said. 'I believe I read somewhere that Hesky has an ex-wife. It might be an idea to have a chat with her and get some more background before we do anything else.'

Mariner nodded solemnly.

'I see that you are very well informed. The divorce wasn't exactly harmonious, and there is a son that Hesky tries to see from time to time, so you might get something useful from her.'

'Did you interview her?'

'Not about his possible involvement in the shooting. As I told you, we didn't focus much on locals. I have had dealings with her on other matters, though. She hates the police almost as much as she hates Hesky. After Hesky she took up with someone else and we nicked him for armed robbery earlier this year. She's not very good at choosing her men.'

He finished his coffee.

'Thanks for the drink. Take care of yourselves. You need to watch your backs where Bridger is concerned.'

'We'll be careful,' Julie promised. 'Thanks for your help.'

Mariner got to his feet and picked up his briefcase.

'My help? I don't know what you mean.'

* * *

After Mariner had gone, they sat and read through the information from the copied file. The home and work addresses for Hesky's ex-wife were listed. Hesky and Jarvis shared the same home address, a flat in the south of the city. They decided to leave visiting the prime suspects until they had talked to the ex-wife. If she disliked Hesky as much as Mariner suggested, they might get some useful information from her.

April Thornton, formerly Hesky, worked at City Taxis, a radio taxi company in Kings Road — not to be confused with the London thoroughfare of the same name. Kings Road, Havenchester was long and winding and felt perpetually grey. Even when the sun came out, the light seemed filtered through dirt. The road was lined with a variety of shops and shop front businesses. The brickwork was dirty, the paintwork generally peeling and most windows looked like they could do with occasional contact with clean water. The pavements were cracked and narrow, but there were permitted parking spaces in the road. Most of the cars parked around City Taxis were presumably plying their trade from the establishment, but Tanner managed to find a space fifty yards further along.

The décor inside the shop matched the outside, with drivers sitting around on a padded bench inside the door and a partitioned area towards the back which led to the control centre. A woman's voice could be heard on the phone taking a pick-up instruction. An elderly man with a pronounced beer gut wearing an open-necked striped shirt sat behind the counter.

'Help you?' he asked in a rasping voice.

'We'd like to speak to April Thornton, please.'

He gave them both a curious look, but didn't object. He swivelled round to face the rear of the shop and the woman who sat at a desk with three telephones and some radio equipment.

'Hey, Api, couple 'ere want to talk to yer.'

Tanner wondered, not for the first time, why even the shortest of names often had to be shortened even further.

Mrs Thornton finished giving instructions on the pick-up into the radio, got to her feet and walked across to the counter.

'Yes?' She was tall with a round face, short, curly hair and sharp blue eyes. Her clothes hung a little loosely, as if she had recently lost some weight.

'My name's Alec Tanner and this is my colleague Julie Cooper.' In view of Mariner's comment on her opinion of the police, it didn't seem prudent to give Julie's official title. 'I'm a private investigator and I'd like to ask you a few questions about Sam Hesky.'

Her expression got even sharper as she looked them carefully up and down.

'In trouble is he?'

'Very possibly.'

She nodded.

'I'm due for a ciggy break. Come through and we'll talk in the yard. Take over the phone, will you, Kenny?'

The elderly man nodded, got laboriously out of his chair and moved to the rear of the shop to take over the phone desk. Mrs Thornton opened the door at the side of the partition and beckoned them through. She picked up her handbag from the desk and they followed her to the back of the shop, past a small alcove with a sink and a kettle and an open door that led to a toilet which, judging from the smell, should not have been used without protective clothing and a gas mask. Beyond the staff facilities was another door that she unlocked, taking them through into a small rectangular paved yard. The air quality improved fractionally until she took a packet of cigarettes and a lighter from her handbag, lit up and took in a deep drag on her cigarette, letting the smoke out slowly through her mouth with a sigh.

'Right then,' she said briskly, 'what's all this about?'

'Sam Hesky is your ex-husband?' Tanner asked. She nodded briefly. 'We are undertaking an investigation for a client. The details must remain confidential, but Hesky's name has come up in connection with some activities that have adversely affected our client and we need to look into him further. Do you have much contact with him?'

She shook her head.

'As little as possible.'

'Does he see your son?'

'No.' Mention of the son seemed to have touched a nerve. She took another deep drag at her cigarette. 'Look, why don't you tell me exactly what you want to know?'

Tanner decided that they wouldn't get very far unless he was a bit more informative.

'We are interested in Hesky's whereabouts on a particular day. The eighth February this year. Do you happen to remember that day?'

He didn't have much hope that her memory would be that specific after several weeks, but to his surprise, she gave a snorting sort of laugh and nodded.

'I'm not likely to forget it.' She lit a second cigarette from the stub of the first.

Tanner thought Mrs Thornton might be more open talking to another woman. He gave Julie a glance and she took over.

'Why, what happened?'

'My husband got himself arrested. My current husband, that is.' She shook her head. 'I can certainly pick 'em.' She paused for a moment, presumably to consider her marital track record. It didn't seem to give her much satisfaction. 'They arrested him for armed robbery. Only the idiot tried to make a run for it, jumped over a fence, tripped and broke his ankle. I spent the evening of eighth February in the hospital with him and the copper who was guarding him. Then, when I got home, I found my son had spent the evening with his bastard of a father. I was pretty pissed off, I can tell you.'

Tanner felt a spark of anticipation and sensed that Julie felt the same.

'Was Sam Hesky there?'

'Not likely — he knows better than to come into my house — I've got too many kitchen knives with his name on.' She shook her head. 'No, Jimmy — that's my son — told me. Not that he wanted to, but I caught him at the sink trying to wash blood out of his T-shirt, so he didn't have much option.'

Julie and Tanner exchanged a puzzled glance. If Hesky was one of the two on the motor bike, where had the blood come from? Neither of the bikers had stopped and got close to Julie or her aunt.

'Whose blood was it?'

'His father's. It's a pity the bugger didn't do us all a favour and bleed to death.'

'Did Jimmy tell you what had happened?'

She shrugged.

'Just that his father had rung him earlier in

the evening and told him that he needed his help. Wanted Jimmy to pick him and that prick Jarvis up in his car because they'd been hurt and couldn't drive. I didn't ask any more. Jimmy swore he hadn't been involved in anything criminal himself, so I just told him never to help his father like that again. That's always been my fear — that Sam would drag Jimmy into his world, make a criminal out of him. Jimmy's nineteen now, he's got a decent job, a mechanic in a garage. Not brilliant money, but he's learning a trade. Trouble is, he's always had a soft spot for his dad, can't see through him. He thinks Sam really cares about him.' She thought for a moment. 'I suppose he does care a bit, in a way,' she conceded grudgingly, 'but if push came to shove, Sam would put himself first every time.'

'We'd like to talk to Jimmy,' Julie said gently, aware that they were starting to tread on very dodgy ground.

'No.' The woman shook her head firmly. 'I don't want him involved.'

'It could be very important,' Julie pressed her. 'Please reconsider. We won't involve him with the police, but if he can tell us more about where his father was that night, it could be vital.'

Mrs Thornton paused and looked at them

with a calculating expression.

'If Sam's done what you think he has, would it put him away for a long time?'

'Yes it would; he wouldn't be able to interfere with Jimmy's life any more.'

She nodded slowly.

'I'll need to talk to him first.' She made up her mind. 'Do you know Panters Park — just round the corner from here?'

'I do,' Tanner said.

'Right then. If I can persuade him, we'll meet you there at one o'clock. There are some benches we can sit on.' She thought for a moment. 'I'll tell him that you need to know where his father was so as to clear him from your investigation — if he thinks you're looking to get his father put away, he won't talk.'

Tanner nodded.

'That's OK.'

She wasn't prepared to shop Hesky to the police directly, Tanner decided, but as he and Julie were seen as being one step removed, talking to them was somehow OK within her particular social code; it wasn't like proper grassing. That was one advantage he had over the official police and he certainly wasn't going to complain about it.

'See you later, then.'

She trod her cigarette into the paving

stones, probably wishing it was her ex-husband, and led them back out through the shop.

★　★　★

Panters Park was a rectangular oasis of green in amongst an area of grubby shops and terraced housing. An asphalt path ran round the outside, and at one o'clock it was being used by a couple of joggers who gave the park an appropriate name. As the park was only a line of shops away from a busy main road, the air quality for such exertion was not first class. In fact, as Julie and Tanner sat on a bench looking across the park, they thought they could almost see the air. A few straggly trees reached bare branches up to the now cloudy sky like petrified athletes frozen in the middle of a series of stretching exercises. Some pigeons pecked busily between a set of metal goal posts. The crossbars were bent down in the middle — no doubt, Julie imagined, by some enterprising local youngster.

It was nearly ten past one before Jimmy and his mother arrived and Tanner had started to fear that she hadn't persuaded him to talk to them.

Jimmy Hesky was a lanky lad who seemed

younger than his nineteen years. He wore torn jeans and a scruffy leather jacket over a T-shirt with some sort of rude message on it. His lean, sharp face was spotted with acne and framed by long, curly dark hair and there was a certain animosity coupled with reluctance in his eyes.

'Thank you for agreeing to see us,' Tanner said.

He grunted.

'Mum said it might help Dad.' His voice was a little throaty and, judging from his yellow-stained fingers, he followed his mother's lead in the matter of nicotine intake. As if to confirm Tanner's thoughts, they both lit up as they waited for him to continue.

'We need to talk to you about the eighth February, when your father rang you and asked for your help.'

Jimmy gave his mother a not very filial look.

'What about it? Just between me and my Dad, that is.'

'He's been accused of doing something towards the end of that evening and it sounds as though you know what he was doing.'

'That's rubbish — he couldn't have done anything, he was hurt.' Jimmy broke off and looked down at his hands on his lap, cupped around his cigarette.

'Then that will help him,' Julie put in. 'I think you'd better tell us what happened.'

Tanner thought they were getting quite expert at this good cop, bad cop, business.

'Dad rang me at about eight o'clock.' Jimmy looked out across the park as he spoke. 'Said he and Uncle Harry had been hurt. They couldn't drive, and he wanted me to go and pick them up.'

'Where from?'

'Castle Street. There's a shop there that sells sex stuff, you know?' He gave them a smutty grin. 'He said he'd be in the alley next to the shop. When I got there, I parked by the mouth of the alley and went to get them. They were lying on the ground, out of sight behind some wheelie bins. Harry was unconscious with blood running down the side of his face and Dad was propped up against the wall holding his side. I managed to get them into the car. Harry was still out cold so I dragged him across the pavement and got him in the back. Then I helped Dad into the passenger seat. That's when I got the blood on my T-shirt. I wanted to take them to hospital, but Dad insisted that we went to this doctor he knew. I drove them there, and left them in the car whilst I went and knocked on the door. The doctor didn't want to come at first, but when I told him my father's name, he came out and helped me get them into the house. Harry was coming around a bit by then, though he was still pretty groggy.'

'Did your father tell you what had happened?'

'Not really. He'd been stabbed in the side, that's why he was bleeding and why he couldn't drive himself. He said something about the bastard in the sex shop, but he didn't mention any names or anything.' Jimmy shook his head. 'We got to the doctor's house just after nine. I waited for the doctor to confirm Dad wasn't too seriously hurt and it was half past by the time I left. Dad had a long cut in his side, but it wasn't very deep, it just bled a lot and was very painful and the doctor was going to start stitching it. There's no way either my Dad or Harry was going to be in a fit state to do anything to anybody after that.'

He looked suddenly very vulnerable and pleading. Just a son wanting to protect his dad, even if it was a toe-rag like Hesky.

'That's all I know.'

'OK. Thanks for talking to us,' Tanner said.

'Does it help to clear him?'

Tanner nodded. It wasn't what his mother wanted to hear, but they couldn't please both of them.

'Yes, I think it does.' At least, he thought, it

cleared him of the shooting of Julie and her aunt.

★   ★   ★

'So what do you make of that?'

They had returned to Tanner's car and sat for a moment before driving off.

'It seems to clear Hesky and Jarvis of the shooting,' Tanner said. 'But if so, that poses an interesting question.'

'If Hesky and Jarvis didn't carry out the shooting, why did Bridger send the heavies to attack us?'

'Exactly.'

'So we carry on digging?'

'You're the client, it's your call.'

'I think we need to answer that question, even if it has nothing to do with the shooting. If Bridger is after us, we need to know why.'

'It could be someone else who happens to use the same solicitor.'

'You don't sound very convinced.'

Tanner grinned at her. 'I'm not. Let's pay a visit to Castle Street.'

'You just want an excuse to visit a sex shop.'

Castle Street was a modest thoroughfare of reasonably prosperous shops situated more towards the centre of the city. There was only one shop selling sex aids, books, films and a variety of interesting costumes. It was situated next to an alley, which was a promising confirmation of Jimmy's story.

They went in. The merchandise inside was, as might be expected, far more diverse than that displayed in the window. Julie did a double take at one item hanging on the wall above a rack of DVDs.

'What do you think that's for?'

'Perhaps we should buy one and experiment.'

A young woman was standing behind a long counter reading a magazine and chewing gum. There were no other customers. She looked bored to tears.

'Is the manager around?' Tanner asked.

'He's in the back.' She gave them an uninterested look and gave her gum another chew.

'Could you get him please?'

They didn't seem to be penetrating her boredom. She nodded, turned her head towards an arch behind the counter and called out, 'Herbie, there's someone to see you.'

Herbie turned out to be a short, rotund man wearing tight black trousers, a red frilly shirt and black bow tie.

'Can I help you?' His weak, pale-blue eyes

were hiding behind thick black-rimmed spectacles and he glanced from Julie to Tanner with a half smile hovering nervously round his rather pouting mouth. Tanner couldn't visualize him beating up two street-wise heavies like Hesky and Jarvis.

'We want to talk to you about Vernon Bridger.'

The manager blinked rapidly, came round from behind the counter and shepherded them into a corner of the shop, licking his lips. His assistant didn't look up from her magazine.

'Look,' he hissed in a desperate whisper, 'I'm paying all I can. I can't afford . . . '

Tanner started to get a feel for what the panic was all about. They'd stumbled on to a protection racket. Herbie had misunderstood and thought they had been sent by Bridger. It seemed a good idea not to correct him straight away.

'He's still pretty pissed off by what happened in February,' Tanner told him. Which was probably true, he reflected.

The little man started sweating. Not a pretty sight. Tanner nearly felt ashamed of himself.

'Look, I made a mistake, but I thought that had been sorted out. The other guys said . . . ' His voice rose an octave.

'Hesky and Jarvis?'

'They didn't leave their cards.' The attempt

at mild bravado didn't have much heart in it.

'Who beat them up — it wasn't you?'

'Of course not.' He frowned. 'Don't you know what happened?'

'We aren't told everything.' Tanner hoped Herbie's nerves would keep him talking for a bit longer before his brain kicked into gear and he realized they hadn't been sent by Bridger.

'After they came for money the first time, I asked a friend of mine to come and stay with me,' Herbie said. 'He was a big guy; he worked out at the gym and could look after himself. When they came back the second time, my friend beat the shit out of them and threw them out.'

'How did Hesky get stabbed?'

'Hesky pulled the knife; my friend was just defending himself, he . . . ' The pale eyes widened as he realized what he had been saying. 'Just a minute, who the hell are you?' He tried, very unsuccessfully to sound belligerent. It was like being growled at by a hedgehog.

'Private detectives.' Tanner decided the misunderstanding had got them as far as it could. 'We're looking at the two men for something else that happened that night.'

'My God.' His voice got even squeakier and he started shaking like one of his own products. 'You've conned me. Get out.'

'We know most of it now; you might as well tell us the rest.'

'Bridger will kill me.'

'He won't need to know you've spoken to us.'

Herbie shook his head stubbornly.

'Look,' Julie took over. 'Whatever you tell us, we won't be talking to Bridger. But what you know could help put him out of business, which can only help you. What happened to your friend?'

'I don't know,' he said eventually, shaking his head miserably. 'I really don't. Nothing happened for a couple of weeks and I thought maybe we'd put them off. Then one afternoon my friend went out for a walk and never came back. Those two men came back again that evening and said that I wouldn't see him again and if I didn't pay for protection, I'd disappear too. I was petrified. I agreed to start paying.'

'What was your friend's name?'

'Salvador Sanchez. He called himself Sally.'

'Didn't he have any friends or relatives who'd want to know what happened to him?'

'No. He never saw his family; they washed their hands of him when he came out. His friends here just think he's moved on to London. I was his only really close friend.'

'Didn't you want to avenge him?'

Herbie started shivering again and shook his head.

'We weren't *that* close.'

★   ★   ★

Back in the car again, they had another case conference.

'Well, that makes things a bit clearer.' Julie said. 'Bridger runs a protection racket as one of his many sidelines. He probably focuses on those shops whose trade wouldn't bear too much looking into, so the owners are less likely to go to the police. Hesky and Jarvis do the collecting.'

Tanner nodded.

'When we said we'd look into Hesky and Jarvis, Bridger was afraid we'd find out about what happened the same night as the shooting. He wasn't worried about us proving Hesky and Jarvis killed your aunt, he was afraid we'd find out about Sally. That's why he wanted us taken out of action.'

'So we can cross them off our list.'

'But not before we get them added to Mariner's. Even if Sanchez's body has never been found, we can tell Ancient who did it and when, so he might be able to find some sort of trail.'

7

Of all Harry Milton's employees, it was, oddly enough, Horace Soames who was least afraid of him. Even Jack Pace was more concerned than Soames at ensuring that he did not antagonize his employer. This was not due to any physical prowess on Soames's part — he was a small, dapper man with a perpetually calculating expression and pale-blue eyes behind gold-rimmed spectacles. He was, however, the most irreplaceable of all the employees. Thugs and strong-arm men are easy enough to come by — although those with real intelligence like Jack Pace, perhaps less so — but Soames had brains and a financial acumen that enabled him to assess the potential profitability of any scheme, whether legal or illegal, with impressively constant accuracy. He also knew where Milton's financial skeletons were buried, having interred most of them himself. He was pedantic and fussy, with an abhorrence of both dirt and violence, or, at least, of coming into contact with them himself. Even so, Soames was careful not to upset Milton, whose temper was never the most stable of his attributes.

The morning after Beverly had run away, Soames was being extremely careful, running everything he was about to say silently through his mind before committing it to his mouth. Milton, when he realized what had happened, had gone beyond anger to a quiet but intense rage that threatened to erupt at any moment. One wrong word, gesture or facial expression would be enough. It would be like treading on a sleeping cobra or teasing a shark with tooth ache.

Jack Pace had been the first to realize that something was wrong. He was usually the first in the household to get up and had been in the habit of touring the house as soon as he was awake and dressed to make sure everything was still secure. He had raised the alarm when he had discovered that the alarm was not, as it were, on to be raised. After checking that Milton had not been harmed and that there was no sign of any obvious theft or damage, Pace had returned to the study where Milton, in dressing-gown and pyjamas, his temper already approaching boiling point, sat with Soames, who as always was immaculately dressed and externally calm.

At first, Milton had accused Pace of not setting the alarm, an accusation which Pace had immediately rejected, pointing out that Milton had been standing next to him when he had done so on their way upstairs after their abortive wait for Reggie Gray. It had then occurred to the three men that Beverly Wallace had not yet been roused and Pace was sent to her room to fetch her. He returned a few minutes later to report that the door had been locked and when he opened it with his master key, Beverly was not there.

'Could she have been abducted?' Soames asked.

Pace shook his head.

'I doubt it. There's no sign of a struggle and no note. It looks as though some clothes and suitcases are gone.' He spoke woodenly, careful to let no emotion show on his face or in his voice as he reported to Milton.

That was when Milton's anger began to spill over.

'It looks like the bitch has done a runner then.' He frowned. 'Why would she do that?' He was genuinely puzzled. A man who lived for material gain alone, he judged everyone one else by his own standards. 'She wasn't being mistreated and I give her anything she wants — ' He broke off suddenly and swore.

Soames was only milliseconds behind Milton's reasoning and he looked on in horror as Milton rushed over to the desk, moved the table to one side, almost dislodging the globe in his haste, and knelt by the floor. He could barely control his fingers as they scrabbled at the carpet, but eventually the safe door was uncovered. When the safe was open, Milton sat back on his heels and started swearing in earnest. Soames walked across and stood behind him, looking down into the empty cavity.

'How much?' Milton asked hoarsely.

Soames couldn't speak for a moment and then his brain clicked into gear.

'Half a million in currency, as much again in diamonds, another million in drugs. And in the box . . . '

He didn't need to complete the sentence.

Milton turned his head to look at Pace. His face was stiff and calm, but Pace had never seen such hatred in his boss's eyes.

'I want you to get her back, Jack. I don't care what you have to do, who you have to bribe or trample on to do it. Just get her back.' He looked at each of the two other men in turn. 'If word gets out that I've been shafted by that tart, I'll be a laughing stock and that will never do — it will affect business.' He focused on Pace and his voice got even colder. 'But it's more than that, Jack, this is personal. No one does something like this to me. You get my stuff back and you bring her to me.' He closed the safe and got slowly to his feet. 'And I want her alive. I don't care if you have to damage her a bit, but I want her alive so I can finish her off myself, slowly.'

'Right.' Pace nodded. 'I'll get the word round to keep an eye out for her. Then I'll go and see her sister. She works for Bridger, so I won't have any trouble if — '

He broke off as his mobile phone rang.

'Sorry, Harry.'

For a moment, Soames thought that might be the spark to set Milton off, but Milton just nodded and Pace took the call.

'Yes?' Pace frowned and then rolled his eyes. 'He's what?' He shook his head. 'Right. Which hospital? Yeah — I've got that, thanks for ringing.' He switched the phone off and looked across at Milton. 'That was Reggie's sister. He crashed his car on his way back here last night. They took him to the Royal Hospital. Nothing's broken, but he was unconscious and he's only just come round. He'll probably be in hospital for a couple of days.'

'Stupid pillock.' Milton was more worried about losing someone who could help in the hunt for Beverly Wallace than he was about Gray's health.

'At least if he was coming back into the city he should have finished his job,' Pace commented.

Milton grunted.

'There's only one job that's important now,' he said. 'Find Beverly Wallace and bring her in.'

⋆　⋆　⋆

At the moment when Harry Milton was expressing a wish to find her, Beverly rolled over in bed and opened her eyes. Sunlight was coming into the small bedroom through thin curtains, illuminating the low-beamed ceiling, the simple furnishings and the thin mat on the floor by the bed. There remained a faint musty smell from the cottage being locked up and unused, even though she had left the bedroom window ajar. She always slept with the curtains drawn and a window open and she suddenly realized that she had no idea whether Jeffrey did too. She could hear the soft sound of his breathing beside her and deeper sound of the sea beyond the window forming a background to the sharp, constant call of the gulls that she knew would be circling the cliff top, hunting their breakfast. The thought of breakfast made her feel suddenly hungry herself. She stretched and turned to look at the man lying beside her. He seemed very young, almost boyish lying asleep with a lock of dark straight hair falling across his face. She smiled at him, leant across and kissed him.

Jeffrey Jones, known generally as JJ, opened one eye and yawned.

'Good morning.' He spoke thickly as he rolled over to face her. 'What time is it?'

She looked at the silver watch that she always wore to bed, often with nothing else.

'Nine-thirty.'

Jones groaned and ran his hands over his face. He felt as though he hadn't had any sleep at all. Memories from the night before came flooding back. Waiting in the woods, tense and worried, for Beverly to arrive. Imagining all the things that could go wrong and what would happen if they did. The immense relief when she came, labouring under the weight of her cases. The two-hour drive to the cottage that he had only visited twice before and never in the dark. The constant glances at the rear mirror for signs of pursuit and near panic on the few occasions when headlights got too close. Relief when they finally arrived after twice losing their way. Eventually crawling into bed and tossing and turning for ages despite his exhaustion, reliving what they had just been

144

through and suddenly aware of the import of what they had done and the danger they were in.

At first, the plan had seemed exciting and romantic, a fitting extension of their passionate love affair. He had first met Beverly when she had come to take individual lessons at the dance school where he worked and he had been her teacher. She was a natural mover, but needed to learn the steps and the discipline of the ballroom dances. The first two or three visits had been purely professional. There had been an immediate easiness between them and they talked and joked as they danced. The mutual attraction had developed quickly and, as he held her and took her through the dance steps, they had started whispering to each other, carefully testing to see if each felt the same, making sure that they weren't overheard by the other couples on the floor.

She told him she was living with a man she didn't love, didn't even respect, but whom she feared. She had plenty of material things, but he gave her nothing else and wanted only one thing from her. Eventually, he would tire even of that and she knew that then she would be cast off to end up only God knew where and doing only God knew what — although she could have a pretty good guess.

You didn't put her current occupation on your CV — at least, not on most CVs.

Their whispers had led to the first of the phantom dance lessons, when she had told Milton that she needed extra tuition and had met Jones at an hotel where the feelings they had been developing were consummated. More meetings followed. She learnt her dance steps easily, so she just had to pretend to Milton that she was finding it more difficult than she really was and the extra lessons were justified. Jones found out more about her, more about the man Milton whom she feared so much. Visits to hotels were supplemented by uncomfortable manoeuvrings in the back of Jones's car parked down wooded lanes or behind abandoned factories. Eventually, the surreptitious meetings were not enough and they decided to run away. Jones resigned from the dance school, giving a month's notice and they decided that they would leave at the end of that time.

Jones had an Irish friend from his student days who owned a boat and would be able to get them across to Ireland. The friend also had somewhat dubious contacts who would be able to produce forged passports and other documents. From Ireland, with new names, they would get to America and disappear. One of the reasons they had to lie low in the

146

cottage for a few days rather than try to leave the country immediately by boat or plane was to give the friend a chance to get the documents ready. He and his contacts insisted on cash on delivery and wouldn't start preparing the documents until Beverly had escaped with Milton's money so that she had the cash to pay for them.

Milton himself had many contacts in the US, so it was imperative that they were able to create new identities and have the money to set themselves up with new lives. With the contacts Milton's organization could call upon, using conventional transport links in Beverly's own name would be suicide in either Britain or America. In these days of computerized information, you only needed to grease one or two key palms and the information could be easily accessed. Beverly knew Milton was bound to come after them anyway, so she might as well steal from him as well in order to fund their new lives. It was, she thought, a bit like a witness protection programme except that it would be funded by the person they needed to be protected against. She rather liked the poetic justice of that. At least Milton wouldn't call in the police, although if they had to be found out, better the police than Milton's people. Also, with luck, Milton wouldn't find out about JJ, at least for a while, and that would make it more difficult to track them.

Beverly had lived her whole life under the control of men she had not been able to choose — first her violent father, then a succession of low-life chancers who had only wanted her for her body, and finally Milton, who was the same but with money to spend. Now she had chosen her man herself and that gave her an immense feeling of freedom and release, almost as if she had been reborn, despite the enormous danger that she faced as a result of that choice.

Their refuge was a cottage owned by Jones's brother, who was a financial trader in London and who owned a cottage on the northwest coast that he could use when he wanted to get back to his northern roots — which he did about three times a year. He had been happy for JJ to use the cottage for a few days, without knowing exactly why he needed it, and they planned to stay there until Jones's friend arrived in his boat, which was scheduled for three days' time. Until then, all they could do was lie low and hope Milton wouldn't trace them.

The cottage was a simple wooden dwelling on the top of a cliff above a shallow bay. There were a few other cottages around, but none within sight. A number of trees and thick bushes covered the cliff top, providing natural seclusion for each dwelling. A steep path led down from their cottage to the crescent-shaped beach, which was shallow enough for Jones's friend to pick them up in a dinghy. Beyond the cove to the right could be seen a narrow spit of land with a disused lighthouse on it. The nearest village was nearly two miles away by road. A narrow track led from the cottage to an only slightly wider B-road bordered by thick hedges and woods. There was little chance of anyone stumbling on their hideout by accident.

Jones intended to drive to the village later that morning for provisions and if asked would simply say that he was a keen bird watcher and was staying alone in his brother's cottage for a few days' holiday.

All these events and plans crowded back into Jones's mind as Beverly kissed him again. Yes, it was all going to be worth it. He kissed her back, tiredness slipping away from him. She pulled away with a laugh.

'Down, Fido. Plenty of time for that later. Sorry to wake you, but I couldn't sleep. I'm too excited and too hungry. Do you want some breakfast?'

He smiled ruefully and sat up against the pillows.

'I'll need to go into the village for some stuff — milk and bread and things. There's some tinned food in the kitchen, but nothing perishable. I'll get enough for two or three days, I want to keep the trips to the village to a minimum, just in case. Maybe make one more trip at the most.'

He swung his legs out of bed and reached for where he had left his clothes, hanging over an old wooden chair.

'Don't worry.' Now that she had escaped Milton's house, Beverly was feeling much more relaxed. She put her arms round his shoulders, starting to regret that she had put satisfying her hunger ahead of satisfying other needs. 'We are quite safe now; there's no way Milton can find us here, and he has no idea that you exist.'

★   ★   ★

There were few similarities between Horace Soames and Chief Superintendent Leo Jason, but one was their mutual dislike of hospitals. Although Milton had been less than sympathetic about Reggie Gray's accident, Soames had felt that someone from the organization should go to see him, if only to make sure that there were no adverse implications arising from it for them. It also gave him an excuse to be out of the house and away from Milton's volatile temper.

The Royal was Havenchester's biggest hospital, recently rebuilt on a new site at considerable expense and public disquiet at the closure of two other hospitals with Accident and Emergency facilities. Its glass walls sprawled over a considerable area and contained a maze of corridors that seemed to stretch for miles. By the time Soames had found a space for his car in the massive (and expensive) car-park, located Gray's ward on the fifth floor of the east tower and found his way there, it was well past midday and he was beginning to feel that it would have been preferable to stay at home and risk annoying his employer.

Gray was sitting propped up in bed with a bandage round his head. Not particularly photogenic at the best of times, his pasty face and bloodshot eyes looked even worse than usual. He was never one of the sharpest knives in the drawer, but even so, he wasn't usually as close to the spoon family as he now appeared. His face held a slightly dazed and unfocused look and his voice sounded thick and slurred.

'How are you feeling?' Soames asked, trying to sound as though he cared. He found a green moulded plastic chair with springy metal legs that was presumably for the use of visitors and sat down gingerly. The legs squeaked on the linoleum floor.

'I've got a foul headache and some nasty bruises, otherwise not too bad.' Gray's answer took a while to come, as if his brain was labouring in first gear. He reached across to the cabinet at the side of the bed, lifted a glass of water in a shaky grasp and took a deep swallow. Soames reflected with sardonic amusement that it was probably the first time since his voice had broken that Gray had drunk his water neat.

'What happened?' Soames took the glass from Gray and replaced it on the cabinet, more through fear of his trousers getting drenched than from any desire to be helpful.

'I was trying to get back to the house quickly and got lost on a back road.' Gray considered the question carefully as if it he was being asked for a complex mathematical formula. 'It was dark and raining and I misjudged a turning and hit a tree. I don't remember all that much about it. The doctor reckons I was lucky not to have done more damage.' He leant back against his pillows and closed his eyes.

'What did the police say?' Soames didn't want him dozing off until he had made sure there wouldn't be any comeback to the organization as a result of the accident. Milton had enough on his plate without being involved in some piddling police enquiry as a result of Gray's carelessness.

Gray opened his eyes again and managed to focus on Soames's face.

'I wasn't over the limit and the car was only a couple of years old, so they accepted that it was just an accident in the bad weather. No one else was injured and there wasn't any property damage, so they're not going to take any further action.'

'Good.' Soames sat back in his chair, causing it to rock alarmingly on its springy legs. He leant forward again rapidly. 'Why were you in such a hurry anyway?'

Gray sat up a bit straighter in bed, wincing as the movement aggravated his headache, and leaned forward as if to keep what he had to say confidential. The patients in the beds on either side were asleep. No one was paying them any attention.

'I saw Beverly Wallace in a pub with a bloke. I thought Mr Milton should know as soon as possible.' The bloodshot eyes seemed animated for the first time. 'They looked like they were more than just friends, if you get my drift.'

Soames felt a flutter of excitement. So it had been worth coming after all.

'Did you recognize the bloke?'

Gray shook his head and immediately regretted it. He lay back on his pillows again for a moment with his eyes closed.

'It's all a bit hazy at the moment because of the accident. He was a young guy and I didn't know him, but I can't remember much else. Doctor says I might have a bit of memory loss for a while, but it should come back soon.'

'Make sure it does, it's important.' Soames spoke abruptly. 'Beverly Wallace has done a runner with some of Mr Milton's property and he wants both of them back sharpish.'

'Strewth, I bet he does.' Gray felt a brief surge of excitement at the sudden realization of his importance, followed immediately by concern that he wouldn't be very popular if he didn't regain his memory quickly.

'They're keeping me in today for observation, but I should be let out tomorrow. I'll try to remember the details by then.'

'See that you do.' Soames got up. 'I'll come and pick you up tomorrow morning. Give us a ring if you think of anything before then.'

'Will do.'

As Soames turned to walk back down the ward, Gray's eyes closed again. He was sure that there was something else he had to say, but he couldn't remember what it was and thinking too hard made his head ache even more than usual.

* * *

The Pussy Kat Klub was about as subtle as its name implied and as proper as the spelling. It was situated, along with a number of other similar establishments, towards the centre of the city. Although ostensibly a membership only club, it catered for anyone who paid the ten-pound fee on the door and appeared to the doorman not to be likely to cause trouble at either the price of the drinks or the antics of the performers. The club was owned by Vernon Bridger and it says something about his other activities that it represented one of his more upper-class establishments — provided you did not enquire too closely about the activities in the rooms on the upper floors. It was designed to maximize profits — to charge as much as the market would bear for whatever services its clientele wanted. If a customer was prepared to pay for a service, Bridger was happy for one of his employees to provide it, no questions asked. He was even prepared for others to trade on his premises — drugs and guns being the main commodities — provided he received his commission.

Jack Pace arrived at the club at 5.30. He was feeling touchy and irritable, having spent most of the day contacting people throughout Harry Milton's organization, giving them photographs of Beverly and putting them on the alert to find her. He had spent time not just with those directly employed by Milton, but also with the even bigger group of those with various other occupations who received monthly payouts to be available as sources of information and support when called upon. In between the telephone calls and personal visits, he had also been trying unsuccessfully to locate Beverly Wallace's sister. He knew her home address, but she had not been in when he called and her flatmate had no idea when she would return. Pace was intelligent enough not to unnecessarily antagonize someone who might actually go to the police if threatened, so he had just left messages for Sandi Wallace to contact him. There had been three such messages. He had obtained Sandi's mobile phone number from the flatmate, but the phone had been switched off and the message left there gone unreturned. He had been the target of some biting criticism from Harry Milton as a result and wondered if Beverly had taken her sister with her. The flatmate was expecting her back and Pace didn't think she was lying about that, but she could have been deceived as well.

Pace knew that Sandi Wallace performed at the Pussy Kat Klub most evenings and so, although his temper had been rising steadily with his frustration, unless she was in it with Beverly, he had in all probability only been delayed for a few hours from hopefully getting a lead on her sister.

The doorman at the club knew Pace, took one look at his face and made no effort to stop him from entering or to enter into conversation with him. The young woman at the counter just inside the door made no attempt to ask for the membership fee; she too recognized Pace. Harry Milton easily trumped Vernon Bridger in the gangland pecking order and they did not want any trouble. When Pace asked for Sandi Wallace's dressing room, he was directed there without question. If Sandi was in trouble, she might get some mild sympathy, but nobody in the club would be helping her against Pace.

Sandi Wallace was sitting alone in front of the mirror in the dressing room that she shared with three other dancers, putting the final touches to her make-up. She worked from 6 p.m. to 2 a.m., with some short breaks. It was physically tiring but she loved dancing and was content enough with her life. She had a good figure, danced well and was popular with the clients, which meant that she was also popular with Bridger and the other senior staff in the club. She always took care of her appearance so she studied her reflection carefully. Her costume required little attention since there was very little of it. It consisted of gold bikini briefs that looked as though they had shrunk in the wash, several times, and a pair of strappy gold sandals with very high heels.

When the door opened she expected to see one of her three fellow performers reflected in the mirror, or possibly the club manager, who had taken to visiting her for non-professional reasons. When she saw Jack Pace, her feeling of contentment vanished. One look at his face was enough to tell her that it wasn't a social call. She turned round in her chair and tried a not very convincing smile, her brain racing with a jumble of panic-stricken thoughts.

'Hi, Jack.' She had met him a couple of times with Harry Milton and Beverly and hoped briefly that she had got a wrong impression.

She knew that she hadn't when he stepped up in front of her and placed his powerful hands on her bare shoulders, squeezing painfully. She gasped and tried unsuccessfully to squirm away.

'What are you doing? That hurts.'

'Where's Beverly?' he asked softly.

A lump of fear formed in the pit of her stomach.

'Isn't she with Harry?' She tried to look puzzled.

Pace turned away from her for a moment without speaking. He locked the dressing-room door, then, in one motion, turned back and hit her. The crack of the slap echoed in the room and Sandi cried out, lifting her hand to her cheek.

'Don't piss me around, ducky, I'm not in the mood.' He stared at her with a flat lack of emotion that was almost more frightening than anger. It was the look of someone who didn't care how far he went. 'Where is she?'

'I don't know, really I don't.' She started to tremble.

Pace swung his arm again. Sandi raised her hands and cringed down in her chair, looking up fearfully into his stony face.

'Mr Bridger won't be very pleased if you hurt me or mark me so I can't perform,' she said. Even as she spoke, she knew it would be no protection.

Pace snorted

'Bridger will just have to grin and bear it,' he said. 'He'll probably blame you for being a silly cow and not telling me what I want to know straight away.' He paused for a moment. 'Still, maybe I should try not to make a mark.'

He bent forward, one hand holding her shoulder, forcing her down into her chair, whilst the other suddenly gripped her again. Sandi screamed out, almost losing consciousness. For a brief moment, she imagined someone hearing her scream and coming to help her, then she realized that was stupid. They'd know Pace was in with her and no one would interfere.

Pace moved behind her and his big, strong hands started to move over her body, one moment almost caressing and the next causing acute pain.

'When did you last see her?' His mouth hovered by the side of her head as he breathed the question into her ear.

'Two weeks ago.' She screamed again, tailing off into a sob as she hung her head. 'I swear it's true.'

'Where has she gone? Is she with someone — is someone hiding her?'

The questions kept coming, alternating with a jagged pain that seemed to jab through her body. She kept denying that Beverly had told her of any plans to run away. Eventually, Pace stepped back and looked at Sandi, hunched over in her chair, breath rasping, tears rolling down her face. His face remained impassive, uncaring. He looked round the room and saw her handbag on the shelf under the mirror. He picked it up and emptied the contents on to the counter. Make-up, comb, mobile phone, her keys and her purse dropped out with a cascade of other items. He looked in the purse, there was only money. He picked up the keys.

'I'll assume for now that you're telling the truth,' he said, cupping her chin in one of his hands and forcing her face up to look into his. 'I'll go back to your flat now and search it. If I find anything to suggest you know where she is, I'll be back and then you'll wish you'd talked, understand?'

She dragged in a sobbing breath.

'I don't know where Beverly is, I swear I don't. She hasn't told me anything about going away.' She met his gaze, blinking through her tears.

Pace grunted and his fingers squeezed her face.

'If she contacts you, then you contact me — right?' He pushed her face away.

'Yes, I will.' She nodded her head like a crazy puppet. 'I'll tell you straight away.'

He nodded.

'Make sure you do. You'd better clean yourself up before you go on stage — you look a mess.'

He unlocked the door and it slammed behind him.

Sandi sat for a while trying to get back her composure. Eventually she looked up at her reflection in the mirror, staring at the pain in her face and her red, tear-filled eyes.

'Oh, Bev,' she said, in a low, shaky voice, 'I hope to God he's worth it.'

* * *

Whilst in the village shop that morning, Jones had mentioned that he was staying in his brother's cottage, the binoculars round his neck hopefully providing support to his twitching credentials. The shop also served as the post office and he was confident that word of his arrival would circulate pretty rapidly. He hoped that would satisfy any curiosity if lights were spotted in the cottage. There had been one other customer in the shop and he nodded politely to two other people that he passed in the main village street, other than that he met no one on his travels.

Arriving back at the cottage, he had prepared a late breakfast which they ate in the kitchen. After that they had sat dozing and watching daytime TV for a while on his brother's small set in the living room that was the only other downstairs room. They had

162

gone back to bed in the afternoon, revelling in the novelty of being able to make love in comfort and without the fear of being traced to a hotel room. Afterwards, Jones prepared an early evening meal. Beverly had not cooked since she had taken up with Milton and even before that she had never achieved much more than cheese on toast or warming up a TV dinner.

After the meal had been cleared away and the plates washed — Jones insisted that they keep his brother's cottage clean — Beverly started pacing the living room floor, stopping occasionally to peer out of the window across the darkening bay and trying unsuccessfully to relieve the feeling of restlessness. She hated being cooped up and although she accepted that she needed to avoid even the faint chance that someone associated with Milton might be around the village and recognize her, she knew that after two or three days in the cottage, she would be climbing the walls.

'Let's go out for a walk after dark.'

'I'm not sure that's a good idea,' Jones looked at her dubiously.

'Oh, come on, there's no risk. You said yourself that the people in the village would accept that you are just using your brother's cottage for a few days. No one is likely to come spying on us.'

'Supposing someone sees you? I'm supposed to be here on my own.'

'So you've brought a girl with you to while away the time — that's not a crime, is it?'

She sat down on his lap and put her arms round his neck.

'Come on, we can go down to the cove. We'll wait until it's completely dark. No one is going to be down there at night.' She grinned at him and kissed him. 'I've never done it on a beach before.' She paused. 'Well, not all the way, anyway.'

He laughed at her, momentarily forgetting the ball of fear that had lived inside him, getting steadily larger, ever since they had first worked out their plans. He gave in, as they both knew he would.

'All right then.' He paused. 'We'd better take a blanket.'

8

As if to demonstrate that beatings and assassinations are equal opportunity professions, Angie and Findon Wilson were a brother and sister team who made themselves available for general hire. According to Mariner's file, they lived together in a large barge on the canal that ran through the north of the city for several miles and had originally formed the veins through which its life-trade had flowed, leading from the docks to the factories and warehouses that lined its banks.

The morning after Tanner and Julie had cleared Harry Jarvis and Sam Hesky of shooting Julie and her aunt (if not of various other criminal activities), Tanner contacted Mariner from his office and suggested that investigation into the disappearance of one Salvador Sanchez might prove rewarding. Mariner seemed happy enough with their progress, even if they were back where they started. They exchanged a few amicable insults about gifted amateurs and hung up.

Having done his civic duty and helped the police with their enquiries, Tanner went through the day's post whilst Julie spread the file notes on the Wilsons on the coffee table and started going through them. There was nothing requiring his immediate attention in the post and having enjoyed delegating various tasks to his staff, Tanner sat at the table and looked at the Wilsons' file as well. It made interesting, if not particularly helpful, reading. Neither of them had ever been arrested, let alone sent to prison. They worked freelance and had been employed by both Bridger and Milton in the past, as well as others with similar interests.

The Wilsons' bread and butter work seemed to be debt collecting for a number of less than scrupulous bookies and loan sharks. They were suspected of a long list of assaults of varying degrees of seriousness, including two that had resulted in the death of the victim. It was unclear whether or not it had been deliberate. They had occasionally been questioned about these events but had never been charged, allegedly because they were quite prepared to widen their activities to include the family of their victim, regardless of age or sex, if anyone made a complaint to the police. Listed at the bottom of the file were three disappearances that could be linked circumstantially to the Wilsons, although there was nothing remotely resembling evidence that you could take to court. Judging by the list of alleged activities, the hit on Julie and her aunt would fit perfectly logically within their CV.

Tanner sat back in his chair and took a swig of coffee.

'Any thoughts as to how we can find out what they were doing on the evening of eighth February?'

Julie collected the file pages together neatly and passed them across to Tanner to lock away again, retaining the two photographs of the brother and sister for reference on their travels. She shook her head.

'Nothing very precise. We could start off by taking a look at where they live and see if that gives us any ideas.'

Tanner nodded.

'According to the file they don't socialize much but their local is a pub called The Tow Path down by the canal. If the barge or the canal doesn't give us any inspiration, we could call in there and see if we can pick up any local gossip. Someone might have seen them on the night in question riding a motor bike down the tow path and waving a silenced handgun.'

'That would certainly constitute evidence.'

'If only circumstantial.'

'Don't you just love our legal system?'

Julie stood up and reached for her shoulder bag and her coat.

'Still, we might get a decent pub lunch out of it.'

★   ★   ★

Tanner knew the Havenchester canal well, having walked and fished along it quite often in his early years. It took them some time to negotiate the city traffic, which seemed to have developed a permanent rush hour from around eight in the morning to eight in the evening, not helped by a recurring cycle of road works. Tanner eventually got them to their destination and found, remarkably, a parking space in a nearby side street of neat terraced houses with small paved front gardens. There was no one about; even the kids bunking off from school appeared to have found somewhere else to go.

Tanner took Julie's hand, leading her across the neighbouring main road to where it formed a bridge over the canal. They descended the narrow stone steps by the side of the bridge on to the tow path. The council and local community groups had spent some time gradually clearing the less appetizing lengths of the canal and there was now a considerable strip of tow path that formed a pleasant walk alongside the water. High blank walls of factories and warehouses, some abandoned, some still in use, and others converted or being converted into much sought after apartments, lined the canal at intervals. In other places, there were areas of tangled bush and trees. Occasionally, a narrow, dank tributary led off to the side into a dim wilderness as yet untamed by the renovators.

The sun was shining and it would have been a pleasant, almost warm, walk if it were not for the long stretches of shade and the chill wind that blew along the path, rippling the grey-green water at its side and setting Julie's hair flowing in raven dark waves.

Tanner squeezed Julie's hand and smiled at her. They were hoping to be taken for lovers having a romantic stroll by the canal — a disguise that was at least partly accurate.

'The Wilsons' boat should be round the next bend,' Tanner murmured, after they had walked slowly for fifteen minutes or so along the asphalt path, 'and the pub is about a hundred yards further along.'

His memory of the geography of the canal proved accurate and they followed the path round to the left where the waterway widened out to allow about ten barges permanent berths. To the left of the path was an open, rectangular, grassy area and beyond that a narrow alleyway between two warehouses that led back into the noise and bustle of the city. Even though Tanner knew that city traffic flowed only a short distance away, he was still struck by the illusion that they were in the depths of the country, almost in another world of calm and serenity.

The Wilsons' barge was called the Fandangle, which suggested a moderate understanding of the art of anagrams on their part. It looked well tended, with gleaming brass and polished wood and an intricate painting of a horse drawing a barge on the side of the cabin area. They strolled on past it, trying to look like casual walkers admiring the painting and the barges. There was no sign of occupation, but that didn't mean very much as both brother and sister were creatures of the night.

Angie was two years older than her brother and the natural leader. From the descriptions in the file, they were both tall and solidly built and both spent time weight training at the gym. Both had shoulder-length blond hair, sported hoop ear-rings and had tattoos on their left arms between elbow and shoulder. Findon's was a panther and Angie's a grizzly bear — Tanner presumed that was to demonstrate her cuddly feminine side.

None of the Wilsons' neighbours was around, although shadows moved behind lace-curtained windows as they walked by, suggesting that the local equivalent of neighbourhood watch was alive and well. Once they had passed all the barges, they stopped and Tanner glanced at his watch.

'It's nearly twelve. Shall we risk the pub food and see if we can eavesdrop on any interesting gossip?'

'Sounds like a good idea.'

'Well, it's an idea, anyway.'

The Tow Path had a small garden area running back from the canal to its rear entrance with four wooden seats and tables for the more hardy clientele who liked al fresco in all weathers. They were all currently unoccupied. Tanner and Julie followed a paved path along the side of the building and arrived at the front entrance. There was parking for a few cars at the front of the pub and a few spaces were already occupied, suggesting either popularity or committed drinking. Boards leaning against the wall by the door advertised a variety of delights for the patrons — pub lunches, a live band on Tuesdays, Fridays and Sundays and big screen sport.

They found the inside a pleasant surprise. There was gleaming, light-wood panelling, a long bar at the rear and a number of tables and chairs set round at intervals. A small stage stood to the left of the door, presumably where the live music was performed. There were a couple of obligatory gaming machines flashing brightly. The atmosphere was generally welcoming and there was a pleasant smell of food cooking. Four or five of the tables were occupied and three people sat at the bar, but no one paid them any particular attention as they walked in. The customers wore a mixture of suits and casual dress and none of them resembled the Wilsons.

They walked up to the bar where a young woman in a T-shirt and jeans was chatting to a middle-aged man who sat nursing a beer. She turned towards them with a smile.

'What can I get you?'

Tanner looked enquiringly at Julie.

'Ploughman's lunch and half of bitter,' she said.

'Same for me please,' Tanner told the barmaid. Equality in all things, he thought.

The barmaid nodded and called the order through to the kitchen area behind the bar.

'Just be a few minutes,' she said, having poured their drinks and taken the money.

'I see you have live music,' Tanner said, more to keep the conversation going than through any great interest in their musical repertoire. With a bit of luck he could steer things round to a discussion about their regulars.

'Yes.' She nodded enthusiastically. 'This Sunday it's The Eternal Sinners, they're a heavy rock group. They're absolutely brilliant. They play here regularly. If you're free on Sunday, it would be well worth trying them out.'

'I hope we don't get a repeat of the trouble we had last time,' the man raised his head and made the observation to the barmaid. He had the complaining air of a regular who was not best pleased at his local being turned into a rock venue.

She gave him a sharp look.

'That wasn't their fault,' she protested. 'The guy was drunk.'

'What happened?' Julie asked.

'One of the customers accused Glen, that's the band's lead singer, of trying to get off with his girlfriend. Mind you, Glen is pretty dishy; I wouldn't mind spending some time with him myself.' Her face took on a wistful look. 'It was after their first set. The band was having a drink at the bar and this guy started on at Glen. Glen was just chatting to the girl, who had obviously enjoyed the session, and her boyfriend got nasty. He told Glen to leave her alone, even though she seemed to be making all the running. Glen told him to chill out and the guy broke his glass and swung at Glen with it. It could have been really nasty. Fortunately, a couple of our regulars stopped him. One caught his arm before he connected and the other one decked him.'

'A useful couple of guys to have around,' Julie commented.

The barmaid smiled.

'One of them is a woman — they're a brother and sister who live near here.'

Julie looked at her with interest. There couldn't be many brother and sister acts around where the sister could deal with a man wielding a broken glass.

'And she helped to sort out the trouble-maker?'

The barmaid grinned.

'She's the one who decked him. Elbow in the side of the jaw: *pow.*' She imitated the action with her own elbow, causing the regular to rear back in his seat in alarm. 'He went down flat.' Fortunately, she didn't try to demonstrate that part of the performance. The ploughman's lunches arrived and she put them on the bar. 'They're big fans of the group, always come to see them when they're playing here.'

That sounded promising to Tanner. Maybe they should expand their musical education on the coming Sunday.

'We're fans of rock music, perhaps we will come on Sunday,' Julie said, echoing his thoughts. 'What time do they start to play?'

'About nine o'clock, but get here early, there's always a good crowd. They're good value; play two one-hour sets with a half-hour break.' She was clearly a fan herself — although possibly mainly of the lead singer.

Tanner had a sudden thought.

'You said the band play here regularly?'

'Yeah — at least once every couple of months, sometimes more.'

'What date was the last gig — can you remember?'

She frowned.

'I think I saw an old flyer round here yesterday.' She fumbled around under the bar. 'Here it is — eighth February.' She looked at him curiously. 'Why?'

Julie put her hand on Tanner's arm and smiled at him with enough syrupy sweetness to cause a diabetic coma.

'Why, darling, that was our anniversary — we could have come here instead of going to see that terrible film.'

Tanner just managed to keep a straight face.

'So we could,' he managed.

175

The romantic comment caused the bar-maid to smile at them and nod, erasing any curiosity she might have had as to why Tanner had been particularly interested in the date.

They took their lunches to a quiet table in a corner well away from the other customers.

'If the band started playing at nine, the first set would have ended at ten. If the Wilsons were here breaking up a fight soon after-wards, it lets them off the hook for the shooting,' Tanner commented.

Julie picked up a piece of cheese, took a bite, added a grape and chewed them thoughtfully.

'Looks very much like it,' she agreed. 'So that just leaves us with Jethro Harper and Kevin Winston.'

'And their boss — Harry Milton,' Tanner added. 'He's got quite an organization behind him, and he makes Vernon Bridger look like a pussy cat.'

Julie spread some butter on her French bread.

'He sounds delightful.' She took a sip of beer. 'At least we won't have to tangle with Ms Muscle.'

'I was going to leave her to you to sort out.'

'Always the gentleman.'

* * *

They got back to the office just before two and settled down with the last part of Mariner's file. They were starting to run out of options, and Tanner was beginning to worry about the impact on Julie if they drew a blank with the last two possibilities. It had undoubtedly helped her mental balance to be actively doing something that might lead to her aunt's killer and he wasn't sure how much it would knock her back again if she didn't have that to focus on. He had blithely talked about trying another tack if Ted's choices didn't pan out, but if the killers were an outside professional contract, he wasn't sure where to start. In any event, that angle was already being covered by the police and they weren't likely to be more successful than the official investigators had been with all the resources at their disposal.

On the positive side, Tanner was certain that their relationship was helping her as well, but it was still in its infancy and although it felt pretty strong at the moment, whether it was powerful enough to pull Julie through such a set-back remained to be seen. Still, there was nothing to be gained by speculating at that point, so he hid his anxiety and concentrated on the job in hand.

Jethro Harper and Kevin Winston were much younger than the other pairings they had been looking into. They were both graduates of the youth justice system, having started with ASBOs and worked their way up — or down, depending on how you looked at it. They had spent time in the same young offenders' institution for violent muggings, had been released at the same time and had teamed up. After that they had got themselves a reputation for violent crime and general unpleasantness, none of which had led to any charges. They had been on Milton's payroll for less than a year.

Harper lived with his mother on a council estate not renowned for the pro-social behaviour of its residents. Winston occasionally stayed there too, but although it was not thought to be his permanent residence, there was no other address for him. The rest of his family, none of whom had been in trouble with the police, had moved out of the city when he was in his late teens and were now living in London. There was not thought to be much, if any, contact between them and Winston.

Julie and Tanner spent the afternoon trying to trace an alternative address for Winston, but without success. Tanner got Danny Worenski roaming the ether to try to find some trace, both officially and unofficially, but even he couldn't find anything. Knowing

Danny's ability to track down the most elusive of prey, it suggested that Winston was not the registered owner or lessee of any property he might be occupying. He also didn't appear to have filled in any official forms recently, or to have had any contact with any agencies whose records Danny could access — which was most of them.

At five, when Worenski came in to report his lack of success, Julie yawned and sat back in her chair.

'Why don't we call it a day? Don't forget, we're going out for dinner tonight.'

Tanner nodded. They might get some fresh ideas in the morning and a break would do them both good.

Julie had received an invitation to dinner that evening from Archie and Laura Tilling. When she told them about Tanner, he was immediately included. Tanner suspected that was both to satisfy their curiosity and because they were genuinely concerned about Julie and were happy that she had someone to bring.

'I suppose I'll have to wear a suit?'

'And a shirt and a tie. You'll also have to wash behind the ears — I shall be making an inspection.'

Tanner dropped Julie off at her flat and drove back to his own to shower and change.

Suitably suited and with shirt and tie (and polished shoes — he didn't do these things by halves), he drove back to Julie's apartment. Tanner gave her a long kiss that she responded to eagerly for a moment before pushing him away gently.

'Not now; I've spent too long on my make-up and we don't want to crease your suit — or my dress.'

'Later then.'

She kissed him again, quickly.

'Later you can crease as much as you like.'

Tanner helped Julie on with her coat and they took the lift down to the car-park beneath the apartments. Julie knew the way so it was easier for her to drive them in her car.

Tanner was welcomed warmly by the Tillings and was taken for a tour of the house by Archie whilst Julie chatted to Laura in the kitchen. He genuinely admired the rooms and the views and was particularly impressed with the boat that could just be glimpsed in the evening gloom, rocking gently in the river from the jetty at the end of the long, tree-lined garden.

'You like boating and water sports?' Archie Tilling asked, his face brightening with the light of the true enthusiast given an excuse to talk about his favourite subject.

'I spend as much time as I can on the water — or under it.'

'We'll have to take you both out sometime. There are plenty of good spots for fishing along the river.'

Tanner admitted that he was more into swimming and diving.

'There's plenty of scope for that, as well.' Tilling beamed at him. 'Laura and I both swim, but we haven't tried diving yet.'

'You should,' Tanner grasped the opportunity to be enthusiastic about one of his favourite hobbies. 'It's incredible, being down there with the fish and exploring the sea bed. It's like a completely different world.'

'Perhaps you could teach us,' Tilling suggested, as they moved away from the window and back downstairs.

'Any time,' Tanner assured him. He knew that Julie shared his love of diving, so that promised to be an enjoyable excursion.

Dinner matched the expectations raised by the splendour of the house and grounds and conversation turned — not unexpectedly — to the progress they were making investigating the shootings. They told them about their abortive investigations into Bridger and his men and that they had crossed the Wilsons off the list.

'We've only got one more line of enquiry at

the moment, if that doesn't pan out we'll have to rethink,' Julie said.

'Who's that?' Laura asked.

'I don't suppose it's anyone we know, darling,' Archie Tilling said with a smile.

'It's a couple of guys employed by a man named Harry Milton.' Tanner said. 'You might know him — he's supposed to be something of an art buff.'

'Doesn't mean anything to me,' Tilling said, but his wife nodded enthusiastically.

'Why, yes, I do know him, as a matter of fact. We've sold him two or three paintings. He likes nineteenth- and early twentieth-century artists. He's got quite good taste and a keen eye. He also collects nineteenth-century porcelain; we've sold him one or two pieces of that as well.'

Her eyes gleamed with excitement.

'Do you mean that he's a crook? How thrilling. You'd never know it to meet him. I thought he was just a successful business-man.'

'Sometimes there's not a lot of difference,' Tilling commented drily.

'Don't be so cynical, darling.' She turned back to Tanner. 'But this is fascinating, Alec. What sort of crimes does he commit?'

'He's into drugs, gambling, high-class prostitution and he funds major robberies as well as some more legitimate stuff.' Tanner took a sip of the excellent wine. 'Not that I could repeat that outside this room without risking being sued for slander.'

Laura smiled.

'I promise I won't mention it next time he comes into the shop. It seems incredible. To think that the things he's bought from us have been funded from crime. And, as I said, he's actually quite knowledgeable about art. You've never met him Archie?'

Tilling shook his head.

'Can't say I remember him, but next time he comes in to buy something, you must let me know.' He sat back in his chair and smiled fondly at his wife. 'An accountant's life is a very sheltered one — I'd like to meet a real live villain.'

'I'll make sure I tell you,' she promised. She thought for a moment. 'He's actually rather charming.' She looked faintly surprised.

Tanner grinned.

'I'm sure he can be if he wants to, but knowledge of and interest in art doesn't necessarily mean respectability. I can assure you that his real personality is something much less appealing.'

Laura shivered and got to her feet.

'Oh well, enough of this talk of crime, shall we have coffee in the lounge?'

Over coffee, whilst her husband was showing Julie a recent acquisition of which he was particularly proud, Laura took Alec Tanner to one side.

'I'm so pleased to see Julie looking so much better,' she said. 'You are obviously doing her the world of good. We were quite worried about her when she came earlier in the week.'

She paused for a moment and glanced across the room to make sure Julie was out of earshot.

'I hope you won't take this the wrong way, but she has very few people to turn to and I was her aunt's best friend, so I'll have to risk sounding impertinent.' She looked closely into Tanner's face, as if trying to read his fortune. 'You know that Julie is emotionally very fragile at the moment. I wouldn't want to see her hurt if things didn't work out.'

Tanner smiled at her.

'Don't worry; I have every intention of making it last for as long as Julie wants me.'

Laura looked relieved, both at his answer and his failure to take offence.

'I'm sure you'll be very good for each other.'

Tanner looked across at Julie, who caught his eye and smiled.

He hoped she was right.

9

If Jack Pace had hoped that Harry Milton's temper would start to improve when Beverly Wallace had been gone for more than twenty-four hours, he would have been sorely disappointed. However, Pace knew Milton much better than that and when he was summoned into Milton's study he saw without surprise that his boss was clearly in, if anything, a worse frame of mind than the day before. Milton and Soames had gone out on a long-standing business engagement the evening before, involving the purchase of certain substances frowned upon by the authorities, and had left Pace to follow up the suggestion passed on by Gray that Beverly had run off with a lover. Since the trail had turned as cold as an Arctic blizzard, and shed about as much visibility on the matter, Pace had made sure that he had not been around for Milton to interview on his return. In the morning, he had snatched a quick breakfast in the kitchen rather than sit in the dining room with Milton. He disliked being the focus of a disagreeable atmosphere at meal times; it gave him indigestion, although he had no qualms about imposing such an atmosphere himself on others.

Pace sat in one of the comfortable armchairs facing the desk and waited for instructions.

'Where's Horace?' Milton asked gruffly.

Soames rarely had more than coffee and a slice of toast for breakfast and he, too, had joined Pace in the kitchen.

'He said he had some errands to run following your meeting last night. He needs to raise some funds to cover the initial outlay.' Pace considered adding that this action was necessary as a result of the lack of cash resources in the safe, but, sensibly, decided to omit reference to the obvious. 'Then he's going to pick up Gray from the hospital.'

Milton snorted. He reached across to the ivory office tidy at the rear of his desk top, picked up a silver paper knife and started stabbing at his blotting pad. Pace had little trouble imagining whose skin was represented in Milton's mind by the pristine blotting paper.

'What does he think we are, an ambulance taxi service?'

'Doesn't hurt to show a bit of support to the soldiers; it helps morale generally.'

'Morale?' Milton spat the word back at him. 'What about my morale?' He stabbed once more, sharply, as if it was the *coup de grâce*, before tossing the knife down in disgust.

'Horace is bringing Gray straight here,' Pace added. 'He might have remembered something else that will help lead us to the man Beverly was with, so we thought it would be a good idea to question him more thoroughly as quickly as possible.'

Milton grunted and leant back in his swivel chair. He stared sourly at Pace's square, boxer's face with the faint tracery of scars round his eyes and the broken nose which dated from his brief but interesting career in the ring. The man who had broken Pace's nose had been the victim of a vicious assault as he was walking home a couple of evenings later. The man's assailant had come at him from behind out of the darkness of an alleyway wielding the ubiquitous blunt instrument and had never been identified. Pace had given up his boxing career shortly afterwards and joined Milton's organization. His opponent had not boxed again either — it had taken him three months to walk properly again.

'What happened when you went to the pub where Gray saw them together?'

'I spoke to the landlord and the bar staff. No joy there. It was a busy night and nobody paid either of them any particular attention. One of the barmaids remembered them vaguely, but she didn't hear what they were saying to each other, or remember when they arrived, or when they left. She clearly thought they were lovers. I made out he was married and I was a private dick working for the wife, I thought she'd be more sympathetic if she thought a woman was being wronged.'

'And was she?'

Pace shrugged.

'I think so, but she didn't remember having seen them before and I don't think anyone in the pub had anything else much to tell us. I couldn't press the questions too much, or they might have got curious. The car-park's at the back of the pub, so no one saw what car they were driving. Like I said, they weren't thought to be regulars so no one remembered them from another night.'

Pace stared woodenly at his boss after giving this report. Hopefully, he would remember the old adage about not shooting the messenger.

'Sod it.' Milton got to his feet and walked over to the window, staring out across the front drive. 'We've got to find them, Jack; I'm not going to let her get away with this.'

Pace nodded, glad that he was not being blamed for finding nothing when there was nothing to find. Milton wasn't usually unreasonable, but this was not a usual situation. In a detached way, Pace rather admired Beverly for what she had done; he hadn't thought she'd got the balls, in a figurative sense, of course. Not that that would make any difference to his reaction when they caught her.

'I've put the word out with everyone I can think of: we should get a response soon.'

Milton turned back towards his desk.

'You're certain the sister doesn't know anything?'

'I don't think she's the sort to value loyalty above pain. I thought I'd let her stew for a while, then go back and see her this evening. If she does know something and she's relaxed thinking I've bought her story, a second visit should do the trick.'

Milton nodded. For all his raging, he trusted Pace's judgement, particularly when it came to making people talk. It galled him not to be taking action, but he accepted that there wasn't much else they could do. They'd spread the net, now they needed to wait for the fish to swim into it.

It was gone midday before Soames arrived with Gray. Milton and Pace were having sandwiches in the dining room when they heard the car pull up in the drive. They were

189

joined by the other two men a few minutes later.

'What took you so long?' Milton was not a student of the bedside manner.

'Sorry, Harry.' Soames helped himself to a couple of sandwiches and sat down at the table with a sigh. 'We had to wait for a doctor to confirm Reggie could be discharged.'

Reggie nodded solemnly. He still had a pad of bandage taped to the right side of his head as if someone had lobbed a snowball at him and it had stuck.

'Said I was lucky not to have brain damage.' Gray tried his martyred look, but just looked self-important.

'Got a bruise on your arse as well then, have you?' Milton growled at him, singularly unimpressed. Soames smothered a grin and Gray had enough sense not to push his injury any further.

'Have you remembered anything else about the bastard?' Milton took a bite out of his sandwich as if he was tearing the head off a chicken, and glared at him.

Gray shook his head. He felt distinctly hard done by. After all, if it hadn't been for him, they wouldn't have known about Beverly Wallace's fancy man, or had any idea what he looked like.

'We need a more accurate description,

what you've given us so far could fit half the population.'

That was, perhaps, a slight exaggeration, but Gray took the point.

'Well, I took his photo on my phone.' He looked round the table proudly.

This announcement wasn't quite greeted with the expressions of delight he had expected. Indeed, Pace and Milton looked singularly annoyed. Milton glared at him. For a moment he was speechless, but not for long.

'Why in buggery didn't you say so before?'

'I only just remembered. My head . . . '

Gray was lucky that he didn't sustain a matching injury on the left-hand side of his face. Milton took a deep breath and snapped his fingers.

'Well, don't just sit there, you stupid bastard, show it to us.'

Gray fumbled in the inside pocket of his coat and produced his phone. His palms were sweaty and his fingers kept slipping on the keys as he switched it on. Fortunately, the battery was still charged. The other three men gathered round as he eventually called up the picture.

'I know him!' Pace exclaimed.

'What?' Milton swivelled to stare at him. If the bastard was actually in his own organization . . .

'Yes, it's her dancing instructor.' Pace nodded slowly. He found a good memory for faces invaluable in his job, particularly as he was often under instruction to rearrange the features. 'When Beverly's car was in for repair a few weeks ago, you got me to take her to the dance studio and pick her up again a couple of times. I had to wait for her to finish the lesson both times. That's the bloke who was teaching her — I'm positive.'

Pace met Milton's eyes.

'It makes sense. I was wondering how Beverly had met someone; I couldn't see anyone in the firm being stupid enough and I couldn't see how she could manage to spend any length of time with an outsider.'

Milton nodded and his eyes hardened.

'It makes sense all right. Now we're getting somewhere. Go over to that dance studio and see what you can find out. Take Gray with you. I don't suppose he'll be there, but you should be able to get a proper lead on him, and her.'

He looked across at Gray.

'Are you sure they didn't spot you?'

Gray nodded.

'I'm positive, boss. I was on the other side of the pub and they only had eyes for each other.'

'Good. That means they won't expect us to

know about him, so he might not be so careful about covering his tracks. Find out where he is and you'll get both of them.'

For the first time in thirty-six hours, Milton allowed himself a small smile.

'Then you take him out and you bring her to me.'

★　★　★

Beverly Wallace was starting to feel like a prisoner, having swapped the mental restraints of living with Milton for the physical restraints of not being able to leave the cottage.

They had gone to bed soon after their walk to the beach the night before. As a result, they had woken early that morning, the gulls screaming their morning alarm call outside the bedroom window, and had breakfasted much earlier than they had the day before. This was a mistake, as it just made the morning seem longer. Daytime TV had not improved; indeed any novelty that there was had rapidly warn off. They were restricted to the four terrestrial channels, and two of them were intermittently fuzzy. Jones made a mental note to advise his brother to invest in a satellite dish. Still, to be fair, he didn't use the cottage in the same way. His brother and sister-in-law wanted the cottage as a base for walking and swimming and from which to drive out to explore the surrounding countryside. It was a place to sleep and to have morning and evening meals; it was not intended to be lived in for the whole day.

Beverly and Jones had an early lunch and spent an hour or so in bed, which, admittedly, did pass the time much more enjoyably, but now the rest of the afternoon and evening stretched before them interminably. They started a game of Monopoly, but playing those sorts of games was not Beverly's forte and she soon tired of it. Nor was she a great reader.

Indeed, she was just beginning to appreciate the reality of what she had done. Not that she had changed her mind and regretted leaving Milton, she still adored JJ and she wouldn't have returned to Milton even if she had been able to and keep breathing. However she was an outdoor person, she loved going out shopping, going to clubs and the cinema, or even just taking a car ride and she felt horribly boxed in. She had, she admitted to herself, not thought through in detail exactly what running away from Milton would entail. It had at first just been a wonderful plan with the promise of freedom at the end of it, something she had dreamed about for weeks, but the reality was proving to be far less romantic. Even the threat of Milton, forever in the background, could not overcome the boredom. She had pictured in her mind the two lovers running from the pursuing villain, but had not pictured sitting around doing nothing in a cottage that was barely equipped even for twentieth-century living.

And there were at least two more days of this. JJ had contacted his friend by mobile phone that morning and had been told that it would be at least forty-eight hours before the friend could arrive with their papers and there was a distinct possibility that it would take another day after that. She didn't think she could stand it.

Getting suddenly to her feet, she pulled on her waterproof jacket and tucked her jeans into a pair of short boots.

'What are you doing?' Jones, sprawled in an uncomfortable armchair trying to find something he had yet to read in the paper he had bought at the village shop the day before, looked across at her in concern.

'Let's go for a walk.' She put her hands in her jacket pockets and turned towards him with a determined expression.

Jones stayed where he was, dropping the paper by the side of his chair.

'It isn't safe, darling. What if — '

'Rubbish.' She over-rode his objections briskly. 'There is no way that anyone in Harry Milton's organization knows anything about you and it is absolutely impossible that they could find out about this cottage.'

'It's still risky.' He had no experience of serious crime or criminals and he had sometimes felt that Beverly exaggerated Milton's influence and activities, but her nervousness had nevertheless affected him as well, particularly since they had actually taken the irrevocable step of flight. He read the papers and saw the news and knew that such people did exist. 'You said that his organization is pretty efficient.'

'It's not that efficient. He doesn't have a crystal ball or magic powers. I'm not going to sit around here jumping at shadows and pulling my hair out. I'm going out — are you coming with me, or shall I go on my own?'

He got reluctantly to his feet and went to get his coat. As he put it on, Beverly gave him a bright smile and a deep kiss.

'Thanks, lover boy.'

He managed a smile in return and opened the front door. He had to admit that he was feeling quite claustrophobic himself, and Beverly was probably right, how could Milton trace them?

The air was sharp and clean and felt refreshing as they followed the narrow path from the small, scrubby cottage garden towards the cliff edge where it branched out, one arm leading to the steep but reasonably negotiable route down to the beach and the other curling round to the right and disappearing into the thick woodland.

'Let's stay up here and go through the trees.' Beverly slipped her hand through the crook of his arm and steered Jones along the right-hand path.

There was no one around and the trees and bushes formed a natural barrier from the wind that gusted along the cliff top. The sun was still quite high in the sky and some warmth penetrated between the branches of the trees. Some were still bare, but there were sufficient firs and other evergreens together with tall, tangled bushes to provide that feeling of cut off seclusion to be found in most scarcely populated woodland areas.

'Tell me more about Milton and why you got mixed up with him.' Jones put his arm around Beverly's waist and hugged her to him. Over the period of their affair, he had gathered a brief picture of her former lover and his organization, but it had come in fragments, short comments at different times, tagged on to another part of a conversation;

she had never spoken of Milton at any length. Nor had she spoken much about her earlier life. He had met her only sister and liked her, knew that Beverly had run away from her abusive father, who was now dead and that she despised her mother for staying with her husband and taking his side against her daughters.

'You're better than he is in the sack, if that's what's worrying you.' She turned her head to grin at him and saw his serious expression. She decided to answer his question; after all he deserved that much at least after what he was risking for her.

'When I left home, my only real male role model was my father and he wasn't much good in that respect — or in any other.' She spoke softly and reflectively, returning his hug and holding it, drawing on the strength of contact with his body as she mused on the past. 'There was a series of men after that, none of them wanting as much from me as I wanted from them; none of them worthwhile. I suppose I was desperately looking for a man who would give me the affection I couldn't get from my father and I ended up having a string of men who just wanted to control and manipulate me as much as he did. They weren't all as violent as him, but that's about all you could say about them. None of them amounted to very much, or had any money. I'm not saying I've got a brilliant mind or anything, but I needed a man to want me for more than my body.' The relief of having someone who cared for her to talk to made her pour out her story in a fast-flowing stream of words.

'When Harry Milton came along I knew he'd want to manipulate me even more than the others and was far more dangerous, but at least he was rich and didn't mind spending money on me provided I did what he wanted. By then I'd given up on the idea of finding anyone who cared about me for myself. I figured that if I could only have men who wanted to use me for one thing, I might as well live in luxury while they were doing it. Harry wants to own things, he wants to make money and he always wants to win — he doesn't care what it costs or how he cheats to do it. I was just another possession that he owned and could do what he liked with. The only things he really loves are his paintings and antiques. He's got them all over the house, but the really precious ones he keeps locked away in a room on the second floor. No one but him is allowed in there, not even Jack Pace or Soames. He even cleans the room himself. When he's at home, he goes in there at least once a day, presumably just to sit and look at them. I asked to go in there with him one time to see them and he went really quiet like he does when he's angry and said that if I ever tried to go in there he'd kill me. And when Harry Milton says something like that, it's not just a figure of speech.'

She shivered.

'He gave me the creeps, and he knew it — and liked it. Then you came along and I realized I could have a real life with someone who loved me and cared about me and I had to get away from Harry at all costs.'

She snuggled closer to him.

'That's enough about Harry Milton; even talking about him gives me the willies.'

They walked on for a while in silence. Occasionally they saw another cottage, once they heard the sound of a car in the distance and once somebody calling to their dog in another part of the wood, but otherwise they could have had the world to themselves. They followed a series of barely defined paths through the trees and managed to loop round so as to arrive back at the path by their own cottage about an hour after they had set out. Beverly felt completely refreshed and cheerful, looking forward now to an evening in with the man she loved. She stopped them by the front door and kissed him happily.

'Thank you for coming on the walk, it was

great. And, you see, there was nothing to worry about. Like I said, we're quite safe. Nobody can possibly find us here.'

★ ★ ★

Veronica Ambrose, owner and chief instructor of the Dance 'Til You Drop dance studios did not know what to make of Jack Pace. He certainly did not look like a representative of the Inland Revenue; despite what his identification card said. Jones was not the only one with friends who specialized in forged documents. Pace had used the identification before and as well as finding it amusing, he had also found that people were generally unwilling to antagonize someone they thought would be able to look into their tax affairs and would provide the information he wanted without questioning why he wanted it. She thought his companion looked more like the sort of person who would be involved in tax evasion rather than inspection. Or was it avoidance, she could never remember?

Still, Pace had a certain persuasive charm and she saw no reason to challenge his right to ask questions about her former employee. Indeed, she had a generally unsuspicious nature as well as a talkative one. She took Mr

Pace and his companion, Mr Gray, into her small, cluttered office at the rear of the spacious dance floor and closed the door on the music and the four couples who were dancing to it with fierce concentration under the critical eye of a young male instructor.

'No, no, no, it's four basics and a *back* step . . . '

Mrs Ambrose motioned her visitors into two rather rickety chairs and sat behind a desk littered with piles of assorted paperwork, two or three of the top sheets of which showed evidence of having been used as coasters. She was a tall, erect woman with short grey hair and an amicable expression. Before speaking, she inspected her visitors through a pair of large blue-rimmed spectacles which gave her a slightly owlish look.

'As I was saying, Mr Jones left last week. We were very sorry to see him go, he was an excellent instructor. He knew exactly how to get the best performance out of his students.'

Gray seemed to find this amusing, but Pace ignored him and kept the discussion on a professional level.

'He has applied to us for self-employed status and has sent the relevant form to our local office, but there appears to be an error in his address. When we wrote to him there, the letter was returned.' Pace took out notebook and pen from his jacket pocket. He hoped she wouldn't ask any technical questions. Horace Soames had briefed him on what to say, but if they went off script, he was going to have to play things by ear and might say the wrong thing. 'He put you down as his employer, so as we had to be in the area on another matter, we thought we'd call in and get his address from you. I assume you do have it?'

'I have his home address, but he said he was going to move out of the area, so he may not be there.' She opened the bottom drawer of a battered grey filing cabinet behind her desk, flipped through a few files and withdrew one. She opened it on the desk and inspected the papers inside. 'Here we are — it's 76 Tollpuddle Gardens, Havenchester West.'

'Thank you,' Pace consulted his notebook and pretended to check the information with the open page, which was, in fact, blank. 'We had it as Havenchester East, which may explain the problem. Do you have a telephone number for him?'

'I only have a mobile number. He told me once that he lived in rented rooms.' She gave him the number.

'Thank you. That is the number we have,

but there was no reply when we tried it. Do you happen to know where he was going after he left you?'

She shook her head.

'I'm afraid I have no idea. I did not even know that he had applied for self-employed status — perhaps he is intending to set up as an instructor on his own. He was friendly and personable enough, but not very communicative about his private life. You might want to check with his landlady. He was a sensible young man, so I would imagine that he probably left a forwarding address with her.' Her tone suggested that she would not give such a testimonial for every young man that she knew.

'I'll do that.' He nodded, started to close his notebook, paused and added a final question. 'Do you happen to know if he has any relatives in the city?'

'He has a married brother in London whom he gave as next of kin; he never mentioned anyone else. I believe that the brother has done very well for himself; he works for a bank, as far as I remember. I suppose Mr Jones might have gone to stay with him. He might have felt that there were more opportunities in London.'

'Do you have an address for the brother?'

Mrs Ambrose consulted her file again. Had

she been of a more suspicious nature, she might have wondered whether providing that information was strictly necessary, but, like many people who were faced with apparent officialdom, once she had accepted Pace's story and started answering his questions, she continued to do so automatically.

'Kenneth Jones, Apartment 7C, Kingsway Towers, Barbican. I have a telephone number for him, as well.'

Pace duly wrote the information into his notebook, put it away and got to his feet. The chair swayed a bit, but remained intact.

'Thank you for your help.' He smiled at her.

'My pleasure.' She smiled in return; he really was a very nice man, even though his colleague was a bit odd. Still, he had clearly suffered a head injury recently so perhaps that explained it. She saw them out of the building and turned back to watch the class, the visit disappearing into the depths of her memory as she concentrated on the steps being performed in front of her with varying degrees of expertise.

★   ★   ★

76 Tollpuddle Gardens was part of a four-storey Victorian terrace that had seen

better days but still held a hint of former glory, like an out-of-work former soap star opening a supermarket. It had been divided up into separately rented rooms. There was no Jones on the list of tenants inside the archway over the front door, and Pace rang the bell marked 'A Kemp — Landlady'.

The door was opened by a short angular woman with a sharp expression, wearing a pinafore apron and with her hair in curlers. She could have stepped straight into the role of landlady in a black and white British comedy of the fifties or sixties.

Pace didn't bother to use his tax inspector persona; he gave no explanation, just said that he was looking for Jeffrey Jones and was he in?

'Mr Jones? He moved out two days ago.' Her voice rasped from gossip and cigarettes.

'Did he leave a forwarding address?'

'No, he didn't. He paid his rent up to date and said he was going travelling and didn't know where he'd be. He asked me to keep any post for him and said he'd call back in a month or so to pick it up, although he wasn't expecting anything.'

'You've no idea where he went?' Pace was starting to get irritated by Jones and his disappearing act.

'No, he loaded his cases into his car and off he went.'

'What sort of car was it?' Pace seized on the new information eagerly.

'It's a Volvo, I don't know the exact make. A small one, silver colour, it was.'

'Registration?' he asked, without much hope.

'Starts with a Y.'

Pace sighed.

'Do you know if he has any relatives or close friends in the area?'

The landlady thought for a moment. She took a packet of cigarettes from her apron pocket and lit one, presumably as an aid to thought.

'He's got a brother who came to see him once. He works in London for one of those big accounting firms or something. Nice man.'

'Kenneth?' Pace thought that if the woman started having any doubts about answering his questions, the fact that he knew the brother's name might help to allay any suspicion.

She nodded, apparently happy to tell him all she knew.

'Kenneth. That was it, Kenneth Jones.'

'Did he stay here when he visited?'

'No, my Mr Jones went to stay with him.

The brother owns a cottage somewhere up around here. It's not in the city; it's on the coast north of here. He said it was about an hour's drive or so away.'

'Where is it exactly?' That was more like it, a cottage hideaway sounded very promising.

'I don't know, he didn't tell me.' She seemed disappointed not to be able to help. 'He said it was a nice quiet spot, well away from the beaten track.'

This was sounding better and better.

'When did they go?'

She pondered for a moment.

'Sometime last summer — July, I think. It was about the time of my Alf's birthday.'

Pace didn't bother to find out more about Alf, whether he was husband, brother or son. He nodded his thanks and motioned to Gray that they were leaving.

'What do we do now?' Gray asked, as they walked back to where Pace had parked the car. Although impressed with Pace's interrogation techniques, he was starting to get bored. He preferred extracting information with the aid of a razor.

'We need to find out where that cottage is. If they didn't try to get right away immediately, they'll be lying low somewhere and that sounds just the place.'

'So how do we find it?'

Pace looked grim.

'I think it's time we paid another call on Beverly Wallace's sister. And this time, we'll make sure we get the truth out of her.'

Gray smirked. That sounded more promising. Maybe he'd get to use the razor after all.

10

When Julie and Tanner arrived at the agency the following morning they found Ella was already there looking calm, neat and efficient as always and wearing her usual combination of skirt and top that were tight and short in all the right places. Tanner thought it amazing that she didn't have a permanent cold all through the winter. They smiled good mornings at each other and, as Tanner followed Julie into his office, he caught Ella's eye. She gave him a wink and a big grin that probably constituted insubordination. Tanner grinned back at her.

Ella brought in two strong coffees which Tanner hoped would get his brain cells working. He went through the post as he waited for inspiration, but the coffee didn't seem to be very effective. Julie sat at the side of his desk at his PC trawling through various internet sites to pick up details of any companies or businesses Harry Milton was involved in. She was also trying to see if she could find any trace of Harper and Winston. Her frown indicated that she wasn't having much success in either enterprise.

Tanner thought that it was beginning to look as though they were going to have to use the same tactics with Milton that they had with Vernon Bridger — go charging in and see what happened. The trouble was that Milton was both cleverer and more dangerous than Bridger. He might react, but just as likely he would deny everything, sit tight and wait for them to make another move. And Tanner wasn't sure that there was another move for them to make. He felt as though he was trying to plan an attack in chess with all his opponent's pieces out of sight on another board altogether.

After half an hour, Tanner had sorted the post and was deliberating whether to see if another coffee might be a help or a hindrance. He was just going to ask Julie for her opinion when there was a light tap on the door. Ella came in and closed the door behind her.

'There's a woman just come into the office. Her name's Sandi Wallace and she says she wants to see you and Miss Cooper.'

Julie looked up from the screen, rubbed her eyes and looked across at Ella with puzzled interest.

'She asked for both of us?'

Ella nodded.

'Yep. I thought that was interesting enough

for you to be interrupted. I asked her what it was about, but she says she'll only talk to the two of you. She looks pretty het up about something.'

'You'd better bring her in then, please,' Tanner said.

In view of their lack of progress in the department of bright ideas Tanner thought it wouldn't do any harm to see Sandi Wallace. If she specifically wanted to see Julie as well, it might lead to something. Besides, he was supposed to be running a detective agency, so he couldn't just limit himself to one client, no matter how involved he was getting.

Ella opened the door again and stepped aside for Sandi Wallace to walk into the office. Tanner and Julie's first impression was of the barely controlled nervousness in her round, attractive face. She wore a high-necked dark-green jersey and knee-length black skirt with a brown suede coat and brown boots. Her eyes were covered by a pair of enormous sun glasses, even though it was a cloudy day. Tanner jumped to an immediate conclusion as to the reason for that — it wasn't likely to be because she thought she needed protection from his sunny disposition.

'Please sit down, Miss Wallace. I'm Alec Tanner and this is Julie Cooper.'

'Thank you.' She spoke without opening

her mouth very far, as if afraid of spilling out too many words, and sat down with a stiffness and care that was not in keeping with either her age or her looks. Tanner's guess about the glasses was starting to look more and more probable.

'What can we do for you?' he asked.

Sandi Wallace sat without speaking for a moment, her small shapely hands gripping the shoulder bag that she had placed on her lap, the knuckles gleaming white. She looked to be one nervous shock away from breaking down completely. Tanner thought for a moment that she was reconsidering her decision to come, but she must have been gathering her thoughts because when she spoke her voice was low but firm and determined.

'I want you to help my sister Beverly; I think she's in terrible danger. I want you to find her and warn her; help her if possible.'

'Why did you specifically come to Miss Cooper and me to help?' Tanner asked gently.

'I work in the Pussy Kat Klub as a dancer. The club is owned by Vernon Bridger, so I know a bit about what goes on in the city, the people who run certain things. I heard people talking at the club. I heard them say that the two of you had threatened Mr Bridger and that when he sent a team out to teach you a lesson, you taught them one. That sounded as though you wouldn't be afraid to help me. And that you might be able to succeed.'

'Is it Bridger that your sister is in trouble with?' Tanner asked.

She shook her head.

'No, it's a man called Harry Milton. Do you know him?'

Julie and Tanner exchanged a startled glance. Perhaps this wouldn't turn out to be a separate case after all.

'I know him,' Tanner confirmed. 'I've met him a couple of times, although not, as it were, in a business sense — either his or mine.'

She looked blank for a moment, and then dipped her head in a brief nod, like a nervous bird spotting a fast worm.

'Why is Milton a danger to your sister?' Tanner asked.

Sandi Wallace gathered her thoughts again.

'Beverly has been Harry Milton's permanent live-in girlfriend for more than two years now. For the last few months she's also been seeing someone else — a man who was giving her dancing lessons. His name is Jeffrey Jones. Two days ago she ran away with him.' She paused.

'And Milton is jealous and wants her back?' Tanner completed.

She shrugged.

'It's partly that, perhaps, his ego doesn't like to be thwarted. But it's mainly because she emptied his safe before she went. I think there must have been a considerable sum in there and not just in money. Beverly told me some of her plans last time we met. I was part of her alibi. Some of the time she was seeing Jeffrey she was supposed to be seeing me, so I had to be in the know in case I met Milton or any one in his organization who might be able to report back. I warned her against antagonizing Milton, but she said she loved Jeffrey and she wanted a new life with him. I can't say I blamed her for that.

'Milton has a minder, a man called Jack Pace. Beverly ran away early Wednesday morning and that afternoon, Pace came to see me at the club just before I was due to go on stage. He tried to find out if I knew anything. I pretended that I didn't, even though he knocked me around a bit and threatened worse if I lied. But I knew what they'd do to Beverly if they caught her. They didn't know about Jeffrey at that stage, so I just played ignorant and he believed me. He took my key and went and searched my flat, but there wasn't anything there for him to find.'

She took a deep breath before continuing.

'Pace must have found out more after that. Yesterday afternoon he came again and he brought a low-life called Reggie Gray with him. They knew about Jeffrey and they think he and Beverly have gone into hiding in Jeffrey's brother's cottage. They thought I knew where it was and they tried to make me tell them. This was the result.' She took off her glasses and looked across the desk at them. There were two massive bruises round her eyes. The right eye was completely shut, the area round it black and swollen. The left was a little better, only partly closed although still so swollen it seemed that she must have had trouble seeing at all. 'There are similar marks all over my body,' she added. 'I won't be dancing for a while.'

'Did you tell them anything?' Julie's voice was soothing, but there was a clear edge to it. She was hoping Pace and Gray might get a dose of that medicine themselves.

'No.' Sandi shook her head. 'I'm not sure I could have held out from telling them, but I really don't know where the cottage is. Beverly wouldn't tell me — she said it was too dangerous for me and if I genuinely didn't know I'd be more convincing because they were bound to question me after she'd gone. I suppose it worked. I must have sounded genuine, because they threatened to break bones if I didn't talk, but in the end they held back from that.'

'Bully for them,' Tanner said in a dry voice.

'Gray wanted to cut me, as a lesson, but Pace stopped him. I doubt if it was for compassionate reasons, I suppose they didn't want to risk involving doctors and hospitals unless it was absolutely necessary.'

'What exactly do you want us to do?' Julie asked.

'Find out where the cottage is and get there before Pace and Gray. Warn Beverly and Jeffrey that Milton knows where they are and that they have to leave and find somewhere else to hide.'

'The police could find them more quickly,' Julie pointed out, omitting to mention that she was the police, albeit on extended leave.

Sandi looked really frightened for the first time.

'No, we can't involve the police. If Milton or Bridger found out I'd gone to the police, they'd kill me. If you do it, with any luck they need never know that I've come to you. Please help me.'

Tanner nodded.

'We'll do what we can. What can you tell us about Jeffrey Jones's brother?'

Sandi gave a sigh of relief and some of the anxiety seemed to fade from her face. Tanner thought that she had more faith in them than he did. If Milton's people had already found out about the cottage the day before, they could be there and gone before he and Julie had even located it.

'His name is Kenneth. He works for a finance company in London and travels abroad quite a lot. He's married and lives in the Barbican somewhere — I don't know exactly where.'

'What about the firm he works for?'

'They haven't mentioned it to me.'

Sandi twisted her slim fingers together on her lap.

'Thank you so much for agreeing to help. If Milton gets to Beverly he'll kill her. I've got to do all I can to help her.' Despair was starting to creep back into her voice.

'Do you know where Jones worked and his home address?' Tanner asked.

'Yes.' She took a notebook from her shoulder bag, wrote on it and tore off the page. 'That's the dance studio where he worked and the place where he rented rooms. I've never been to either of them, but Beverly mentioned the studio when she first went there for lessons, before the affair with Jeffrey started. She told me where he lived when I started covering for her. If Milton had ever contacted me when she and I were supposed

218

to be together, I could have left a message there; not that I ever had to.'

Tanner nodded. Beverly seemed to have thought some things through quite thoroughly, even if her love life was pretty complicated — and dangerous.

'We'll do what we can.' He gave her his card. 'Ring the office if you need to contact us or if Pace comes back. If we aren't around, you can leave a message, you can completely trust everyone who works here.' He paused. An idea had been nagging away at the back of his mind as they were talking and the more he thought about it, the more likely — and unpleasant — it became. 'You said you aren't able to work for a while because of the beating you took, are you intending to stay at home for a few days?'

'I suppose so. I hadn't really thought about it,' she looked puzzled. 'Is it important?'

'It might be better if you stayed somewhere else.'

Alarm flared in her eyes.

'You think I might still be in danger?'

'It's possible. I don't want to frighten you unduly, but one of the reasons they didn't hurt you so much that you couldn't get around might be that they're following you in the hope that you'll lead them to Beverly. They could well have followed you here.

When Pace had your key he could even have bugged your flat.'

Sandi started to shiver. Tanner wondered if he should have been so blunt, but it was more dangerous for her not to be aware of the potential risk.

Julie came round the desk, sat on the edge of the client chair and put her arm round Sandi's shoulders.

'Alec is just speculating,' she said gently. 'It may not be like that but he's right, you need to keep alert. Did you notice if you were followed here?'

Sandi swallowed and shook her head.

'I didn't really look. It didn't occur to me. My flatmate was out when Pace went round with the key, so I don't know what he did there, he just left the key at the club when he finished. He could even have copied it.' She looked forlorn and defeated. 'I'm not much good at this sort of thing. I always try to avoid trouble.'

'Is there anyone else you can stay with — a friend, perhaps?'

She shook her head.

'Most of my friends are connected with my work; they work for Bridger or someone like him. Some of them would probably turn me in, either for money or through fear, and those I can trust would be in danger because of me; I couldn't lay them open to that.'

Tanner thought for a moment.

'One of our former clients might be prepared to help,' he said. 'She's in the Territorial Army and a pretty formidable lady. She wouldn't take kindly to two men beating up a woman; you'd be safe with her. She owns a keep-fit studio and runs defence classes for women in the evening. She said I could call on her if I ever needed a favour. I'll need to speak to her first, of course.'

He gave Sandi Wallace a reassuring smile.

'I'll contact her and see what I can arrange. Someone can go home with you so you can pack a bag.'

'Thank you so much. What about your fees? I have some money.' She fumbled in her shoulder bag and brought out a small wad of notes. 'One hundred and fifty, is that enough? It's all I could get at short notice, but I have some savings I can draw on.'

Tanner nodded.

'That will be fine for the moment. Don't worry about paying more than that for now, this might tie in with something else we're working on. We'll let you know tomorrow when we've had a chance to look into it. If you'll wait in the outer office, I'll start making arrangements for you.'

Sandi got to her feet, wincing as she put

her weight on her left leg. 'Gray's handiwork,' she said in answer to Julie's look. She put the glasses back on and Tanner opened the door for her. Julie watched the new client limp out. She hoped very much that they'd be able to have words with Mr Gray.

★   ★   ★

'If we can help Beverly Wallace, she might be able to give us a lead to Harper and Winston,' Julie commented as Tanner went back to his desk. 'If not, she could give us a useful insight into Milton's organization.'

'Yep, the same thought occurred to me. I think we need to consult the oracle again,' Tanner picked up his desk phone and asked Ted Manning to come over. Manning arrived in a few seconds, full of boundless energy as always, and lowered himself into the spare chair.

'What's up, doc?'

Tanner gave him an outline of Sandi Wallace's story. Manning nodded thoughtfully.

'Could be exceedingly useful, that could.'

'What do you know about Pace and Gray?' Tanner asked. 'Could they have shot Julie and her aunt?'

Ted leant back in his chair, frowned for a

moment and then shook his head.

'I don't think so. Pace is a hard man and he could easily be a killer, but he works directly for Milton who uses him for all the nasty personal chores, presumably on the basis that if all that is done by one man and that's someone he can trust, he can sleep easier. He might have used Pace if Julie had busted one of his own rackets, but he wouldn't risk him by hiring him out. Gray is an even nastier piece of work in many ways. For Pace, hurting people is just a job, Gray enjoys it. Gray tends to use a knife or a razor rather than a shooter; he does debt collecting, puts the frighteners on, that sort of thing. He and Pace don't generally work together; I don't see them as a hit team. I still think Harper and Winston are our best bet if Milton took the hit job.'

'You do know the nicest people,' Julie commented.

'It was worth a thought,' Tanner said, 'it could have simplified matters considerably.'

Manning grinned. 'You know your trouble, you want things too easy.'

'Yeah.' Tanner thought for a moment. 'We need to look after Sandi Wallace first. You remember Annie Thorpe?'

Manning's grin broadened.

'Intimately,' he said. Tanner raised his

eyebrows. Knowing Ted Manning, he meant that literally.

'Do you think she would look after Sandi for a few days if you asked her nicely? Let her stay in her spare room? She said we could call on her for a favour if we needed to. She was very impressed with our service, as I recall.'

'Yes, indeed. And the after-service care as well.'

★ ★ ★

Tanner introduced Sandi Wallace to Ted Manning and left him to arrange matters with Annie Thorpe whilst he and Julie went to visit Jeffrey Jones's last known place of residence. Before they left, Tanner took a look out of the front office window to see whether he could spot someone watching the front of the building who might have followed Sandi. There were no obvious loitering pedestrians, but there were a couple of parked cars that could have fitted the bill. There was also a café diagonally opposite where a shadower could linger and watch the building entrance. A watcher wouldn't know that Sandi wasn't visiting one of the other occupants of the building, of course, but a glance at the sign by the front door would make the detective agency the first choice in the circumstances. Sandi wasn't likely to be interested in either a secretarial career, or having her picture taken. The more Tanner thought about it, the more convinced he became that, with little else to go on, Milton's people would aim to convince Sandi that they believed her story and then watch her to see where she led them. He doubted if Pace or Gray would actually do the watching — apart from anything else, she would recognize them — but they would certainly be within call.

As far as Tanner could make out, no one followed them on the way to Tollpuddle Gardens. Not that it's very easy to tell in the midst of city traffic, but none of the cars behind them when they left the agency were still there when they got to their destination. Of course, Tanner thought, that could just mean that they were better at tailing than he was at spotting.

When they reached the house, Tanner pushed the buzzer for flat 1A, which had a very faded card that he could just decipher as reading: 'A Kemp — Landlady'. After three pushes and no reply, he deduced that she was out (they didn't call him a master detective for nothing). He then tried 3B — T Gorringe. After a few moments a disembodied voice that was just about recognizable as female croaked out of the grille and asked his name and business.

'My name's Alec Tanner. I'm a private detective. I'm trying to locate Jeffrey Jones. I think he moved from the rooms next door to you and I wondered if I could a have word with you about him.'

There was a moment's silence and Tanner thought she had switched off on him. Then there was another crackle from the grille that he presumed translated as some variant of 'OK' and the door buzzed and clicked open.

They walked into a narrow, gloomy hall that smelt of dust and long dead meals, but fortunately nothing more objectionable. They went up the even narrower and gloomier stairs to the second floor where two doors stood facing each other on either side of a small landing with faded carpet and grubby window. A lace curtain that was more lace than curtain hung limply across the window. Both doors sported dark-brown paint that was starting to peel; the door to the right had 3A screwed on to it in gold letters. 3B was already open, with its owner standing waiting for them. Tanner introduced Julie as his colleague; it seemed easier than a more complicated explanation of her official rank-ing.

T Gorringe — they never did discover what

the 'T' stood for — stood aside and invited them in.

The inside of the flat was a pleasant surprise. Although small, the living room was bright and cheerfully furnished with several paintings and ornaments spread around at intervals. There were two armchairs of slightly faded but not threadbare flowered material. Ms Gorringe had clearly stamped her own personality in the room. A TV stood on a table in a corner by the window with the sound turned down. A smiling host seemed to be discussing a burning issue with the studio audience. Tanner thought that the intellectual content was probably improved without the words.

Ms Gorringe's brown eyes stared at them curiously from behind pink-rimmed spectacles. Her nose was as red as her cheeks and that, together with the handkerchief clutched in her hand revealed why they had caught her at home on a workday morning.

'We're sorry to disturb you,' Tanner said, after they had accepted her invitation to sit down.

'That's all right,' she spoke thickly. 'I'm getting pretty bored up here on my own anyway.' She paused to dab at her nose. 'Don't worry, I'm not contagious any more.' She smiled reassuringly.

Tanner wondered if the germs knew that.

'We won't keep you long,' he assured her. 'We're trying to locate Mr Jones rather urgently and, as he's moved, we wondered if you knew him very well and might know where he'd gone.'

'He moved out one evening a couple of days ago,' she said. 'We were quite friendly, living on the same floor here. We used to pop into each other's rooms from time to time for a chat and a cup of tea. He was a good neighbour; I was sorry when he left.'

'Do you know where he went to?' Julie asked.

'No, I'm sorry I don't. He said he was going abroad with his girl-friend, but things weren't fixed up yet and they were taking a short holiday first. He didn't say where.'

'It's to do with his girlfriend's sister that we need to contact him,' Julie said, which wasn't a complete lie. 'We understand that he might have gone to his brother's cottage — do you know where that is?'

She shook her head again.

'I know that he has one, Jeffrey went to stay there last year with him, but I don't know exactly where it is. I believe it's somewhere north of the city, on the coast, but he didn't say exactly where.'

'You wouldn't have his brother's address or

phone number, I suppose?'

'No.' She thought for a moment. 'But I know the name of the firm he works for, would that be of any use?' She seemed delighted to be more positive. 'It's called Kenton Anderson, it's quite a big finance firm in London. Is that any help to you?'

Julie nodded, it was, at least some progress. 'That could be very helpful indeed.'

They left Ms Gorringe to nurse her germs and went back downstairs. As they were already in the building, Tanner tried the landlady's door on the way out, but there was no response to his knocking. He supposed that was what was meant by an absentee landlord.

* * *

By the time they reached the top of the flight of narrow dark stairs that led to the Dance 'Til You Drop dance studio, Tanner was surprised some people had much breath left for dancing.

As they came through the swing doors that led into the studio, several couples were on the floor. A tall woman walked over to them, moving with the smooth grace of the professional dancer and smiling pleasantly. Tanner and Julie walked towards her, keeping to the side wall so as to avoid being trampled by the dancers, and they met halfway.

'Good afternoon. If you are interested in lessons, we have a beginner's class this evening, or more advanced tomorrow.'

'We haven't come for lessons, I'm afraid,' Julie told her. 'We'd like to talk to you about a former employee — Jeffrey Jones.'

She looked startled.

'Are you with the Tax Office as well?'

'No.' It was Julie's turn to look surprised. 'Why should you think that?'

'Well, two gentlemen from the Inland Revenue were here yesterday asking about Mr Jones.' She started to look concerned and glanced at the dancing couples as if suspecting one of them might be a spy. 'Perhaps you had better come into the office.'

They followed her into the rear room and sat down facing her as she moved behind her desk.

'My name is Veronica Ambrose, I am the owner of the dance studio,' she paused expectantly.

'I'm Alec Tanner, a private detective,' he gave her his card. 'This is . . . '

'My name's Julie Cooper. I'm a police officer, but at the moment I'm on leave and I'm working with Mr Tanner.' Julie showed her warrant card. She thought giving Mrs

230

Ambrose her official title would make her more receptive to their questions.

Mrs Ambrose blinked at them from behind her spectacles.

'Is Mr Jones in some sort of trouble?' She asked. 'First the tax inspectors and now detectives.' She shook her head. 'He seemed such a level-headed, respectable young man, but you can never tell these days.'

'I doubt whether the two men yesterday were real tax inspectors. He isn't so much in trouble as in danger,' Julie told her. 'We need to find him urgently to see that he gets protection.'

'Good heavens,' Mrs Ambrose eyed her visitors shrewdly. 'You mean the two men yesterday were the ones wanting to harm him?'

'It seems likely. What did you tell them?'

Mrs Ambrose shook her head in self-reproach.

'I thought there was something odd about them, but one of them, at least was very plausible.'

'What information did you give them?' Julie asked again.

'His home address and mobile phone number and his brother's address and home number.'

Julie and Tanner exchanged glances.

'You have Kenneth Jones's address and telephone number?'

'Yes.' She took out a file from a filing cabinet and gave them the details.

'I do hope I haven't helped them to find him.'

Julie nodded; so did she.

★   ★   ★

When Julie and Tanner got back to the office, Tanner immediately rang Kenneth Jones's home number. He got an answering machine and left a message for him to ring back urgently as they needed to contact his brother. Then he rang directory enquiries and got the number for Kenton Anderson. There were three numbers, one of which was the head office, so he tried that first.

A receptionist put Tanner through to Mr Jones's personal assistant. She told him in a cool, efficient voice that Mr Jones was meeting with a client in the client's office and couldn't be contacted, but he was expected back at their offices soon after five and she'd get him to ring Mr Tanner then. Tanner thanked her and told her to emphasize that it was very urgent. She agreed to do so. The temperature of her voice seemed unaffected by the urgency.

Tanner tried the home number again at fifteen minute intervals without getting past the answering machine, which didn't seem to appreciate the urgency either. Just after five, Ella put through a call from Kenneth Jones.

'Thank you for ringing back. As I told your PA, my name's Alec Tanner; I'm a private detective working in Havenchester.'

'You wanted to speak to me about my brother?' He had a strong, no-nonsense, voice with a distinct northern accent that suggested life in London hadn't affected his roots.

'Yes, I need to contact him urgently. I believe he is staying at your cottage up here and I was hoping you would give me the address.'

There was a moment's silence whilst this was digested.

'My brother specifically stated that he did not want to be disturbed.'

At least, Tanner thought, he wasn't denying that his brother was at the cottage.

'Do you know why your brother wanted to use the cottage?' Tanner asked.

'He wants a few days' holiday with a friend.' The tone was still cautious. 'And I still don't know why I should be discussing my brother's private affairs with a stranger.'

'Your brother is in serious danger, Mr Jones. He has run away with the girlfriend of a very dangerous man called Harry Milton, a man with serious criminal connections. I believe that they are intending to lie low in your cottage; they believe they are safe there because they don't think Milton knows about your brother. However, I have discovered that Milton does know about him, and that he is staying at the cottage, but he doesn't yet know exactly where it is either.' Tanner hoped that was still true. 'I have been hired by the girlfriend's sister to find them and warn them to change their hiding place.'

The pause this time was even longer.

'Supposing this remarkable story to be true, how do I know that you do not represent these people who are trying to harm my brother?'

Tanner closed his eyes and swore under his breath. Kenneth Jones was right, of course, but there was only one way to convince him, and that meant further delay.

'If you ring Detective Chief Inspector Richard Mariner at the Havenchester City Police serious crime squad, he'll vouch for me. Could you ring him straight away and then phone me back?'

'Very well.' The offer to involve the police seemed to impress him.

'I'll give you the number.'

'Don't worry — I'll get my PA to find it.'

Tanner sighed; there was so little trust these days. Still, Jones was right again, Tanner could have arranged for someone to answer the other number and call themselves the Havenchester City Police.

It seemed to take hours, but it was only just over ten minutes before Jones rang back. This time his voice was less restrained and more concerned about his brother.

'Chief Inspector Mariner has vouched for you,' he said, 'and confirmed what you say about this man Milton. My cottage is situated on the west coast near the village of Lower Winkley. It is not immediately on a main road and it is quite difficult to find, I'll give you precise directions.'

Tanner wrote them down.

'Thank you. Have you been contacted by anyone else?' he asked. 'I think Milton's people found out about the cottage yesterday and they were given your home number at the same time.'

'No one else has contacted me. My wife has been away for a few days and there were no messages last night on the answer phone at home. I have been with a client all day and have had no messages other than yours that were not work related.' He paused and the business-like tone crumbled a little. 'Please do all you can to help Jeffrey.'

'I will,' Tanner assured him. Whether they could do anything was another matter. 'We'll leave for the cottage now. I'll get him to call you later.'

That was assuming Jones would be in a fit state to ring his brother later, Tanner thought. The fact that Kenneth hadn't been contacted was worrying; it suggested that Milton might have other ways of locating the cottage and could be hours ahead of them. They could easily get there and find it empty.

11

Harry Milton had cultivated many and varied contacts in many and varied walks of life and he owned every one of them in some way or other. Some he had let off gambling debts in return for present or future favours; some had asked him for help and had received it, not realizing that they had put themselves into a similar position to Dr Faustus, their devil being somewhat less immortal, but no less demanding. All were expected to repay their debt at some point and most of the things he required meant that once you had done them Harry Milton had a hold on you for life. Sometimes when he cultivated one of his contacts, he had no specific idea of the use he would be able to make of them; he just felt that it might be useful in the future to have access to whatever they might be in a position to provide.

One such contact was a man called Simon Joiner, an employee in the Havenchester City Council tax offices. Mr Joiner was too fond of risking his salary on the performance of horses that seemed incapable of finishing a race unless they had other horses ahead of them and, as a result, he had run up significant debts in one of Milton's businesses. It had occurred to Milton that someone working in the council's tax department would have access to the sort of personal information that could well prove helpful and he had accordingly cleared Joiner's debts from his books.

Now was the time for that debt to be called in.

At nine a.m., Harry Milton was on the phone to the council offices. There were occasions when he felt that the personal touch obtained maximum co-operation.

'I'd like to speak to Simon Joiner, please.'

'I'm sorry, Mr Joiner is not available this morning.' The female voice sounded genuinely disappointed for him. 'Can someone else help?'

Milton's voice grew slightly less pleasant.

'No, I need to speak to him personally. Can he be reached?' Milton usually had others making initial telephone contact for him, so that by the time he came on the line the person he wanted was already there and ready to speak to him. He was not used to being frustrated.

'He's at a seminar this morning at our training centre.' The voice told him brightly. 'We have some new performance indicators to meet and all the senior managers have to — '

'Yes, I see,' Milton cut in. The only performance indicator he was interested in at the moment was the length of time it would take to get his hands on Beverly Wallace. 'When do you expect him back?'

'There's a lunch laid on, so it will probably be after two. Can I ask him to ring you?'

'No, I'll phone back later.'

He slammed the phone down and scowled. His working life was being disrupted and that annoyed him. Worse than that, the longer things dragged on, the more time there was for word to get round that Harry Milton had been shafted by his own girlfriend. Such stories undermined his position in the sort of businesses he was mixed up in and that affected his influence, which could have a detrimental impact on both his profits and his control over his empire. He was very conscious that it could take just one young bright spark to think that Harry Milton was an easy target and things could get very messy indeed. He was completely confident of his ruthless ability to win through, but it was a waste of time and effort he could well do without. Things were nowhere near that stage yet, of course, but he needed to get the matter sorted quickly and that meant making an example of Beverly Wallace.

His mood was not improved an hour later when Jack Pace came in to report that the man he had watching Sandi Wallace's flat had followed her to an office building in the centre of the city.

'One of the occupants is Tanner's detective agency.'

Milton swore and added further stab marks to his blotter with his letter opener.

'That's not a coincidence.'

'Hardly,' Pace agreed. 'Do you want us to pick her up again when she leaves?' He too was feeling the pressure of them not having located Beverly Wallace yet. Any doubts about Milton's authority would inevitably reflect back on him, and that could be dangerous.

Milton thought for a moment. It was tempting, but he was aware that he needed to keep police interest out of his affairs and taking out his anger on Beverly's sister, although temporarily satisfying, would not achieve their main aim and it could lead to complications.

'No,' he decided reluctantly, 'just keep having her followed. This doesn't necessarily mean that she knows where her bitch of a sister is; she could have hired Tanner to locate the cottage for her so that she can warn her sister that we're on to her.'

'So do you want us to keep tabs on Tanner as well? In case he finds them before we do?'

Milton frowned. Important as this was, he didn't have unlimited manpower, certainly not of the calibre needed for smart on-the-spot decisions.

'We don't know he'll be looking into it personally.' He killed his blotter twice more. 'But if he is and he gets lucky he could lead us there.' With a final stab, he made up his mind. Being so indecisive irritated him. This thing had really got under his skin. 'Do we have someone who knows Tanner by sight?'

'Yeah, we can use Lenny Kelly. Tanner got his brother sent down for theft a couple of years ago.'

'Good.' Milton nodded. Kelly was someone who could use his initiative. 'Put him on to it. And tell Lenny not to let himself be seen.'

'Right.' Pace nodded, his face impassive. Giving unnecessary instructions like that showed just how rattled Milton was becoming.

After Pace had left, Milton tried to concentrate on the papers in front of him. Looking at details of the money coming in from his various enterprises and assessing the profit-making potential of new activities usually focused his mind totally, but today he couldn't concentrate. Images of Beverly kept coming into his mind, of how she must have duped him over the past months, laughing at him behind his back. For someone who got a lot of his pleasure out of controlling other people, to discover he had been manipulated himself was hard to bear.

Finally, he gave up. He needed to relax; there was too much going round inside his head. He took his key ring from his trouser pocket, selected a small key that had no duplicate and unlocked the top right-hand drawer of his desk. He removed another key from inside, closed the drawer and locked it again, pushed back his chair and got up. He left the study and walked upstairs to the door of the room on the top floor that was always kept locked. Using the key from his desk, he opened the door, went inside, switched on the carefully placed lighting and turned to lock the door again. Then he sat down in the comfortable leather swivel chair that stood in the centre of the room. He sat for a few moments, closing his eyes and breathing deeply to relieve his tension. Then he opened his eyes again and started studying the painting on the wall in front of him, one of several that hung at intervals around the room. Each painting was by a master, each lit by its own soft spotlight. The room's only window was covered by a thick blind that was never raised. Behind the blind was a secure grille. Beneath three of the paintings were small display cabinets, each holding a few exquisite pieces of porcelain. This was his sanctuary, the one place he could come to relax fully.

After a few moments, he felt the inner peace and almost sensual pleasure that always came to him when locked away with his treasures and a smile crossed his face. As always, it added an extra dimension to his pleasure to know that he could never bring another person into this room, because everything in it was stolen property.

*   *   *

Lenny Kelly had been lucky. He had reached the junction with the road in which the detective agency was situated and he was just about to turn right towards it when he saw Alec Tanner driving past, accompanied by an attractive brunette he assumed was Julie Cooper. Kelly changed his indicator from right to left and took advantage of a brief gap in the traffic two cars behind his quarry to pull out smoothly in pursuit. Tanner had been concentrating on the traffic ahead and had not seen him; the woman had glanced incuriously at his car as he reached the junction and then turned her attention elsewhere.

Kelly was a tall, thin man of mixed Irish and Afro-Caribbean parentage. He had curly dark hair, a complexion of milky coffee and an almost permanent expression of humour and goodwill in his green eyes. He found humour in nearly every situation, but could be cold, calculating and totally ruthless when he needed to be. He had worked for Milton for several years and although he could turn his hand to a number of activities when required, it was behind the wheel that he felt most at home. His driving skills were exceptional and his assessment of traffic, timing and space was the equal of most motor sport drivers. He had acted as getaway driver on several occasions in the past, but as Milton's activities started to assume a veneer of respectability, he was now employed more for general driving, as Milton's chauffeur when necessary and for following people.

The city-centre traffic was heavy with the usual congestion caused by road works, vans unloading and the sheer volume of cars and Kelly was able to keep three or four vehicles between him and his target car without fear of losing it. They moved through the business area of the city and then out to more residential areas. Traffic thinned a little and speeded up to over twenty miles an hour. He saw Tanner's car turn down Tollpuddle Gardens, and followed. There were no other cars between them now, which was a nuisance, but when Tanner pulled over and parked, Kelly drove on past and turned down the next side road on the left. He spotted a space on the opposite side of the road and quickly turned his car and parked facing back up towards Tollpuddle Gardens again.

Kelly left his car and moved cautiously to the end of the road. He saw Tanner and the woman standing by the entrance to a house twenty yards away on the other side of the road. When they went inside, he sauntered casually along the street and walked up to look at the door. None of the names meant anything to him. He made a mental note of the number and strolled back to his car. Unless Tanner did a U-turn in the road, which considering how narrow it was with cars parked on both sides seemed unlikely, he would have to drive past the mouth of the road Kelly was parked in. Kelly could then start up and resume his tail. It would be a bit of a risk, but he'd be certain to be spotted if he just loitered in the street and if he took refuge in a doorway, someone might get suspicious and ring the police.

He got out his mobile and reported back to Pace.

'They're at 76 Tollpuddle Gardens.'

'That's where Jones lived. Keep following them. Don't let them see you.'

Kelly grunted. He hardly needed telling that. He reached over to the back seat and picked up the official-looking clipboard that he kept there. The front sheet was a form he had picked up from his local council office. He pretended to be making notes on the form whilst keeping a watchful eye on the T-junction ahead. He had found that a single person sitting in a car might look suspicious, but someone sitting and filling in a form on a clipboard was always accepted without question as being on official business.

Half an hour later, Tanner drove past and Kelly started his engine and moved out after them. Again, he allowed a couple of cars to get between them as soon as possible.

Tanner's next stop was a public car-park. Fortunately, Kelly had already pulled further back and two other cars entered ahead of him. He drove in behind them without being spotted by Tanner and parked in the next row of spaces. He backed in so as to get a quick start if necessary.

Kelly followed Tanner to the pay and

display machine and got a ticket for an hour. He knew Tanner by sight because he had seen him in court when he had given evidence against Kelly's brother. However, as far as Kelly was aware, Tanner did not know him, so there was little risk.

From where he was parked, Kelly could sit in the car and look across the street. He watched Tanner and Cooper cross the road and go through a doorway at the side of a shop. He peered across at the notice over the doorway and frowned. What on earth were they doing going to a dance studio?

He shrugged to himself mentally and got out his mobile again.

$$\star \quad \star \quad \star$$

It was ten past two when Milton telephoned the council again. This time, he was successful and Joiner was available. Milton identified himself and could hear the alarm in the voice of the man at the other end of the line. Those moments gave him almost as much pleasure as his art collection.

'I need you to do me a favour.'

'What is it?' Joiner asked cautiously.

'A man called Kenneth Jones owns a cottage somewhere on the west coast north of the city. He's bound to be registered as the council tax payer and I want you to get me the address.'

Joiner paused. The phrase Data Protection Act sprang into his mind, but he didn't feel there was much point mentioning that to Milton. He briefly considered refusing, then recalled stories of what happened to punters who failed to pay gambling debts to people like Milton.

'I'll try,' he said eventually, 'but it sounds like it isn't in my council's area.'

'I'm sure you have contacts with colleagues in other authorities.' Milton's voice was silky smooth.

'Yes, but — '

'Here's my number,' Milton had no wish to mess about; they both knew Joiner was going to do what he wanted. 'I'll be waiting for your call.'

Milton hung up; he hoped the clown wouldn't take too long over it.

Pace knocked lightly and came into the study as Milton finished his call.

'Lenny's reported back a few times. He picked up Tanner and a woman — presumably Cooper — just as he got to the agency. He was lucky, he saw them driving past as he got there. He followed them to Jones's flat and to the dance studio. Now they've gone back to the agency.'

Milton grunted.

'What happened to the sister?'

'She was taken back to her flat by Ted Manning, the guy who works for Tanner. They came out with a suitcase and drove off.'

'Where to?'

Pace hesitated.

'We don't know, Manning spotted our tail and lost him.'

Milton snorted.

'Sometimes I think I'd do better employing a gang of monkeys.'

'I don't think it matters. Tanner wouldn't be going to Jones's flat and the dance studio if he knew where the cottage is, he'd have gone straight there. Sandi Wallace must have been telling the truth about that, even if she lied about knowing Jones himself.'

Milton considered that for a moment and then nodded.

'Yeah, you're probably right. Let's just hope my contact in the council comes up with that address.'

It was after four o'clock when Joiner rang back and Milton was starting to get edgy again.

'I've found the information you wanted. The cottage is in the West Linton council area. It took a while to track it down.' He paused, but didn't receive any acknowledgement of the difficulty of his task. 'The cottage is called White Cove View and it's near the village of Lower Winkley.'

Milton hung up with a grunt of thanks and called for Pace.

'I've found out where the cottage is.' He gave him the details. 'Get Gray and go over there. Contact Lenny Kelly and take him as well. We don't need to follow Tanner any more and with three of you there shouldn't be any slip ups. Bring Beverly and Jones to the garage.'

The garage was an old building situated on the edge of a decaying industrial estate, away from prying eyes and ears. It was well soundproofed and had often been used by Milton in the past when he wanted a quiet word with someone.

'Ring me when you're on your way back and I'll meet you there. Bring both of them there if you can, but if that's a problem, finish Jones on the spot and just bring her. She's the one I really want. And make sure you bring my property back as well.'

'Yes, boss.'

Pace was already on his way out.

★ ★ ★

Jeffrey Jones got the call that they had been waiting for on his mobile shortly after breakfast. Beverly, who was clearing away the cups and plates, could hear the relief in his voice and she was already smiling to herself in anticipation.

'That's great, Sean. Thanks for all you've done. Yes, I know exactly where you mean, we'll see you there at nine.' He turned to Beverly with a big grin, swung her around in his arms and kissed her.

'We're on our way at last. Sean has our new papers and he is going to pick us up from the jetty by the disused lighthouse at nine tonight. We'll have to walk there but that shouldn't be a problem. He says it will be easier for him to find us by the jetty than trying to pick us up from somewhere in the bay. He knows this stretch of the coast well and, as there's a full moon tonight, he says the old lighthouse should stand out clearly. In any case, he can take a bearing from the new one.'

The old lighthouse that stood beyond the right-hand point of the bay had been taken out of commission in the late eighties and replaced by a new, fully automated version further along the coast.

Beverly pulled him close and hugged him. She was starting to feel almost light-headed thinking that the nightmare might nearly be over.

'That's brilliant.'

She thought for a moment.

'Couldn't we drive the car over there?'

'I'd rather leave it here out of sight. I'll ask Kenneth to dispose of it once we've got away. If we leave it exposed by the lighthouse and someone reports it, it might alert Milton too quickly.'

Beverly nodded.

'I suppose you're right. I can't always have the easy option.'

Jones smiled at her.

'Once we're home and clear, I'll make sure you always have the soft option.'

Beverly looked at him seriously for a moment.

'Don't make promises you can't keep. I don't mind roughing it in a good cause. Is it deep enough by the lighthouse for him to be able to get his boat up to the jetty?'

Jones shook his head.

'No, he'll anchor his boat off the coast and pick us up in a motor dingy. Do you mind that? The sea might be quite rough in a small boat.'

Beverly laughed.

'I think I can put up with a bit of sea sickness if it gets us out of the reach of Harry

Milton.' She hugged him again. 'I can't believe that we're on our way.'

'Nor can I.' He looked at her. 'We need to think of a way to celebrate.'

'What do you suggest?'

'Well, we can either watch television, or we can amuse ourselves upstairs.'

'Do you mean to take advantage of a poor helpless female?'

'Unless you can think of something better?'

She grinned and took his hand.

'The old ideas are usually the best.'

When they came down again, even the TV that they spent the rest of the morning watching didn't seem as tedious as before.

After lunch they went for what had become a regular walk through the woods. Beverly stood for a while at the edge of the cliff, arm in arm with her lover, and looked out across the bay. She was starting to feel quite attached to the view, although she would be glad to be away from it. The broad curve of the cliff followed the sweep of the bay below with the pale sand that gave the cottage its name. Looking along the cliff top to the right, the woodland came almost to the edge of the cliff and she could not see any of the three cottages she knew nestled like theirs a short distance back from the cliff edge. Beyond the cottages, the woodland thickened and spread backwards, forming a natural barrier between the village of Lower Winkley and the sea, before thinning out again as it reached the point of the cliff above the far side of the bay. Beyond that point, out of sight, the cliff fell away sharply to merge into a flat broad spit of land that jutted out like a natural pier into the sea. The old light-house, dirty white now from the weather and the spray, stood at the end of the spit of land like a long-forgotten sentry still doing its duty. The end of the spit and the lighthouse could be clearly seen from where they stood. On their side of the spit of land, poking out at the foot of the lighthouse towards their bay, was the old grey stone jetty from which they were due to be collected that evening. Beyond the lighthouse, five great jagged columns of rock called the Devil's Claw thrust up from the sea like the fingers of a massive hand lying cupped below the surface ready to drag down any unwary ships that drifted into its clutches. The new lighthouse was out of their sight, further along the coast.

Looking at the rocks, stark and hostile against the grey-green sea, white foam breaking at their bases, it was easy to see how they had got their name and to imagine an ageless, malevolent being lurking beneath the churning water.

Beverly shivered at the fancy and pulled Jones on along the cliff. Perhaps she wouldn't miss the view quite so much after all.

As usual, they saw no one on their walk and got back to the cottage cold but invigorated by the crisp country air.

When they got back indoors, Beverly rubbed her gloved hands together.

'We need to warm up.'

'And how do you suggest we do that?' Jones raised his eyebrows in mock enquiry.

Beverly grinned at him.

'You weren't short of ideas this morning.'

Laughing, arms around each other, they went upstairs.

When they came down again Jones went into the kitchen to start to prepare dinner.

'Blast, we need some more eggs, butter and milk.'

'Can't we make do?' Beverly, in jeans and a thick jumper came to the kitchen door.

'This will be our last meal here; I want it to be a good one.' He closed the door of the small refrigerator. 'I'll walk into the village; the shop should be open for a while yet. It won't take long if I cut through.'

'OK, darling, hurry back.'

He grinned.

'We're starting to sound like an old married couple already.'

He followed the short-cut through the wood to the village that came out just by the edge of the village green. He walked quickly, feeling really happy for the first time in days and he was at the shop in less than fifteen minutes.

The single village shop seemed to hold far more goods inside than the outside appearance indicated, rather like a commerce-related Tardis.

The shop's owner was a friendly widow who, as a result of her position as sole provider of sustenance apart from the pub, knew everyone in village. Although assisted by her son and his wife, she was almost always in the shop herself and she had remembered Jones from when he had stayed at the cottage with his brother the year before. His visit to the shop earlier in the week had resulted in several minutes of conversation about his brother, the weather and village life in general. Although on this occasion he was eager to make his purchases and get back to Beverly, he liked the lady and when he saw that she was alone in the shop, he prepared himself for some necessary small talk.

Her opening words sent all thoughts of small talk, and of dinner, from his mind and a cold shaft of fear running through his body.

'Good evening Mr Jones.' She seemed surprised to see him. 'You've only just missed that friend of yours who's coming for dinner. He was in here not five minutes ago asking for directions to your brother's cottage.'

*   ★   ★   ★

'I can see where Lower Winkley is, but how do we find the cottage?' Reggie Gray peered at the map book in front of him as if expecting the information to suddenly appear on the page.

Jack Pace spared a quick sideways glance to glare at him. They had picked up Lenny Kelly on the outskirts of the city, where he had left his car in a quiet side street, before taking the main A-road that roughly mirrored the line of the coast northwards. After forty minutes, they had left the dual carriageway and branched off on to a B-road, before turning again to follow the signpost to Lower Winkley. They were now driving along a narrow country lane bordered on both sides by a combination of woods and hedges. A number of narrow tracks led off on each side of the road, some had signs but others did not. None of the signs was for White Cove View Cottage.

'If we don't see anything,' Pace said, 'I'll

drive into the village and ask for directions.'

Gray frowned.

'Is that wise? They'll be able to identify us.'

Pace's glare grew stronger. He did not like his ideas to be questioned, particularly by a goon he regarded as having the IQ of a retarded squirrel.

'If we do this properly, there won't be any evidence left that anything happened that we could be accused of. Besides — how else are we going to find the bloody place if it defeats even your map reading skills?' Even as he spoke, he knew Gray wouldn't respond to the sarcasm — he'd probably take it as a compliment.

Pace peered ahead through the windscreen. Although it had been a clear day, the sun was dipping to the horizon and the hedges and trees were throwing deep shadows across the road. 'Besides, if we don't get there soon, it'll be dark and if Beverly and her bloke try to make a run for it we could find it difficult to spot them. They know the area better than we do. Unless you've got a better idea?' Again, the sarcasm was completely wasted on Gray. Pace glanced in the mirror and saw Lenny Kelly grinning as he sprawled across the back seat. At least he had a bit more gumption.

They reached the village less than ten minutes later, having turned left on to a surprisingly broad road that twisted through a short avenue of trees before leading them past the inevitable church and pub. A number of picturesque cottages stood round the small village green. There were a few people about and the village shop was still open. Pace parked the car by the side of the green and walked across to the shop. An old man walking his dog across the grass stopped and stared at the car and its occupants with undisguised curiosity. The dog sat and looked bored. Pace turned and smiled at the man as he walked into the shop. No point in antagonizing the locals.

'Good evening, sir,' the shopkeeper stood alone behind the long, cluttered counter. 'What can I get for you?'

'I'd like some directions please.' Pace gave her his most charming smile. 'I'm an old friend of Jeffrey Jones. He's staying in White Cove View Cottage, his brother's place. He's asked me over for a meal this evening, but I've mislaid his directions and I seem to have lost my way. Do you know where it is?'

'Yes, sir. You've come a bit too far; the cottage isn't actually in the village itself.' The shop owner accepted his story without question.

'You go back up through the village to the T-junction and turn right. Then you take the fourth turning on the right. That leads straight to the cottage; there's no other property down there.'

He repeated the directions, thanked her and returned to the car.

Pace drove to the end of the green, turned the car round and went back the way they had come. The villager stopped again to watch them and even his dog seemed to be taking more of an interest.

Back on the narrow road, Pace counted the turnings on the right. The first three had signs with cottage names, the fourth did not. Pace grunted. That was promising; it suggested someone might have removed the sign to make the place more difficult to find.

The side road was little better than a track, a bumpy and narrow combination of stones, grass and mud. It sloped slightly downhill; Pace was able to keep a minimal touch on the accelerator and the evening was still light enough not to need headlights, so he could minimize any advertisement of their approach. After a short distance, they came to a flat grassy area on the left-hand side of the track. Pace pulled over on to it and turned off the engine.

'We don't want to warn them that we're coming. Come on.'

They went the rest of the way on foot,

moving carefully and keeping to the side of the track, ready to dodge back out of sight when they came into view of the cottage, just in case they were spotted from a window. Pace didn't want any slip ups, he could imagine Milton's reaction if they let their quarry get past them. After twenty yards, the track turned sharply right and opened out on to the flat open area that held the cottage and ended at the edge of the cliff. The cottage stood unlit in front of them. There was a car parked at the left-hand side, which suggested both that the cottage was occupied and that they weren't expected.

Pace held them back out of sight for a moment by the turn of the track.

'Lenny, you wait here in case they try to make a break for it. You'll be able to cut them off if they run for the car. Reggie and I will go round to the other side. Reggie can watch the outside there while I go in. If I miss them, you two can get them when they come out. Remember, Harry wants the woman alive; the bloke can get the chop now if it's easier.'

'What if they overpower you?' Gray asked.

'A civilian and a woman?' Pace didn't bother to answer the question.

Leaving Kelly where he was, and keeping inside the edge of the tree and bush line, Pace and Gray moved carefully round to the other side of the cottage. There was no indication that they had been spotted by anyone inside the cottage. Leaving Gray crouched behind a bush, Pace ran quickly across the few yards of open ground to the edge of the cottage wall. There was still no response from inside. Keeping flat to the wall, and ducking under a window, he edged round to the front door, which had a glass panel at the top. He picked up a loose stone from the path and gave the window in the door a sharp tap. A piece of glass fell inside and he was able to lever out two more pieces. He had made very little noise and the cottage was still silent. He took out his gun, put his hand through the hole in the glass, turned the latch, opened the door and stepped quickly inside.

The door led straight into the living room. One glance told him it was deserted and there were no hiding places. He paused for a moment to listen and heard nothing. He glanced at the newspaper on the coffee table. It was only a couple of days old, so someone had been there recently. The living room ran the whole length of the house and there were two doors in the right-hand wall. He opened the nearest and stepped through into the kitchen. It was empty. Plates were laid on the table but there was no sign of food being prepared and the cooker was cold.

With a sudden feeling of concern twisting his stomach, he stepped back into the living room and went through the second door. That led to a small hallway and a narrow flight of stairs. He checked the cupboard under the stairs and found only dust, an old coat and a couple of pairs of muddy Wellingtons. With his concern rising, he rushed up the stairs. There were only two rooms, both leading off from a narrow landing. The bathroom door was open and it was immediately obvious that the room was empty, although the toiletries, toothbrushes and paste on the shelf over the sink were fresh. The final door was closed. He flung it open so that it banged back against the wall and stepped quickly inside. Unsurprisingly, it was the bedroom. The door of the single wardrobe hung open, a few clothes hanging inside. There was no one there. There were three suitcases, two on the floor and one on the bed. The case on the bed was open with clothes hanging out of it as if someone had been frantically searching for something at the bottom. Someone who had definitely left in a hurry.

Pace swore and went back out on to the landing. He paused and looked up at the ceiling. There was a small hatch and a ladder attached to the blank wall below it. It was just possible someone might be hiding up there. He went up the ladder and pushed open the trap, aware that his head would make a good target when he poked it through, but too annoyed to care. Before risking his head, he fumbled round with his hand and found a light switch. There was only three feet of space to the roof, so very little room for an attacker to manoeuvre. He thrust his head up through the hole, gun ready just in case. No one was laying in wait up there, just the water tank and another quantity of dust.

He went back down the ladder again and into the bedroom, his mind running through the options. Their quarry had obviously bolted. It was possible that they were coming back, but he doubted it. He checked the cases; there was no sign of the money. He was sure he had only just missed them; there was every sign of a hurried departure, otherwise they would have taken the cases and the car. Where the hell had they gone?

His professional pride was hurt and, more importantly, Milton would have his hide if they got away.

★ ★ ★

Jones stared at the shopkeeper, his brain momentarily numb with fear. Mumbling something, he turned and ran out of the shop, leaving the owner staring after him in amazement. These city folk, always in a hurry.

Once outside by the green, Jones got a grip on his panic and started to think. He took his mobile phone from his jacket pocket, fumbled for agonizing seconds to call up his directory and dialled Beverly's number. He had purchased new mobiles for them both a few days before they had run away and they had disposed of their old phones. Sean was the only outsider who had the numbers, so Beverly would know that any call was safe to answer. He had a frantic few moments before she responded.

'Hello?' Even knowing the phone was secure, her voice sounded nervous.

'It's me,' he spoke rapidly. 'Someone's just been asking directions for the cottage at the shop. It must be Milton's people. They're on their way now. You've got to get away. Don't hang around just leave. I'll meet you by the lighthouse. Keep in the cover of the woods as much as you can.'

'But how — '

'Just go, quickly.'

Beverly felt panic rising and crushed it down. She shrugged into her coat, slipped her phone into the pocket, then she ran upstairs. It was all very well saying go now, but there was one thing she wouldn't leave behind. She rushed into the bedroom, flung open the wardrobe door and pulled out the carry case that held the contents of Milton's safe. She glanced out of the window. It was starting to get dark and they'd have to hang around the lighthouse for a while. She picked up one of her cases, dumped it on the bed and pulled out some of the clothes. At the bottom was the powerful torch that she had bought the week before, anticipating that it might be useful. Then she ran downstairs again, grabbed her shoulder bag from the living-room coffee table, pulled open the front door and ran outside, pulling the door closed behind her.

There was no sign of anyone and she couldn't hear a car.

Although she didn't know it, Beverly reached the shelter of the trees and bushes just as Pace parked his car up the track and switched off the engine. She started to run through the trees, but after a minute her brain started reasoning again and she slowed down. If she tripped and fell it would be catastrophic — the last thing she needed was a twisted ankle, or worse. Also, if someone was looking for her she was likely to make more noise running and her movement would be more noticeable. She slowed down to a swift walk. She looked back once, but saw no sign of pursuit and that calmed her. As she walked, she tried to imagine what could have gone wrong. She could not believe that only that afternoon she had been standing looking across the bay, happy and anticipating her escape from Harry Milton's influence. Now she was literally fleeing for her life. She was grateful for the afternoon walks, which had given her a reasonable idea of the layout of the area.

The best way to the lighthouse on foot was to follow the line of the cliff top through the trees, past the three other cottages, before reaching the top of the cliff at the further edge of the bay. There was a path down the cliff on the far side, out of sight of the cottage. Beverly moved diagonally to her right so that she would pass across the tracks leading to the other cottages rather than passing them in the open. Once past the third track, she entered the thicker woodland that lay between the village and the cliff. There was no defined path, but there were enough gaps between the bushes to enable her to angle back to her left towards the cliff edge. She stumbled once across a rising root that was difficult to see in the gloom and she slowed a little more and trod more carefully. The strap of her case dug into her shoulder and seemed to weigh a ton, but she adjusted its position and moved on. There was no way she was leaving the money behind; it was their only hope for a decent future. She felt a little better now that she was in the final stretch of woodland. With any luck she'd come out by the edge of the wood close to the cliff edge on the other side of the point of the bay.

Beverly reached the edge of the tree-line without mishap and found herself only a few yards away from the narrow but negotiable path that ran down the side of the cliff on the far side. Even more aware of the danger — and appalling consequences — of falling, she scrambled down the path. It was a mixture of rock and scrubby grass, but the light was better outside the trees and she could see where she was going reasonably well.

The path ended at a gentle slope that led down to a patch of open land beside a rocky track that became the narrow spit of land leading to the lighthouse. This was the most dangerous part of her journey. Up until now she had been hidden from anyone looking from the cottage by the bulk of the cliff jutting out like the prow of a great ocean liner. About halfway along the spit of land, the cliff would cease to cover her and she would be in plain view of anyone standing by the cottage and looking that way. There was no cover at all and the distance seemed to grow further and more exposed the longer she looked at it.

As she stared across towards the light-house, Beverly saw a dark figure standing by the side of the tower that was hidden from the cottage. The figure beckoned to her. She felt a surge of relief and ran across the final thirty yards to fling herself into Jones's arms, clutching him tightly. Her heart was thumping and she felt breathless, but at least they were together again and away from immediate danger.

'Did you see anyone?' he asked anxiously.

She shook her head.

'No. Mind you, I didn't stop to look; I just grabbed the money and a torch and ran. What happened exactly?'

'The woman in the village shop said that someone had come in about five minutes before me asking directions to the cottage and saying I'd invited him to dinner. I didn't know whether she meant five minutes literally, or she just meant it was a little while before. I was scared I'd be too late and they were already there when I rang.'

Beverly shivered.

'Thank goodness they weren't. But how on

earth did they find out about you?'

Jones shook his head.

'I don't know and hopefully it's not really important any more. We can lie low here until Sean comes to collect us.'

Beverly nodded.

'Do we have to stay out here though?' She shivered again and dug her hands into her coat pockets. 'That wind's icy cold.'

'We need to get inside out of sight,' Jones agreed. 'I checked the door just now, but it's securely locked. Besides, it's on the side facing the cottage. We'd be in plain view of anyone looking around from up there, so it wouldn't be a good idea to be spending time trying to force the door, even if I could manage it. There is a window about four feet from the ground on the seaward side of the lighthouse. That might be a way in.'

Jones led the way round to the window, which had six square panes of grubby glass. He took out his penknife and opened the blade. Reaching up, he tapped one of the lowest panes of glass hard with the end of his knife. The pane shattered, the noise lost in the whine of the wind. Beverly looked out to sea. There were a few ships, no more than dark smudges on the steadily darkening horizon, but nothing close enough to see what they were doing.

Jones tapped all the glass from the square, careful to leave no jagged edges he might cut his hand on. Then he reached inside and found the catch. It was stiff with misuse and awkward to turn from outside, but he eventually managed it and pulled the window open, despite the squeaky protest from the rusted hinges.

'Wait here a moment.'

He put his knife away, reached for the sill and pulled himself up. The years of dancing had given him good muscle power and he managed to lift himself on to the sill without too much difficulty. He paused, perched on the sill, and looked back at Beverly.

'Hand me the torch, please.'

She passed it up and he switched it on. There was nothing on the floor beneath the window, apart from twenty years of accumulated dust and grime, so he dropped down inside and swung the torch beam round. An old table and three chairs stood by the wall to his left and immediately opposite a flight of metal stairs led up to the next level. He crossed to the front door, but a moment's inspection told him there was no way he could force the lock from the inside. The window would have to be the way in.

Jones lifted the table across to the window and then went back to inspect the chairs.

They all still looked remarkably sturdy, if very grubby. He took two over to the window, placing one by the side of the table before he climbed up and lowered the second chair out of the window to Beverly.

'Stand on that, it will be easier for you to climb through.'

The area of rock at the foot of the lighthouse was reasonably level. Beverly placed the chair against the wall and stepped on it. She handed her case to Jones and then took his hand as he helped her through on to the table.

'You're spoiling me.'

'You remembered the torch.'

He squeezed her hand. Despite the danger they were still in, just achieving the small success of breaking into the lighthouse to find shelter seemed to have rekindled the romance of their adventure. Beverly climbed down on to the second chair and then on to the floor whilst Jones lifted the outside chair back up through the window and pulled the window closed as far as he could. The rusty hinges would not completely close and the broken pane was apparent from close inspection, but at a quick glance it would not be very obvious that the window had been tampered with.

Despite the rather damp atmosphere, they

were disturbing a lot of dust and Beverly started coughing.

'If we've got to be here a while, let's try to get to the top.' Jones put his arm round her and gave her a comforting squeeze. 'That will give us a better view and we should be able to see Sean coming, in case he's early.'

It would also give them a chance to see Milton's men if they approached the lighthouse, but he didn't put that depressing thought into words. He was very aware that although they were well placed to be picked up by the boat, they were also boxed into a trap with no other exits if they were cornered. Night had almost fully fallen, but the stars had already appeared in the clear sky and there was a bright full moon.

'Come on.'

He picked up the bag from the table and led the way over to the stairs. He used the torch sparingly. A little greyish light was coming in through the windows, giving some blurred shape to the rooms and their contents, but that also meant a light might be spotted from the outside. Still, it was better to risk that than to trip and fall down the stairs.

They made their way carefully up each of the flights of stairs. The lighthouse had been cleared of most items when it had been locked up and apart from a few pieces of furniture and some dusty rags and other discarded items of little use, the rooms were empty. After stopping briefly on the way to get their breath, they arrived on the floor immediately below the lamp station. Jones risked another quick circuit of the torch. There was an open (and empty) storeroom to their left and straight ahead a metal spiral staircase led up to a trap door and the platform above.

Jones went up the stairs and tried the catch. It moved more freely than the window catch and he lifted the hatch and laid it back on the floor above. The lamp level of the lighthouse consisted of the old lamp mechanism in the middle of the floor and curved glass windows all around. Beyond them, accessible through one of the windows, an open walkway followed the circumference of the building. The windows were grimy on the inside, but the outside had been kept cleaner by rain and sea spray. Jones found an old cloth and wiped an area on two or three of the windows so that they had a partial view of the spit leading to the lighthouse, the bay and the sea. He had thinned the dust to a smear rather than actually cleaned the glass, but at least they had some sort of a view.

As they stood looking down toward the land, the moon slid behind a block of cloud and night suddenly closed in. Jones looked up at the sky ruefully.

'Well, that was a good idea while it lasted.'

The cloud formed a thick wedge, but with clear sky beyond, the moon would be out again before long.

They sat on the floor, ignoring the hardness and the dirt, put their arms round each other for warmth, and settled down to wait. The wind howled round the top of the tower, but at least it was dry and the glass seemed to have kept some of its insulation. Although it was cold, they were under cover and protected from the most severe effect of the elements. It was, Jones reflected, by no means the worst position they could be in.

Fifteen minutes later, that complacency was shattered by the voice that spoke suddenly from six feet away.

'Hello, Beverly,' said Jack Pace. 'We thought we'd never find you. Harry is most anxious to see you again.'

★ ★ ★

Pace came out of the cottage, ignored Gray's puzzled enquiry, and ran to his car. He opened the glove compartment, grabbed the powerful binoculars he always kept there and raced back to the cliff top. Making sure that he kept away from the edge, so as not to be standing out against the skyline if anyone looked his way, he surveyed the woods and the bay below.

Nothing.

Fighting down the irritation that rose within him, he started again, traversing slowly along the edge of the woods, looking for a glimpse of colour or activity that shouldn't be there. As his inspection reached the far point of the cliff, there was a flash of movement just beyond that caught his eye. He focused on the old lighthouse just in time to see Beverly race across the end of the spit and disappear behind the far side. He stepped back quickly from view, lowered the binoculars and smiled thinly.

'Got you,' He muttered, under his breath.

He turned back to Gray and Kelly who were standing by the front of the cottage. Kelly had his usual half amused look and Gray was still frowning.

'Given us the slip, have they?' Kelly asked.

'Not for long.' Pace walked over to them. 'They must have heard us coming or something and made a run for it. They're in that old lighthouse over there.' He jerked his thumb over his shoulder and looked at Kelly. 'Go and get the map from the car.'

When Kelly returned with the map, they

bent over it together and looked at the road layout around the village.

'We can get there easily by road.' Pace's finger stubbed out the route. 'We go back up the road towards the village, drive past the village turnoff and take that next road on the left. That takes us down to the track that leads across to the lighthouse. We can park back there off the track somewhere and go across after them.'

He looked up at the sky.

'It'll be fully dark soon and there's some cloud to cover the moon. We should be able to get near them without them spotting us.'

'Do you want us to sabotage their car in case they get past us again?' Gray asked, eager to start venting his violent feelings on something even if it was inanimate.

Pace thought for a moment.

'It's tempting, but no. If we get hold of them without too much trouble, we can bring them back here and collect their cases and stuff from the cottage. One of you can then drive their car back. If we dispose of them and their car and there's nothing at the cottage linked to them, there won't be any evidence pointing to us either.'

Gray nodded. He always admired those who could think and plan ahead better than him — which covered most of the people he came into contact with.

The three men walked back up the track to their car. Pace drove down to the cottage, turned round and went back up the track. The headlights swung across the trees and bushes, creating long shadows that swayed and danced as they passed. He retraced their route along the narrow B-road, drove past the road to the village and then took the next turning left down towards the coast.

The side road was steep and twisting for a few hundred yards before levelling out. There was a clear, harsh silvery light from the moon and Pace risked switching off the headlights as he coasted round the next bend.

The old lighthouse lay before them at the end of the long spit of land. The track widened into a flat stony area and Pace pulled over on to that and parked. The only sounds were of the wind and the sea. To their right the new lighthouse sent a strong beam sweeping out across the water, giving it fluctuating silvery highlights. There were lights further along the coast, but nothing close to them. The lights of two or three ships could be glimpsed on the horizon.

Pace nodded in satisfaction. Whatever was about to happen, there shouldn't be any witnesses — apart from those directly involved, of course. He glanced up at the sky.

The area around the lighthouse was bathed in light; if anyone was watching for them they would be clearly seen. A bank of cloud was moving sedately across the night sky and would cover the moon in a few minutes. Pace decided to wait and move in under cover of the darkness that would bring. Their quarry was boxed in, but it would be better to catch them unawares and capture them without a struggle than to risk alerting them. There was nowhere for them to run, except into the sea, but there was no sense in making life unnecessarily difficult.

Once the cloud had drifted across the moon, Pace led the way along the track and on to the rocky trail that led to the lighthouse. Kelly and Gray followed without speaking. They paused by the curved wall of the tower and Pace walked to the front door. He had a small flashlight in his pocket and risked a quick inspection of the door. It showed no sign of being tampered with so they must have found another way in. He briefly considered that Beverly and Jones might have gone back inland again, but dismissed the idea. There was no point in coming all the way out there unless they were going to take shelter in the building.

His reasoning was confirmed when they reached the window and discovered the empty square. Pace got the window open without too much noise and lifted himself up over the sill. When he found the table against the window, he was certain he was right. He turned and beckoned the other two in. Kelly's tall and wiry frame easily made the journey, but they needed to help Gray, whose shoes scrabbled at the wall as he was hauled up.

Standing in the dark, they waited and listened. There was no sound other than the wind and the crash of the sea against the shore and the rocks. Pace used his torch again briefly to locate the stairs and they moved upwards carefully.

As they reached each floor, the three men checked it quickly before moving on. When they got to the floor below the lamp, a murmur of voices drifted down from above. The speech sounded soft and undisturbed; they hadn't been alerted by the raiding party from below.

Pace had already drawn his gun. He looked upwards and saw the square of paler grey in the ceiling above the spiral staircase. Slowly, careful not to make any noise on the metal steps, he walked up and through the hatchway with Kelly and Gray close behind him.

When Pace stepped out through the hatch,

he saw Beverly and Jones sitting on the floor a few feet away, engrossed in each other and not looking his way. Pace stepped forward to allow the other two to come up behind him, switched on his torch to illuminate the two figures on the floor and spoke with great satisfaction.

'Hello Beverly. We thought we'd never find you. Harry is most anxious to see you again.'

While Beverly and Jones sat stiff with shock, Kelly moved quickly round the lamp to come up on the other side of them and cut off any movement they might have made in that direction. Sitting on the floor, they had no way of finding the momentum to take any action, even if they had not had two guns focused on them.

'Get up, very slowly,' Pace ordered. 'Don't try any heroics, we're quite happy to hurt you if necessary. Harry doesn't mind what condition you're in when he sees you.'

Pace and Kelly kept them covered whilst Gray carried out a body search — taking an unnecessarily long time over Beverly's. He pocketed Jones's penknife, picked up the case, Beverly's shoulder bag and the torch and moved back behind Pace.

'The money's in the case,' he reported after a moment.

'Good.' Pace nodded with satisfaction. It

was all coming together nicely. Harry would be pleased. 'Right then.' He inspected the prisoners impassively. 'We're going back downstairs and out to our car. Reggie will shine the torch on you and Lenny and I will cover you with our guns. Walk nice and slowly.'

Jones gave Beverly's arm a squeeze to try to give her some comfort, although he was feeling none himself. They had been so near to getting away with it and now . . . If there was the ghost of a chance he'd sacrifice himself to give Beverly the opportunity to run, but at the moment, any action would just harm both of them. He felt Beverly stumble as she tried to move and put his arm round her briefly.

They walked back down the flights of stairs in the order of procession that Pace had dictated. Pace went first, walking backwards and keeping his gun trained on Beverly and Jones who followed him. Kelly came next, with his gun on their backs and Gray was at the rear, shining Beverly's powerful torch down on the whole line, but careful not to shine it in Pace's eyes.

When they reached the ground floor, Kelly went out of the window first, then the two prisoners. He kept them against the wall at gun point whilst Pace and Gray climbed out.

Nobody bothered to shut the window after them.

Jones had considered making a dive for Kelly whilst the other two were still inside the lighthouse, but the gunman kept several feet away and would have had no trouble in shooting both of them before he could be reached. Whilst Jones was considering the idea, Pace dropped to the ground and even that faint opportunity had passed.

The moon was out from hiding again and the whole area was flooded in silvery light. Gray moved up to Beverly's side, put his arm round her and gripped her wrist. She tried to pull away from him in disgust and he showed her the wicked stiletto in his other hand, its silver gleam matching the moonlight.

'Just keep next to me, nice and cosy,' he smiled at her.

Jones swore and started to move towards them, but Kelly's gun dug into his side.

'Not advisable.' The pleasant Irish lilt was amused. 'You'd have a bullet in the gut before you got two feet.'

Jones stopped and glared at Kelly, which only made him smile wider.

'Off we go then,' Pace directed them with his gun. 'The car's just up the road.'

When they reached the car, Pace opened all the doors. Jones was put in the front passenger seat with Kelly behind him, his gun pressed to the back of Jones's neck. Beverly was pushed into the back next to Kelly with Gray beside her, still holding her wrist and with his knife pressed against her neck.

'Fasten your seat belt,' Kelly told Jones. 'You don't want to bump your nose if Jack has to stop suddenly do you?'

'Better not brake too sharp, then,' Gray said with a snigger. 'Don't want me to jab my knife in her accidentally, do we?'

Pace turned the car and drove up the track.

They were back at the cottage in little more than five minutes. This time, Pace drove right up and turned round, parking next to Jones's car. He took out his gun and covered Jones.

'Lenny, go in and pack the cases while we wait outside. Have a quick look round and bring out anything that looks like theirs.'

'OK, boss.' Kelly slid out of the car and disappeared round the side of the cottage. After a few moments a light came on in the living room and another upstairs.

Beverly made a little moaning noise.

'Shut up.' Pace growled.

Beverly rolled her head.

'I can't, I think I'm going to be sick.'

Pace swore.

'Not in my car, you're not.'

He opened his door and motioned Jones

out. He still wasn't sure if Beverly was trying a con and, as Gray didn't have a gun, he wanted to be in a position to cover both of them if necessary.

'Take her round to the side of the path,' he told Gray. He looked at Beverly with distaste mixed with suspicion. 'And you keep it in until you get out of the car.'

Beverly, clutching her hand over her mouth, was pulled out of the car by Gray. She turned towards the bushes and Gray, understandably not wanting vomit over his trousers, stepped back and eased his grip on her wrist. That was the chance Beverly had been waiting for. She suddenly raised herself from her crouch and shoved Gray away. Off balance, he stumbled and she ran at Pace.

'Run, Jeff,' she screamed.

Pace swung his gun towards her and Jones lashed out with his hand, a lucky blow that knocked Pace's gun to the ground. In the brief moment of confusion, they ran.

They might have got away with it if they could have turned away from the cottage, but Pace and Gray were between them and the pathway, so they had to run towards the cliff. Gray recovered quickly and was running along the edge of the woodland, so they couldn't immediately go off to the right. As they rounded the edge of the cottage, Kelly was coming out, alerted by the noise. He reacted swiftly, moving to trip Beverly as she ran past. From the corner of his eye Jones saw Beverly fall and turned back to help her, walking straight into a roundhouse blow from the hand in which Kelly held his gun. The gun butt smacked into Jones's temple and he went down in a boneless heap and lay motionless. Beverly cried out and, as she scrambled to her feet, Gray grabbed her wrist again, twisting it painfully up behind her back.

'You crafty little bitch.' He was spitting the words with anger. 'I hope Harry gives you to me after he's done with you so I can finish you off. We'll have some real fun, you and I, and you won't be faking sickness.'

Pace raised his recovered gun, glaring at Beverly. She had nearly fooled him and if she'd got away Harry would have taken it out on him. Pace looked round. They were only a few feet from the edge of the cliff. Harry wanted her taken in alive but he hadn't said the same about the boyfriend. Pace looked down at Jones, then across at Beverly. He gave her a nasty smile.

'Change of plan,' he said. 'We'll just take her gear with us. We leave his stuff and the car here. It'll look like he was staying here on his own and had a nasty accident.'

He turned to Kelly.

'Throw him over the cliff.'

'No!' Beverly twisted helplessly in Gray's grasp as Kelly nodded and moved over towards Jones.

Gray chuckled, and with that laugh something seemed to snap inside Beverly's reason and create an almost insane animal ferocity. She swung up her free hand and scraped her long nails down Gray's cheek. Gray cried out at the sudden shock and pain, dropped his knife and lifted his hand to his face, relaxing his grip on her wrist. Beverly twisted towards him and, her eyes alight with hatred, drove her knee as hard as she could between his legs. Gray gave a strangled gasp, his hands dropping to clutch at the affected area. His legs wobbled as he twisted round and bent over, partly in agony and partly to avoid a second attack in the same place. Instead, he presented Beverly with another prime target. She kicked out, all her frustration, rage and hatred of Milton and all he stood for boiling over into the strike. Gray, his legs already like jelly, sprawled forward. His head clipped the side of a coffee-table-sized piece of rock by the cliff edge and he slumped to the ground unconscious.

Pace was reacting almost as wildly and instinctively as Beverly. He came up behind her and swung his gun hand viciously at her head, moderating the blow slightly at the last moment as he remembered that Milton wanted her alive. It still felt to her as if the side of her head had exploded and she fell sideways on to the rock-strewn grass. As Beverly lay barely conscious, she heard Pace's voice, hard edged with suppressed anger.

'Don't just stand there, Kelly, throw the bastard over.'

12

Alec Tanner was feeling frustrated.

By the time Kenneth Jones had given them directions to his cottage and they had got down to the car, the cholesterol of the rush hour was severely clogging the transport arteries of the city. They found themselves in a line of solid traffic. It took five minutes to reach the end of the street. They could have walked it in less, he thought disgustedly. If he had been James Bond, he could have swung out of the line of cars and driven along the pavement, miraculously avoiding injuring any pedestrians, although demolishing at least two barrowloads of fruit and vegetables, before screaming down a narrow alley on two wheels and launching the car off the quayside into the river, flicking a switch to turn the car into an amphibious vehicle in mid air so that they could zoom off up river through uncongested waters. As it was, they just had to sit and wait it out, hoping that anyone sent by Milton would be stuck in the same traffic jam that they were.

Julie spent the time checking the map for their route. Tanner spent the time tapping the steering wheel in annoyance and muttering 'come on' under his breath. Julie, he accepted, was the more productive.

'We want the city ring road, then the A777 north, then there's a B-road. Lower Winkley should be signposted when we get near it, so we can start looking out for the turning to the cottage.'

Tanner nodded. The one thing in their favour was that Jones's cottage was not easy to find without detailed directions. With any luck anyone else looking for the cottage would get lost and waste time driving round. He had plenty of experience of the country lanes in the area north of the city and he knew how confusing they could be, particularly after dark. One narrow road bordered by tall hedges and woods looks much like any other.

After considerable cursing from Tanner and hooting from other drivers, they eventually got through the centre. Tanner felt they had inhaled enough carbon monoxide in thirty minutes to last a lifetime. When they got to the roundabout that led on to the ring road, they found that three cars had had a minor accident. It didn't look as though there were any serious injuries, but the police and ambulance services were on the scene and there was the usual crawl of other traffic going past so that the drivers could absorb every detail of the scene.

Once on to the ring road, Tanner could speed up and the A777 was moderately clear. There was a commuter belt north of the city, but the A-road had been widened to three lanes a few years before and that helped things along. The sun had set and darkness closed in once they were away from the immediate sphere of the city's civilizing influence. As always, the planners seemed to have considered that most roads beyond residential areas do not require lighting, no matter how busy they are. Still, at least they were moving.

Julie was settled back in her seat. She had unzipped her jacket in the warmth of the car and had the map book perched on her knees. Tanner was jealous.

'This next bit should be plain sailing.' Julie was tracing her finger along the open page of the book.

'Wash your mouth out, young lady, haven't you ever heard of Sod's Law?'

She flashed him a grin in the darkness.

'I got my Girl Guide badge for map reading. I'll tell you when we're near the turn-off.'

For once, Sod's Law didn't apply and they reached the B-road without any more delay.

There was little local traffic about and after ten minutes of steady driving, their headlights carving a steady glow through the darkness, the sign for Lower Winkley gleamed white in the lights.

Once on to the narrow meandering road that led towards the village, Tanner slowed down a little, partly so as not to lose their direction and partly in case they met anything coming the other way. If they did, someone was going to have to travel in reverse for some distance.

A sign on the right indicated that Upper Winkley lay in that direction.

'There we are,' said Julie, sitting forward, 'the cottage is down the next but one turning on the left.'

'OK.'

Tanner glanced to their right. They were passing an area of open woodland that ran level with the road, with trees and bushes dotted around randomly. He slowed right down and drove off the road into the woodland. The car bumped a little over the rough ground and Tanner stopped with a couple of trees between them and the road. He switched off the lights and the engine. Darkness drifted in around them, diffused by the glow from the moon. There was the faint sound of a car engine ahead of them, but it was impossible to tell the exact direction and distance.

'From what Kenneth Jones told us, the track to the cottage is pretty narrow. If Milton's men are around, we don't want to meet them head on. They've no doubt got guns, which would put us at considerable disadvantage. I suggest we walk from here.'

Julie nodded.

'Good job I also got my Girl Guide badge for woodcraft.'

They got out of the car and walked to the edge of the road. They were both wearing black jeans and jackets, so there was little chance of their being spotted from any distance. Tanner had a heavy torch and he knew that Julie had her shoulder bag, which no doubt contained one or two useful articles. Tanner didn't want to risk the torch except in an emergency in case Milton's people were about. Although, he thought, blending into the darkness as they did, until they reached the turn off to the cottage they were probably more at risk from a car being driven too fast down the narrow road.

Now that the car's headlights were off, their night vision improved, helped considerably by a reasonable amount of light from the full moon. They moved along by the trees until they reached a point where the road bent round to the left before straightening again. As anticipated, there was a narrow track leading off to the left just ahead of them.

'I hope you are impressed by my intrepid navigational skills,' Julie murmured.

'I'll buy you a new woggle when we get back.'

Tanner saw a brief glimpse of a smile before they moved forward and down the track, treading carefully and watchful of the area ahead in case they met any of the opposition coming the other way. The moonlight was still strong enough that he didn't need to use his torch to avoid their bumping into trees, although they needed to be wary that they didn't trip over any ground level hazards.

They reached a bend in the track and could see a light ahead standing out in the darkness, sharper than the moonlight. Moving forward they saw the cottage, framed against the sky. There were lights on upstairs and down. Two cars were parked outside, apparently both empty. Tanner touched Julie's arm and motioned to the right. They moved forward again slowly, keeping close to the fringe of trees and bushes on that side. There was no sign of anyone standing at either of the lighted windows, and the light would destroy their night vision anyway, but two cars suggested that Milton and/or his minions had located their quarry and there could be people lurking in the bushes.

Suddenly a shout echoed from the other side of the cottage and there was the sound of struggling and curses. Ignoring the cautious approach, Tanner and Julie ran forward and stopped by the side of the cottage, looking round it towards the edge of the cliff.

They were just in time to see Beverly Wallace launch her kick into Reggie Gray's backside, causing him to lose his head-butting contest with a nearby lump of rock, followed by Jack Pace knocking Beverly to the ground and turning to the lean man who stood a short distance away.

'Don't just stand there, Kelly, throw the bastard over.'

Tanner and Julie decided it was time for them to get involved.

'I'll take Kelly,' Julie muttered and moved forward.

There was no time to argue. Besides, Pace was armed and Kelly's hands seemed to be empty, so Tanner was happy to tackle the bigger man, particularly as Pace didn't know he was there yet.

The ignorance didn't last long. Tanner swung his torch down on the wrist of Pace's gun hand and he dropped the weapon with a cry of pain. From the corner of his eye, Tanner saw Kelly look up and then he had his own problems as Julie launched a flying kick at him. After that, Tanner had to concentrate on his own battle.

Pace recovered from the pain and shock remarkably fast. Tanner aimed a punch at the hinge of the big man's jaw that should have ended matters, but Pace managed to evade it and get in a punch of his own that, even though he turned away from it, hit Tanner in the chest with enough force to send him sprawling.

Tanner started up again quickly. There was no way he could afford to give Pace time to look round for his gun or weigh in with his feet whilst he was on the floor. Pace tried a follow up kick, but Tanner rolled clear and caught the raised foot in his hands, lifting and twisting as he came up off the ground.

It wasn't a particularly elegant effort, but Pace was very conscious of the edge of the cliff and tried to fall inland as much as possible. Tanner moved in to finish things off, but Pace managed to trip him up, and a moment later Tanner was on his back with Pace on top of him. As Pace was both stronger and heavier, that was not good news.

Fortunately, Tanner had learnt a lot of his

fighting skills from his uncle, topped off by instruction from Ted Manning, and both his mentors were of the opinion that fighting dirty was far more acceptable than losing.

Risking a small earthquake around the Marquis of Queensbury's grave, Tanner twisted Pace's ears and, as he pulled back, Tanner was able to heave himself up a little and head butt his opponent. Tanner thought it probably hurt him as much as it did Pace, but it gave him the opportunity to roll out from under. As Pace got to his knees, half blinded, Tanner kidney punched him and that exposed the thick neck for the finishing strike.

Tanner considered kicking Pace while he was down, but it didn't seem necessary, so instead he looked round anxiously to see how Julie was doing.

Kelly was laid out on the ground unconscious and Julie stood over him looking as calm and poised as ever, in contrast to Tanner's gasping breaths.

She gave him a salute.

'Mine weighed more than yours,' Tanner said, when he'd got enough breath back.

Julie grinned and knelt down to take a look at the crumpled form next to Kelly.

Tanner turned to the woman he assumed was Beverly Wallace, who was kneeling up, still dazed, but looking at him with a mixture of hope and fear. He spotted Pace's gun a few feet away, picked it up and gave her what he hoped was a reassuring smile.

'Beverly Wallace?'

She nodded.

'I'm Alec Tanner and the attractive young Amazon over there is Julie Cooper. Your sister asked us to come and help you.'

'Sandi sent you?' The dazed look was starting to fade.

'Yes; she thought Milton had found out where you were hiding.' Tanner glanced around the battlefield. 'It looks like she was right.'

'How is Jeffrey?' Beverly had managed to get to her feet and walked unsteadily across to Julie.

'He'll be OK; he's starting to come round.'

Tanner looked down at Pace. He was still sleeping, but that desirable state might not last long.

'We need to get Pace and his mates tucked away somewhere before they wake up. Is there anywhere in the cottage we can put them?'

Beverly shook her head.

'I don't think so.'

'How about a strong, lockable cupboard?' Julie asked.

'There's the cupboard under the stairs, but I don't think it's got a lock on it.'

'That might do.'

Five minutes later they had transported Pace, Gray and Kelly, all still unconscious, into the house and dumped them in the cupboard under the stairs. A line of blood ran down the side of Gray's face, but his skull seemed intact and he was starting to mutter. There was just enough room in the cupboard for the three of them, provided they were good friends and didn't get cramp. Tanner and Julie brought the kitchen table through into the narrow hallway, turned it on its side and jammed one end against the cupboard door and the other against the opposite wall. The panel in the centre of the door was thinner than the outside, but the table edge was across the middle and they lodged two of the kitchen chairs in between the door, the table legs and wall so that they couldn't be shifted very easily. The three men certainly couldn't get out without making a lot of noise, providing plenty of reaction time. Tanner had emptied their prisoners' pockets and taken their guns and Gray's knife, so he thought the arrangement was good enough, at least in the short term.

By the time they finished incarcerating Milton's men, Jeffrey Jones had recovered consciousness. Beverly had helped him into the living room and she sat beside him on the settee, dabbing at the side of his head with a damp cloth she had found in the kitchen. They were both complaining of blinding headaches — which was not surprising, Tanner thought, considering they had both been hit on the head with the blunt end of a gun. Beverly had some aspirin in her shoulder bag. Tanner fetched some water for them to swallow two tablets each and Julie followed him out of the kitchen with mugs of strong tea.

Beverly took a sip of her tea and seemed to revive a little more. She looked at her watch, put her mug down on the coffee table and started to get up.

'We've got to get back to the old lighthouse; we're being picked up by boat in less than an hour.'

'You're not going anywhere for a moment,' Tanner said firmly. 'You need to finish your tea and give the aspirin a chance to work. And we need to have a talk.'

'But . . . ' Beverly subsided back on to the settee and looked at Jones in concern.

'We need some information from you,' Tanner said. 'I think you owe us that much at least.'

Beverly seemed disposed to argue, but

Jones put his hand on her arm.

'He's right, darling. Let's just answer the questions, the sooner we do that, the sooner we can get going.'

He looked at Tanner for a nod of confirmation and Tanner gave it to him. In fact, he wasn't quite sure yet what they were going to do with the two runaways, but there was no sense telling them that before he got the information he wanted.

'Why is Milton so keen to get hold of you?' Tanner asked. 'Surely he hasn't sent his main man after you just in a fit of jealous rage?'

Beverly hesitated and looked at Jones again.

'We'd better tell them everything.' Jones told her. He looked across at Tanner, his eyes tired and his face drawn. Tanner got the impression he was still a little bewildered and close to giving up. He supposed that coming within seconds of being chucked over a cliff could do that to you. 'Beverly emptied Milton's safe as well,' he said.

'Yes,' Tanner nodded, 'that would do it.'

'It's our stake money,' Beverly put in quickly. 'I earned it, putting up with him for two years.'

'Where is it?' Tanner asked.

Beverly didn't reply, but Jones clearly wanted the questioning over and was too exhausted to play games. Tanner nearly felt guilty at taking advantage of his weakened state, not that it would stop him doing so.

'It's in a carry case in the boot of Pace's car.'

Tanner took Pace's keys from the side table where he'd put them, went out to the car and came back with the case. He unzipped the top and lifted the contents out on to the coffee table. Tanner studied the collection for a moment before returning the cash to the case and putting it on the sofa next to Beverly.

'I suppose you think that's a reasonable payment for saving us.' There was a thread of contempt in Beverly's voice as she viewed the items left on the table.

'That's not the payment,' Tanner told her. 'That lot is being handed over to the police. The figure and the diamonds could well be stolen property and there are enough drugs on the streets already without adding to them. No, our price for helping you is something different.'

He paused. There were bumping noises coming from outside the room.

'Sounds like our prisoners are getting restless,' Julie said.

Tanner got up and went out into the hallway.

'Shut up and keep quiet in there,' he said.

There was a pause and then a gruff voice snarled through the woodwork, 'Let us out, now.' It was not the tone of one used to being disobeyed. Tanner assumed it belonged to Jack Pace.

'No.'

There was another thump against the door.

'We can't breathe in here.' That was a different voice, less assured and more plaintive. Tanner guessed it meant that Gray had woken up completely now.

'If you want ventilation, I can always put a couple of bullet holes in the door,' Tanner told them. 'Of course there's no guarantee where the bullets will go.'

There was silence. He guessed they'd decided there was enough air after all.

Tanner went back into the other room. Julie's eyes crinkled at him.

'Way to go, tough guy.'

'I hope they do suffocate.' Beverly spoke with some force. She looked across at Tanner. 'So what is your price for helping us?' The fact that Tanner had threatened Pace and his colleagues seemed to make her more disposed to co-operate.

'Do the names Jethro Harper and Kevin Winston mean anything to you?' Tanner asked.

She looked surprised at the change of tack.

'Sure, they work for Harry — at least, they used to.'

'What do you know about them?'

'Not a lot. They joined the organization sometime last year, just a couple of gofers, I think. Jethro was a weirdo, but I liked Kevin, he was cute.'

From what they had heard about Harper and Winston, 'cute' was not a description that sprang immediately to Tanner's mind, but he supposed that was the feminine perspective.

'They came to Harry's house a few times and I used to talk to Kevin a bit. Sometimes I was just hanging around and it got boring, so I chatted to the help. Harry didn't mind so long as we didn't talk shop.'

'Have you seen them lately?'

She thought for a moment.

'Not for a few weeks. I heard that they'd moved on elsewhere. That was just a rumour, though; it doesn't pay to be curious about Harry Milton's business affairs.'

'Do you know how we could find them?' Julie asked her.

'I didn't really talk to Jethro. I think someone said that he lived with his mum. Kevin has a girlfriend.' She frowned in thought. 'Her name is Connie, Connie Preston and she lives on the Yarrow Estate

— I don't know exactly where. Reading between the lines, I think she's a hooker and it sounded as though she likes a good time, but he used to talk about her as if he cared, you know? I suppose she might know where he is.'

'Thanks.'

It was a lead, at any rate, better than nothing.

'What's the significance of the figurine?' Tanner asked.

'Harry collects them, and paintings. There are a number round the house, but he has a special collection locked away in a room on the top floor. He's the only one with a key and no one else is allowed in there. The rumour is that the stuff in there is all stolen and he enjoys gloating over it. Maybe that was meant for the stolen collection.'

'So why was it in the safe?'

She shrugged.

'Perhaps he only got it that day and hadn't had time to put it in the room.'

Tanner nodded; it was a reasonable assumption. That could give them a hook into Milton's affairs, although he couldn't see immediately how it might work.

'There's nothing else you remember about Harper and Winston?' Julie asked. 'Nothing else he told you? It could be important.'

Beverly seemed genuinely anxious to help them now. There's nothing like threatening someone's enemies to get into their good books, Tanner thought. She looked quite disappointed as she shook her head.

'No, I'm sorry.' Her face was strained and she sounded near to collapse; she seemed very young and vulnerable as she sat on the settee holding Jones's hand.

Tanner looked across at Julie and raised his eyebrows. Julie shrugged her shoulders.

'You're the boss,' she said. 'It's your call.'

Tanner thought for a moment.

'I take it the other car out there is yours?' Jones nodded.

'Yes, the Volvo.'

'And you know the way to the lighthouse by road?'

'Yes.' Hope glimmered in his voice and Beverly suddenly perked up.

'I have to tell you,' Tanner said in his most formal voice, 'that in my opinion it is your duty to stay and give the police the information they need in order to prosecute Pace and Milton.'

Tanner knew perfectly well there was no way they'd agree to that, but at least he wouldn't have to lie to Mariner — not too much, anyway.

Beverly looked at Tanner as if he'd

suggested they all go outside and jump off the edge of the cliff. He thought she probably considered the end result would have been the same.

'No way,' she said. 'I'm not giving evidence against them. Besides, we'd never survive long enough to get into court. Harry's got contacts everywhere.'

'Police protection . . . '

She gave him a look.

Tanner nodded. 'OK, then. I've said my piece. We can't stop you leaving if that's want you want to do.'

They both got up with alacrity. The aspirin seemed to be working.

'As soon as you drive away, I shall be phoning the police and I'll tell them exactly what's happened,' Tanner said. 'I'm sure they'll want to interview you, so if your friend's late picking you up, the police will probably do it instead. If he's on time, I expect you'll be out at sea before they get here.'

Jones nodded.

'Thank you, for everything.'

They collected their cases and Julie and Tanner sat looking at each other without expression until they heard the car start up. Headlights swung past the window and the car bumped off up the track.

'You old romantic softy, you,' Julie smiled at him.

Tanner pulled a face as he took his mobile phone from his jacket pocket.

'Let's hope Ancient shares your opinion. I think it's time we roused him from his comfy armchair.'

13

Mariner was, predictably, not best pleased. He arrived shortly after ten o'clock, having the advantage of a police siren to ease his way, and brought with him a police van and four officers. Julie had gone to collect Tanner's car while they were waiting and the front of the cottage was starting to resemble a car-park.

Pace, Gray and Kelly had been evicted from their cupboard and placed in the police van, where they were receiving rudimentary first aid. None of them seemed unduly damaged by their imprisonment and they said nothing when they were taken outside. The looks they gave Julie and Tanner made any verbal comments superfluous.

Mariner sat with Julie and Tanner in the living room. His sergeant sat to one side taking notes and Mariner was staring down at the items on the table. Julie and Tanner had taken Beverly and Jones's position on the settee.

'So you just let them walk away,' Mariner said for about the third time.

'Drive away actually,' Tanner corrected

him. 'I didn't think we had any right to detain them. Besides, we'd run out of cell space. We didn't want to add to the prison overcrowding statistics.'

Mariner wasn't amused.

'That didn't stop you dealing with Jack Pace and his pals.'

'That was different,' Julie put in, looking wide eyed and innocent. 'We were frightened of them.'

Mariner snorted.

'It looks like it. With any luck, they'll sue you for assault and false imprisonment.' He seemed to relish the idea.

'I don't think that's very likely,' Tanner said. 'Apart from the fact that Milton won't want the publicity, we have Sandi Wallace and Kenneth Jones to call on in our defence. Besides, those weapons on the table will have their fingerprints on them.'

'Anyway,' Julie said,' we had no real grounds for holding Beverly and Jeffrey. Milton isn't likely to admit to being robbed, is he? So what evidence is there of any crime committed by them?'

Mariner grunted again.

'You mean apart from a small fortune in heroin, an assortment of deadly weapons and some possibly stolen property?'

Julie and Tanner looked at him in silence.

He sighed.

'You're quite right, of course. I don't suppose we'll even get very far with a case against Pace and co. With Beverly Wallace and Jeffrey Jones gone and not available to press charges of assault and kidnap we have very little evidence that would actually stand up in court. Milton's solicitor will have his soldiers back on the street in five minutes; in fact his pet poodle could probably do it in less than ten.' He sounded disgusted.

'Meanwhile, we have a clue,' Tanner pointed out.

'So it was all worthwhile, then?'

'Come off it, Ancient, we've undoubtedly saved two lives, you've got some drugs off the street and some stolen goods to return and Milton is, at the very least, severely embarrassed. You've also got the chance to give three of Milton's men a night in the cells before his brief springs them. Not a bad night's work. You might even make the firearms offences stick.'

'They'll probably suggest you planted their fingerprints on the weapons after you'd knocked them out.' Mariner grinned suddenly. 'Still, as you say, it's better than a couple of murders. And Milton losing face with the criminal fraternity won't be unhelpful.'

'Is Bridger likely to make things tough for Sandi Wallace?' Julie asked.

Mariner shook his head.

'That's one bit of good news. We got a statement from the owner of the sex shop and a neighbour has come forward who might have seen the abduction of his friend. Bridger's going to have enough to worry about without going after Sandi Wallace. Particularly as he knows if anything happens to her, we'll be breathing down his neck for it. The same goes for Milton. I shall make very sure Pace and his friends get that message before they're released.'

'You could let them know, in passing, that we got the details of the cottage from Jones's brother and not from Sandi, so she wasn't holding out on them in that respect,' Julie suggested.

Mariner nodded and looked across at his sergeant.

'Have you got enough to type out their statements, Bob?'

'Yes, sir.'

Mariner got to his feet.

'Let's call it a night, then.' He looked at Julie and Tanner. 'Come in sometime tomorrow and sign them.' A thought occurred to him. 'We'd better let Jones know his brother's safe.'

'I called him while we were waiting,' Tanner said. 'And Julie spoke to Sandi.'

'Good.'

They followed him out to the cars, leaving the cottage locked up as best they could. Kenneth Jones had told Tanner that he would drive up the next day to secure the cottage and pick up his brother's car.

As they watched the police van drive away Mariner paused and looked at Tanner and Julie across the roof of his car.

'You've annoyed some very nasty people,' he said. 'Watch out for yourselves.'

'Don't worry,' Tanner told him, 'we'll be very careful.'

★   ★   ★

They slept in late the next morning and it was nearly ten before Tanner and Julie were ready to leave her flat. Tanner had spoken to Danny Worenski at the office an hour earlier and he had rung back twenty minutes later with Connie Preston's full address. Tanner didn't ask how the information had been obtained. After all, he thought, sleeping with a policewoman carried some responsibilities.

The phone rang again shortly after Danny's message. Tanner thought it might be Worenski with some further information, so he answered the call. In fact, it was Mariner to tell them that Milton's solicitor had got Pace and the others released. Preliminary discussions with his superintendent also suggested that they would be unlikely to pursue charges against the three men unless further evidence or more eager witnesses came to light.

'I did get him to agree,' Mariner went on, 'that the position will be reviewed if Pace and co try to play silly buggers and claim assault against you and Julie.'

'I take it 'silly buggers' is a technical legal expression?'

'Yes. Mind you, their solicitor indicated that if we did nothing, they wouldn't either, so it looks like they want to call it quits.'

'Forgive and forget?'

'I think that would be putting it too strongly,' Mariner said drily. 'You still need to watch your backs.'

'Yes. Thanks for letting us know.'

'In the light of this, there's no rush for you to sign your statements, though I'd like to have them on record, they might come in useful.'

Tanner promised they'd call in when they could and rang off.

He hadn't expected much else, but it would have been nice if they could have kept at least one of Milton's minions in a cell for a little longer.

Ten minutes later, they were ready to go. Julie had just picked up her shoulder bag and they had reached the front door when the telephone rang again. Julie pulled a 'what now' face and walked across to answer it.

'Oh, Hi Laura. Yes, we're making progress, we think we might have a lead on one of the shooters — a guy called Kevin Winston.' She paused. 'No, we haven't located him yet, but we've found out that he has a girlfriend and we're on our way to see her. You just caught us.' She listened for a moment. 'Thank you, I'll ask him.' She moved the phone away from her ear and looked across at Alec. 'It's Laura. She'd like us to go to dinner again this evening. I think they're rather enjoying getting first hand information about crime.'

Tanner nodded.

'That's fine by me.'

Julie spoke back into the phone.

'Yes, we'll both be there. Seven-thirty. See you.' She hung up. 'Let's see if we can make it through the door this time.'

★ ★ ★

The Yarrow Housing Estate was named after a Cromwellian Commander who had defeated the Royalists on that very spot in a significant and very bloody battle midway through the Civil War. According to some sources, bloody civil war was still raging on the site, with guns and knives superseding muskets and pikes and various illicit substances instead of the dream of republicanism. The estate consisted of five high-rise blocks that, as they arrived, soared against the grey, rain-swollen clouds; huge ugly grey dominoes crying out for someone to flick them over with a celestial finger. Connie Preston lived in the West block, the towers being named, rather unoriginally, after the points of the compass — the fifth block being called Central.

Tanner parked just beyond a small muddy rectangle of grass containing two upturned shopping trolleys and, he suspected, several needles that had never been near a ball of wool. A frame for swings — minus the swings themselves — and a forlorn seesaw stood at one end, enclosed by rusting railings with a gap where the gate should be. Tanner's ancient car fitted in nicely with the others parked there. He had decided long before that as he was never sure where he was going to be leaving it unattended, a tatty vehicle which looked as though it had only just scraped through its MOT was more likely to still be there without further damage when he returned.

Running alongside the parking area in front of the flats was a wide slip road and beyond that the Yarrow Road, a three-lane highway leading to the Yarrow Roundabout. Tanner assumed that the planners must have been running out of names when they reached the area. The roundabout was a junction on the ring road and one of the major transport routes into and out of the city.

Connie Preston lived on the fifth floor of her block. There were two lifts, but as neither seemed to be working, they took the stairs. By the time they reached their destination, Tanner, deciding that there was only so much of the aroma of stale urine that you can stand to inhale, was very glad they were going to the fifth and not the twenty-fifth floor. Flat 54 had a blue door that was accessed by way of a graffiti-covered concrete walkway that over-looked the Yarrow Road and was open to the elements from the waist up.

Julie rang the bell. According to Beverly, Connie was a lady of the night in both senses of the phrase, so whether she had been earning or partying the night before, she should at least be at home at eleven o'clock in the morning and hopefully not too comatose.

At the third ring, the door was opened and

a young woman with tousled blonde hair around a heart-shaped face peered out at them as if her pale-blue eyes were having trouble focusing. She was wearing tight white trousers, a very tight sleeveless pink top with the motto 'two of a kind' and, rather incongruously, bunny slippers.

'Yeah?' Her voice was thick with sleep or alcohol, or, probably, both.

'Hi, I'm Julie Cooper and this is Alec Tanner. We're trying to find Kevin Winston and thought you might know where he is.' They had dressed for their visit in jeans, T-shirts and scruffy jackets and hoped they looked suitably like people who might want to offer Winston a job.

'Who sent you?'

'A guy called Jake Reaper; he's a friend of Jethro Harper.' They had decided that making up a fictitious friend of Harper's was less likely to be challenged than using a real person, or claiming friendship with Winston directly, which might have made her suspicious. As it turned out, it was a wasted strategy since she accepted them without question. 'We haven't seen Jethro lately, either,' Julie added.

'They've gone away.' Connie stood leaning her head against the edge of the open door, showing no inclination to invite them in, but equally none to slam the door in their faces.

'Do you know how we can get in touch with Kevin?'

She shook her head and winced slightly. Julie assumed that the fuzziness was hangover rather than sleep induced.

'No, Kevin just said that he might need to get away for a while and a couple of days later he blew. I haven't heard from him since.'

'When was this?'

'I dunno, about six weeks ago, maybe.' She paused and decided to trust them with her opinion. 'If you ask me, he isn't coming back.' She didn't appear exactly devastated by the prospect, Julie thought, it sounded like Winston was the caring half of the relationship.

'What makes you say that?'

'He was always talking about going down to London; he said it's where the big money is. I expect he's there now, shacked up with someone else. Bastard.' She spoke without heat. 'At least I can sell his stuff.'

'He left some things when he went?'

'A few clothes, stuff like that.'

'You didn't know he was going, then?'

'He had a job on and said he might have to lie low for a while afterwards. Maybe he had to nip off a bit sharpish.' She tapped her nose and nearly missed.

'Can you think of anyone else we could ask? We've got a bit of business to put his way; there should be some useful money in it.' Julie thought she had better reintroduce the criminal element before Connie wondered why they were so curious about Winston's previous activities.

She shrugged.

'Jethro's his only real friend. You know they both worked for Harry Milton?' They nodded. 'I suppose you could ask him, but Kevin says he isn't too keen on people asking questions, so I wouldn't recommend it. Sorry I can't help any more.'

She obviously considered the matter closed. With a brief dip of the head, she closed her door.

'We must have caught her on a good day.' Tanner remarked, as they walked back towards the stairs. 'Winston and Harper disappeared around the time of the shooting and they definitely worked for Milton. It'll be well worth following them up.'

'We still don't have any real lead on where they are now, though.'

'No.' Tanner scrunched his brow. 'We might have to transfer our attention to London, or at least ask Ancient to get his colleagues down there to make enquiries. Ted has some people there he can talk to as well.'

'I've got some good contacts in London too, don't forget,' Julie reminded him. 'I'd rather stay up here and concentrate on Milton, though. If he did take the job, we need to find a way of linking him with Jarrow.'

They came out through the double doors at the bottom of the flats. Tanner decided that going down the stairs was considerably easier than going up. Apart from anything else, they didn't need to breathe so deeply. The edges of the doors scraped on the chipped concrete path as they pushed them open and walked across the pavement towards their car. Tanner saw a movement out of the corner of his eye. A car was racing along the slip road towards them. He caught a glimpse of a pale face in the back seat, an open window and the shape of a gun barrel and reacted instinctively.

Tanner shoved Julie to the ground and sprawled on top of her as bullets struck the building, the path and the cars in front of them.

As the car raced past, heading for the main road, Tanner felt a blow on one leg and a sharp pain over his right eye. He put his hand up to his face and it came away sticky with blood. He rolled off Julie and looked down. There was blood seeping on to his jeans as well and pain stabbed through his leg.

Julie leaned over him, her eyes wide with horror.

'Oh, my God, no, not again.'

Tanner laid his head back against the concrete and watched the grey cloud swirl dizzily above him as the pain in his leg pulsed and grew. So much for being careful.

14

It was mid afternoon when Julie reached the antique shop. She was obviously in distress as she asked to see Laura.

'I'm afraid she is out at the moment, but Archie is in, I'll tell him you're here.' The assistant, who recognized Julie from her previous visit, looked at her with curiosity. 'Please wait there a moment.'

Archie came out from the back office, his smile of welcome fading as he saw the look on Julie's face.

'Come through, Julie.'

He followed Julie into the office and closed the door. A spreadsheet glowed on the computer screen. Archie pulled a chair across for Julie and sat in his own chair by the screen, swivelling round to face his visitor.

'What on earth has happened?' He studied Julie's face with concern. 'Laura said you thought you had tracked down the girlfriend of one of the killers.'

'Yes. We were just leaving her flat when a car drove by and they opened fire on us.'

Julie took a deep shuddering breath and Archie noticed for the first time a patch of dried blood on the front of her jeans.

'My God. Are you hurt?'

Julie shook her head.

'I'm OK, but Alec was hit. He pushed me to the ground and shielded me. He got shot in the leg and a head wound. He's going to be all right, but it was a near thing. He had mild concussion and he'll be in hospital for a few days while they sort his leg out.' She shook her head, her face twisted with self contempt. 'Anyone who gets close to me seems to get hurt.'

'Don't be silly.' Archie reached across, took her hands in his and squeezed them. They felt icy cold.

'Did you get the car number?'

Julie shook her head.

'It happened too quickly. They sped off and out of sight in the traffic.'

Archie nodded.

'Yes. It would be difficult to trace them. They could get anywhere from the Yarrow Roundabout, north, or east or back into the city.'

'The police found a car of a similar make and colour abandoned a couple of miles away, nowhere near any CCTV cameras, of course.'

'You didn't see who it was in the car?'

'No, but it isn't difficult to guess. Someone

connected to Harry Milton. I can think of three potential candidates straight away.' Her voice was bitter.

'Is there anything we can do?'

'I just came to tell you about it — I didn't want to do it over the phone. I need to get home and change and then I must get back to Alec at the hospital, so I won't be able to do dinner tonight, but I'd still like to come and see you later in the evening, if you don't mind. I want to ask you and Laura to help me.'

'Of course, if we can.' Despite his offer of help, he looked surprised. 'What can we do?'

'Like I said, we are pretty sure that the man behind all this is a gangster called Harry Milton. We told you when we came to dinner before that one of his hobbies is collecting paintings and other antiques. I've come up with an idea for getting at him through his hobby, but I need you and Laura to help.'

'What exactly do you want us to do?'

'I'll explain tonight when you're both there.' Julie managed a shaky smile. 'Thank you.'

Archie squeezed her hands again.

'You know we'll both help you however we can.' He paused. 'I'm sorry; I should have offered you coffee, or something stronger. The look on your face drove everything else out of my mind. What would you like?'

Julie got up.

'Don't worry, I'm fine. I just need a shower and a change of clothes and I'll feel better. At least Alec isn't too badly hurt. I'll be with you about nine o'clock this evening, will that be all right?'

'Yes, that's fine. You can have that drink then.'

Julie nodded, her smile more normal.

'Thanks, I'll look forward to it.'

★ ★ ★

When Julie arrived at nine, Archie opened the door and welcomed her in. She looked much fresher and more relaxed than she had at the shop that afternoon. She was wearing a short leather jacket over a black satin blouse, open at the neck to reveal a thick gold chain, and a tight-fitting knee-length grey skirt that was slit up one side and just reached the tops of her high-heeled black leather boots. He thought she looked superb and said so.

'You look much more like your old self.' He kissed her cheek.

'Thank you, I feel a lot better now. Sorry for the wobbly display earlier.'

'You had good cause, by the sound of it.'

He hung up her jacket in the hall and led

the way to the back room where Laura was waiting.

'It's good to see you.' Laura kissed her and studied her face anxiously. 'I take it from the look on your face and from what you said to Archie that Alec is going to be all right?'

'Yes. They've patched up his leg. He was sleeping when I left.'

'That's good.' Laura poured Julie a glass of wine. 'Sit down, dear. Have you had dinner?'

'Yes, thanks, I grabbed a takeaway after I left the hospital. Not as good as your food, of course, but I didn't feel much like eating.' She sat in one of the deep armchairs and took a sip of her drink.

Laura and Archie sat on the sofa opposite her and Laura looked at her expectantly.

'Archie said that you wanted us to help you catch this man called Harry Milton?'

'Yes. You said before that he'd brought one or two things from the shop?'

Laura nodded.

'That's right.' She looked sideways at Archie. 'We're really thrilled at the idea of being detectives, aren't we darling? What do you want us to do?'

'Milton considers himself something of an art buff and has built up a collection of paintings and other items.' As she spoke, Julie reached into her shoulder bag and brought out the box that Beverly had taken from Milton's safe. She opened it, took out the delicate porcelain figurine that lay inside and leant forward to place it on the glass-topped coffee table.

'What do you make of that?'

Laura reached for the figure and studied it carefully.

'It's a Staffordshire shepherdess. It's very rare, one of a very small number produced with that particular shade of pink colouring.' She looked at the base. 'Yes, the marks are right.'

'Do you remember it from the stolen property list?'

Laura considered.

'Yes, I think I do.'

'In a about two or three days' time, I'd like you to contact Milton and tell him that someone has offered the piece to you and told you that Milton would be an interested buyer. Your story is that you are checking to see if he is interested.'

'Where has this come from, then?' Laura laid the shepherdess back on the table.

'It was taken from Milton's safe earlier this week. We think that he had it stolen for his collection. Milton will assume that the person who stole it from him sold it on and told the buyer that he would probably want to buy it back.'

'So how does that help you?' Laura still looked puzzled.

'Assuming Milton buys it from you, we'll know that he has stolen property in his possession and the police will be able to get a search warrant for his house. We know that there are a number of other stolen items kept in a room that only Milton has access to. Once the police have found that room, they can take action against Milton and, as a part of that investigation, they can access his other records, which should lead to other things.'

Laura frowned.

'We'll do as you ask, of course, but isn't it all rather tenuous? You're assuming Milton will buy the item from us, that a judge will issue a search warrant on the strength of it and that there will be other information brought to light in the search. If one of those doesn't happen, you won't be much further forward.'

'I agree it's tenuous, but even if we just pin a possession of stolen property charge on him, it will be something. It's the best I can come up with at the moment.' Julie paused and finished her wine. 'We need to be as sneaky as he is and catch him off balance. It's no good reacting afterwards; he'll just slip through our fingers. He always plans well ahead, like this morning.'

Archie nodded.

'Yes, like being able to drive straight on to the Yarrow Road and away.'

'That's right, they — ' Julie broke off and looked at him with a puzzled expression. 'I didn't think of it when you said that this afternoon, Archie, but how did you know that Winston's girlfriend lived near the Yarrow Road?'

Archie frowned.

'You told Laura when she rang you this morning.'

Julie shook her head.

'No, I didn't. I just said we were going to see the girlfriend of a man who might have been one of the killers. I didn't say where she lived.' Julie stared at him. 'If you knew where we were going,' she said, slowly, 'that means you knew about the girlfriend and where she lived and that means you knew about Kevin Winston.' She stopped again, staring at him with growing horror. 'But that would mean that you set us up to be shot at today and that you were involved in arranging for Aunt Jo and me to be shot.'

Archie was staring at her in silence, his face impassive, his normally amiable expression wiped away as if he was waiting to see what happened next.

Julie shook her head. 'But I don't understand — why should you have wanted to have me shot? Why should you care that I had broken up a drugs ring in London?'

Laura was sitting forward on the settee, looking at Julie in apparent bewilderment. Julie remained focused on Archie, working through the logic of what she was saying.

'My God.' Julie stared at him in sudden realization. 'I wasn't the target, I was the decoy.'

'What do you mean?' Laura tried to keep her voice sounding normal, but couldn't hide the nervousness she was feeling.

'The connection isn't me, it's the shop. The shooting wasn't Jarrow getting his revenge, it was you murdering Joyce. My being there just gave you the opportunity to lay a false trail. That's why I wasn't killed, they had been told to make sure of Joyce first, which meant they were less accurate with me.'

'Very clever,' Archie said. 'But rather too late.'

As he spoke, Tilling leant forward to open a drawer at the side of the coffee table. When he sat back, he was holding a silenced gun. He pointed the weapon steadily at Julie, showing no sign of nervousness. Laura got up and, careful not to get between Julie and her husband, crossed to the door and turned the key in the lock. Archie stood up and Laura went to his side, calmer now that they were back in control of the situation.

'You are, of course quite right,' Tilling said, dipping his head in acknowledgement to Julie, who still sat looking stunned. 'Joyce was the real target. For some years we have been using the antique shops to launder money for Milton as well as providing him with a selection of stolen pieces. We worked partly through fictitious sales and partly through fencing other stolen goods to and from our less scrupulous clients.

'Your aunt knew nothing of this, but she spotted a stolen piece in the shop storerooms before we could pass it on and she was going to report it to the police. Laura played for time and said we'd got it from a reliable source and she wanted to talk to them first to get their explanation. Joyce agreed to wait, but we knew it was only a matter of time before she went to the police. Any investigation would have been fatal for us, so we had to dispose of her. Your presence made it look like a revenge attack on you.' His mouth formed a thin-lipped smile. 'You were very useful to us and we were actually rather grateful, so you weren't in any danger afterwards provided you found nothing out yourself that was a danger to us. We needed to keep in regular touch with you, of course, to keep an eye on what you were doing — which you most obligingly told us.'

He paused and looked at her reflectively.

'Once you started digging around Harry Milton, we started to get worried. Not only might you find something to suggest a connection between us, but if Harry was in danger of going down, he could well have decided to take us with him. We needed to be mutually supportive, you might say. That's why Laura tipped him off about your trip to the Yarrow Estate this morning. The attack was just to show that someone was still after you. If you had been seriously injured, it would have been a bonus, but it didn't matter too much. Now you are on our home turf, so to speak, we can deal with you much more cleanly. We can't have you running around knowing the truth, can we?'

Julie just sat looking at him, her face frozen and expressionless.

'I'll take that as a yes.' Tilling seemed to be enjoying himself. 'I won't shoot you here, unless you give us any trouble. We don't want any blood on the carpet. We'll take you off somewhere — suitably restrained, of course — and dispose of you. It will appear that

Jarrow's contract was still running and the killers caught up with you again. We'll tell the police that when you got here this evening you told us that someone had contacted you to give you information about the shooting of you and your aunt. They wanted to meet in an isolated spot and would give you proof of who Jarrow had hired. As you were coming to see us anyway you suggested the common at the end of our road. A meeting by the war memorial, perhaps, a suitably isolated spot and not well lit. You were due to meet him at ten when there won't be anyone about, even the most devoted dog walkers are back indoors by then at this time of year. We'll say that you left your car here as it is only a short walk to the common. We can't drive you anywhere in your car in case we leave any unexplained DNA behind. When you don't return by eleven, we'll get worried and call the police.'

'The police will still go after Milton for it.' Julie still seemed to be in shock. She spoke in a numbed way as if slowly working out the solution to a complex puzzle.

Archie shook his head.

'Milton and Jack Pace have arranged watertight alibis for the evening. They involve some members of the police force, I understand, so even your friend Mariner won't challenge them.'

Julie frowned.

'That makes it all sound pre-planned.'

Archie nodded.

'Yes, it is. With Alec temporarily out of the picture, it seemed a good opportunity to get rid of you. I was worried about my little slip this afternoon and, as you seemed to be getting rather too close to the truth for comfort, we thought it would be a safe precaution to dispose of you this evening, even if you hadn't worked things out just now. After you're gone, we'll keep in touch with Alec, of course, offer our condolences and be suitably supportive; make sure he's kept off the right track.'

'Killing someone yourself is a bit different to hiring someone to do it.' Julie seemed to have recovered some of her poise and looked at Archie steadily.

Archie smiled.

'Don't worry, I have previous experience. I have already disposed of your aunt's killers. They only survived her by an hour or two and are currently residing down a convenient mine shaft. We couldn't let them live knowing of our involvement in the murder. Not that you will be joining them. We will be quite happy for your body to be found; after all, Jarrow will get the blame again.'

Julie looked across at Laura.

'And you'll go along with this; you backed what he did to Joyce?'

'Of course.' Laura had shed her kindly, supportive image like a snake shedding its skin and looked at Julie as though she was stupid. 'It was better than losing our lifestyle here and going to jail. No contest at all, really.'

'And of course you inherited her half of the shops.' Julie's voice was peppered with distaste.

'That really wasn't the point; we only had her killed because she was a threat to us. I meant what I said: we'll miss Joyce's contribution to the business.' Laura seemed keener to defend herself against accusations of poor business sense than of murder. 'Joyce knew nothing about the criminal side of our activities, she wouldn't have stood that for a moment had she known, that's why we had her killed. She was boringly honest,' Laura's face took on a sneering expression that made Julie want to smack her. 'All her money came from the legitimate trade, so you needn't worry, your inheritance is clean.' The sneer broadened. 'Not that you'll get a chance to spend it now.'

'And you got the gunmen from Milton?' They seemed disposed to talk for a while and

Julie had no reason to hurry them on to the next phase.

'Yes. You were quite right to suspect Harper and Winston,' Archie told her. 'They were a couple of young lads working for Milton. He didn't want your aunt going to the police, either, and was quite happy to help by providing the cannon fodder. Harper and Winston were a bit too keen on thoughtless violence and that made them rather too unpredictable for his business activities, so he felt that they were expendable. As I said, I disposed of them soon after they had completed their task.'

'That was a bit of a balls up on your part, though, mentioning the Yarrow Road this afternoon, wasn't it?' Julie decided it was time to give his self-confidence a poke.

Archie's smile hardened.

'Not at all, it was a simple misunderstanding. You told Laura that you were going to see the girlfriend of one of the killers. Laura knew who that was and she said to me that you were going to the Yarrow Estate to see Connie Preston. I assumed that you had mentioned the name and the place. Milton told us about Connie Preston; he had been keeping an eye on her in case she raised a stink about Winston's disappearance, but she swallowed the story that he had gone away to look for work. We may need to deal with her eventually, but she seems to have taken up with someone else now, so that probably won't be necessary. No one else is likely to care much when a yob like Winston disappears. When we heard where you were going, we tipped Milton off and he set up the shooting. He was starting to become rather concerned about your activities.'

'As a matter of interest, who did the shooting this morning?'

'I believe Jack Pace had the gun and someone called Kelly was driving. Harry said that they had reason to dislike you both.'

Tilling was still looking calm and amused, perfectly in control of the situation. Julie longed to wipe the smile off his face, but with the gun pointing unwaveringly at her stomach, it was not the time to do it.

'It will make it all the more plausible when you are found lying in the bushes on the common with a bullet in the back of your head. It will be assumed that there was still a contract out on you over your work on the Jarrow case. You were tricked into a meeting, overpowered and then executed.'

'If you take me along the street at gun point, you risk being seen by one of your neighbours,' Julie pointed out.

'That is precisely why we don't intend to

take you out the front way. In fact, I think it's about time to leave.'

Tilling motioned with the gun for Julie to stand up.

'You will be accompanying us on a little boat trip. Laura will get your jacket — you aren't likely to have gone out on a chilly night like this without it and we want our story to look as realistic as possible, don't we?'

Julie said nothing as Laura unlocked the door, went out and returned with her jacket.

'There's nothing in the pockets,' she told her husband.

'Put it on,' Tilling told Julie. 'And don't try anything stupid. If necessary, I'm prepared to shoot you now and clear up the mess afterwards. If you behave, you'll get a nice quick death, if not I'll make it very painful.'

Julie shrugged into her jacket. There was a chance she could have flicked it in Tilling's face and unsighted him enough to go for the gun, but it was risky and she didn't know how Laura would react. The odds weren't good; it was worth waiting for them to improve.

'Bring her shoulder bag,' Tilling told his wife. 'She'd have taken that with her and we can leave it by her body.'

Tilling motioned with the gun and they went out of the living room, Laura leading, Julie next and Tilling at the rear, keeping a safe distance so that Julie couldn't swing round and go for the gun.

They went across the hall and into the kitchen. As they reached the back door, Tilling halted the short procession.

'And now,' he said, 'we just need to make sure you aren't tempted to try something when we get outside.'

He nodded to Laura. She went into the utility room at the side of the kitchen and returned with a length of cord which she used to tie Julie's wrists together behind her back.

'Right, then, I think were ready.' Taking it in turns to cover Julie with the gun, the Tillings put on old coats that were hanging in the utility room. Laura then unlocked and unbolted the kitchen door. Cold air swept into the kitchen as she opened the door and stepped outside.

Tilling gripped Julie's right arm above the elbow, and pushed the barrel of the gun into her side.

'Don't try to call out. We're well away from any of our neighbours and, as soon as I hear a sound from you, I'll use the gun. We're going to take a leisurely walk down the garden to the river. We've got a dinghy moored there next to our boat that's just got room for the three of us. It's only a short distance upstream to where the river runs through the common, so it won't take us long to get there. Don't expect anyone to be messing about on the river at this time of night, either. There will be no witnesses, I assure you.'

Julie didn't bother to respond as he tugged on her elbow and she walked out by his side on to the deep paved patio that ran the length of the rear of the house. The sky was cloudier than it had been the night before and the moonlight much more fitful. The lights were still on in the living room and kitchen, shining through the drawn curtains to illuminate the patio in a soft shadow-filled glow. There was an open balustrade along the edge of the patio, with a gap to their right where a short flight of stone steps led down to the wide lawn. Two stone pots with short, perfectly manicured palm trees stood on either side of the steps. On the far side of the terrace, the statue of an unidentifiable Greek goddess watched placidly over the proceedings.

Laura closed and locked the back door and walked down on to the paved path that led from the patio steps round to the right of the lawn and then on down towards the river. Julie glanced back up over her shoulder. The top floor of the house next door was visible above the trees and bushes that lined the edge of the garden, but the windows were dark and there was no sign of anyone watching.

The moon slid out from behind a line of cloud and spread a strong silvery light across the middle of the lawn, contrasting with the deep shadow created by the trees and bushes on each side.

'I have to say, it's a pity from your point of view that you didn't twig all this before.' Tilling seemed to feel the need to provide a running commentary as they walked along the path. 'If you had been a good enough detective to spot earlier on what I said about the Yarrow Roundabout this afternoon, we could have been in serious trouble. I was also worried that Laura was the only non-official person who knew you were going to see Winston's girlfriend this morning, so you might have realized that only we had time to arrange the ambush.'

Julie turned her head to look at him and for a moment her eyes met his. Her expression did more than simply poke at his confidence.

'I did,' she said. 'End game.'

As she spoke, she raised her right leg and drove the stiletto heel of her boot down hard along Tilling's left shin and into the top of his foot.

Tilling screamed out with the sudden shock of the sharp pain, dropped his gun and bent over, clutching at his injured leg. Laura swung round, her mouth opening in alarm as they were suddenly bathed in bright light from both sides and the garden came alive with movement.

Julie looked down at Tilling, her eyes deep pools of contempt.

'You're nicked,' she said, with considerable satisfaction.

15

Half an hour before Julie arrived at the Tillings' house, a small police boat, its lights having been dowsed some hundred yards back downstream, drifted gently into the bank beside the jetty at the end of their garden. A large beech tree grew close to the edge and a convenient thick branch was used to temporarily moor the boat and allow the four armed police officers, two male and two female, plus Mariner and Tanner to step ashore. Mariner gave a brief signal and the boat was untied again and allowed to float back softly into the night. There was another landing stage on the opposite bank where the boat would moor out of sight, awaiting Mariner's further orders. The dark waters of the river rippled gently in the brief passage of moonlight, chuckling against the jetty as if at some long forgotten joke.

Because Julie and Tanner had seen the garden before, they knew the layout and the small landing party had already worked out its placements, allowing them to move up the garden in silence. They reached the main lawn and split into two groups, Mariner and

Tanner and one policewoman on the right and the others on the left. The fitful moonlight enabled them to keep in deep shadow and out of sight of a casual glance from the house. Occasionally, a shadow would pass across the curtained windows as someone moved round a room, but there was no indication of any alarm being raised. Halfway up the lawn they drew back even further into the shelter of the surrounding bushes and settled down to wait.

Tanner was very unhappy about Julie's plan, but she had insisted that it was the best way to confirm their suspicions, unless he could come up with anything better? Tanner couldn't. Nothing new there, then, he thought. His thoughts drifted back to earlier in the day.

After the shooting, Julie had called for an ambulance and Mariner, in that order, and had accompanied Tanner to the hospital. The bullet had gone through his leg and missed the bone. The head wound had been caused by a piece of sharp flying plastic created by one of the bullets hitting the rear nearside light of the car in front of where they were lying. They had been lucky. As Tanner had pushed Julie to the ground and fallen on top of her, they had been below the initial trajectory of the bullets. By the time the gunman had adjusted his aim, he was nearly past them and was unsighted by the parked cars. Apart from Julie having a few scrapes and bruises from the pavement and Tanner's relatively mild wounds, they were uninjured. The parked cars had suffered more than they had, although, ironically, Tanner's was undamaged.

By the time Mariner arrived at the hospital, Tanner had been treated. There was a thick bandage round his lower right leg, but he could walk on it with care. They had loaned him a walking stick and a severe young doctor who seemed barely out of short trousers was warning him that he risked splitting the stitches if he used the leg too much.

'If I can find someone to lend me a parrot, I'll audition for pantomime.'

Julie hadn't responded to Tanner's smile. She was looking worried and pensive.

'When you're ready, I'll drive you back to pick up your car,' Mariner had offered.

'We need to talk first.' Julie's eyes were narrowed and puzzled, as if she was trying to work out a riddle and the obvious answer seemed wrong.

They went out to Mariner's car, Tanner sat on the back seat with his leg up. Julie got in the front with Mariner and they half turned in their seats to include the invalid in the conversation.

'I'm sorry, but I need to ask you this. Did you mention to anyone that we were going to see Connie Preston?'

Mariner shook his head.

'No, I had no reason to.' He looked at Julie curiously and without offence.

Julie had looked across at Tanner.

'Alec, do you think we were followed this morning?'

Tanner had suddenly realized where her thoughts were leading. He would have thought of it himself, if he hadn't been shot. At least, that was his excuse.

'I'm sure we weren't.' he said positively. Knowing that Pace and his merry men had been released, he'd been particularly conscious of the need to check the surrounding traffic regularly.

Julie nodded.

'That's what I was afraid you'd say.' She had looked away from Tanner and stared out of the side window, her face hurt and bewildered. 'There's only one person who knew where we'd be and who could have set us up to be shot — Laura Tilling.'

Tanner had frowned.

'Laura admitted that she does business with Milton, so there's a connection there.

But you didn't mention Connie Preston by name, or where she lived. Why should — ' He had broken off at the look on Julie's face.

'It's more than just a connection; it raises a whole load of questions. I know it sounds bizarre and I don't know all the answers yet, but there's one way to find them out.' Her voice was grim as she set out her plan.

'But . . . ' Tanner began.

She knew what he was going to say and shook her head.

'If I'm on my own, I'm more likely to be able to prod them into revealing themselves. I'll seem less like a threat, something they can deal with straight away.' She smiled without humour.

'So what will you do if they do react?' Tanner was already starting to have a nasty gut feeling about what she was suggesting.

'I'll play it by ear, see what happens. They won't do anything to me in their own house if they can help it. Don't worry, I'll be careful.'

Tanner's gut feeling began to get a lot worse.

His thoughts returned to the present, loitering in the Tillings' garden in the freezing cold with five police officers, waiting for something to happen. Hoping that something would happen so that the preparations would not be wasted, but dreading it as well. They were not sure what reaction would be provoked when Julie tried to goad the Tillings into betraying themselves — assuming, of course, that there was something to betray. They had the back garden covered and there was a vanload of officers parked a little way down the street outside ready for a possible frontal exit. Other cars were in place to block the street if they tried to take Julie away in a car. Each group of police had torches, battering rams and pistols that fired tear gas and smoke bombs. If Julie seemed to be in danger inside the house, they'd all go in together like the US Cavalry. Hopefully, Tanner thought, not like General Custer. The police were very aware, of course, that if they weren't careful they could end up with a hostage situation.

As a plan, Tanner thought, it had more holes than St Andrews, but it was all they had. And Julie was one of the most resourceful and determined people that he knew. He kept repeating that to himself. It wasn't a great deal of comfort.

After Julie had gone into the house, the ache in Tanner's leg had got worse. The leg had protested about clambering around in the boat and standing around in the cold was not improving matters. He tried a few on the spot exercises to keep it mobile. He had found he was able to get around without the walking stick and had left it behind in case he couldn't resist the temptation to brain one of the Tillings with it.

After what seemed an eternity, they saw movement on the blind over the kitchen window. A short while later, the door opened and a wedge of yellow light spilled out on to the patio. They watched Laura, Julie and Archie come out. Tanner felt his heart leap with relief at the visual confirmation that Julie was unharmed. As Laura closed and locked the back door and led the way down on to the lawn towards them, Tanner could almost feel Mariner tense himself beside him.

They could hear Tilling taunting Julie as they came across the grass, his voice mocking and confident. They heard her respond briefly and then give the agreed code words at the same moment as she stamped down hard on Tilling's foot to distract him.

As the police moved in, Tanner could see from the look on Julie's face that she wanted to stamp even harder on some other part of Tilling's anatomy, but she restrained herself and let Mariner organize the arrests.

By the time Archie Tilling had recovered enough to realize what was going on, his gun had been scooped up and placed in an evidence bag. With a bit of luck, Tanner thought, Tilling only owned the one weapon and if they could locate the bodies of the hired killers, it would add an extra element to the case against him.

Tanner moved round behind Julie and cut her wrists free. Then he turned her round, put his arms round her and hugged her tightly. Her response suggested that, despite her undercover experience, she hadn't been nearly as calm inside as she had appeared to be.

The Tillings were handcuffed and cautioned. Neither had spoken a word. They had gone from complete control and domination of the situation to total defeat in a couple of seconds and were both staring at Julie in a state of starched-faced shock. Julie didn't bother to say anything to them. She simply pulled the bottom of her blouse out of her skirt and lifted it up to a point just below her breasts. It wasn't intended as an erotic gesture; it simply revealed the microphone and wires taped to her body. Mariner and Tanner both had ear-pieces and had been listening to every word spoken in the house and the van in the road outside had been recording it all for posterity and the courts. Julie turned her head to look at Mariner.

'Did you get it all?' she asked.

He nodded.

'Every word.'

Julie relaxed and smiled.

'At least I seem to have done something right.'

'More than just something.' There was considerable satisfaction in Mariner's voice.

The Tillings had switched to staring at Tanner.

'Reports of my injuries have been greatly exaggerated,' he told them. He glanced at Julie. 'Although I will require a great deal of TLC. I have been in agony loitering about in the undergrowth with my bad leg.'

Julie grinned, her eyes completely free from pain of guilt for the first time since Tanner had known her. She tucked her blouse back in.

'Don't worry. As a special treat, I'll let you remove the bug.'

16

Harry Milton was in his study feeling edgy and irritable. The three carefully selected guests with whom they had been playing poker for most of the evening had gone soon after 10.30. Jack Pace had just left the room having announced that he was going to check that the house was secure before going to bed. Milton had grunted, envying his employee the fact that he had Jane Weston to share his bed. Jane might not be the most beautiful woman in the world, or have the sharpest intellect, but she curved in all the right places and walked with a wiggle that could make you cross-eyed. He decided that he needed a woman. He would have to visit his clubs and do something about that as soon as possible.

Milton scowled to himself. Part of the trouble was that he couldn't even go upstairs and spend a soothing hour with his paintings and other art treasures. As soon as he heard that Beverly Wallace had spoken to Alec Tanner and Julie Cooper, he had moved his illegal possessions to a safer location as a precaution against a possible police search of his property. The items were not that far away, but he had kept them crated in case a second move was required.

The telephone cut across his gloomy thoughts and he barked out a sharp acknowledgement as he answered it. The voice at the other end spoke in subdued but urgent tones. The call did not take long, but when it was finished, Milton's mood was several degrees fouler than it had been before.

Jack Pace was halfway up the broad staircase when his boss came out of the study and called out his name.

'What is it, boss?'

'I've just had a call from Den Fletcher.'

Pace's forehead creased. Detective Sergeant Fletcher was one of their best moles in the Havenchester City Police. A call from him after eleven o'clock at night, coupled with the look in Milton's face, did not suggest good news.

'They've arrested Archie and Laura Tilling.' Milton spat the information out.

Pace swore.

'They must have made a balls-up of killing Cooper.'

'Yes.' Milton looked disgusted at such incompetence. 'Fletcher wasn't involved in the arrest and he doesn't have any details, but he says Mariner was looking particularly pleased with himself, so I expect the bitch is still alive.'

'Do you think Tilling will talk?'

Milton snorted.

'Of course he'll bloody talk. He'll do as much as he can to save his own skin. He'll be squawking like a parrot with verbal diarrhoea. The only question is how long it will take him to give the cops enough information on us for them to act.'

Milton clamped down on his anger as he worked out the best next move.

'Mariner will have to get them booked in and questioned and he'll need to get a warrant to raid us here. They're partial to dawn raids, so we should have until early morning.' He thought for a moment. 'Go and tell Horace to come down. There's stuff he needs to sort out before we can leave. Then get Jane to pack you a couple of cases and switch off the lights as if you're going to bed. The cops may not be moving in for a while, but if I know Mariner, he's got a watch on the front gates in case we try to leave, so we don't want to do anything to alarm them. We'll all meet in the kitchen at twelve-thirty.'

'We'll be leaving the same way as the paintings then?'

Milton nodded tersely, his brain already running over the things he needed to do.

'When you've spoken to Jane, ring Reggie at the other house and tell him to expect us.'

As Pace turned and ran up the stairs, Milton went back into his study, his face stiff with rage. He knew who to blame for all this. He might have to go on the run, but if he got a chance he'd deal with Tanner and Cooper first.

*   *   *

'They got away?' Superintendent Mornington was a plain-spoken Yorkshireman who didn't bother to hide either his astonishment or his displeasure. 'There was no one in the house at all?'

Mariner was not happy. Although he was sitting in the chair facing his chief's desk, he felt more as though he was standing to miserable attention in front of an old-style headmaster who was bending a cane in his hands. Not that he could blame Mornington — he felt like giving himself a thorough dressing-down as well.

'Just the cook, sir. She claimed to know nothing about Milton's business activities. That may or may not be true, but I doubt if she knows much that could help us or she wouldn't have been left behind.'

'How on earth did it happen? I thought

you had the place under surveillance?'

'We did, sir. We were watching the front entrance. As far as we knew, there was no rear access. Milton would have needed a helicopter to get out any other way.'

'I take it your surveillance team didn't notice a helicopter landing?' Mornington raised his bushy eyebrows, showing a slightly surprising turn of sarcastic humour.

'No, sir.' Mariner's face was as wooden as a forest. 'He didn't need one. It turns out that there was a rear access that we didn't know anything about.' He paused. 'Nor, to be fair, did the council's planners.'

Mornington sighed.

'What exactly happened?'

'We got a warrant for Milton's arrest and to search his house based on Tilling's statement and an armed team raided the property at five-thirty this morning. When we broke in, there was no one there but the cook. She claims to have gone to bed at ten-thirty last night with everyone in the house as usual and knew nothing more until she was woken up by us. We made a thorough search of the house to make sure there were no hidden rooms or anything, but we found nothing. We located the room where the stolen pictures were supposed to be kept but that was bare too.'

Mariner took a disgusted breath.

'My first thought was that the surveillance team must have missed something, but they swore there hadn't been as much as a stray cat through the gates all night. I organized a thorough search of the grounds. There was evidence of fresh footprints which suggested some activity in the garden last night. We checked right round the perimeter and eventually found it.'

'Found what?' Mornington snapped. 'Don't keep me in suspense, Ancient; this isn't a bloody mystery story.'

Mariner nodded. At least he'd called him 'Ancient' rather than 'Chief Inspector'.

'Sorry, sir. There was a brick-built storage shed at the rear of the garden. It seemed to contain just the usual garden junk, but we spotted that it backed on to a similar shed in the back garden of the house beyond. In fact, they shared a common wall. A section of shelving at the back of the shed swung open and there was a door behind it that led to a similar section of shelving on the other side. They must have gone through there and into the other house, which is in a road two streets away from the one Milton's property is in.'

'I assume there was also no one in when you entered this second house.'

'No, sir. There were signs of recent

occupancy, though. We checked with the neighbours. A couple on one side heard activity sometime after one o'clock this morning. They sleep at the front and were woken by engines starting up and headlights across their window. The husband looked out and saw a small van and a car leaving the house. He went back to bed. He didn't notice the make or colour of either vehicle except that the car was dark and the van was light.'

'No chance of a registration number then.' Mornington's eyebrows did another round of exercises.

Mariner assumed that was a rhetorical question and carried on.

'The neighbours know very little about the occupants of the house, which was last sold about three years ago. We checked the land registry and the supposed owner is no one we know. Either Milton used an alias, or he got a stooge to stand in for him. We're checking into that now.'

'Milton's a careful man if he's had this prepared for some years,' Mornington commented.

'Yes, sir.' Mariner's mouth twisted. 'I suspect the rest of his escape plan has been equally carefully prepared.'

The superintendent grunted.

'Who else is with him, do you think?'

'Jack Pace and Horace Soames without a doubt and probably Jane Weston — she's Pace's girlfriend. They all live in Milton's house. One of the neighbours did spot someone around the second house yesterday and gave us a description that sounds like Reggie Gray, so he could be part of the mix as well.'

'If they had a van, they were presumably moving quite a bit of stuff with them?'

'It was probably carrying the stolen paintings and other artefacts that Milton kept in his secret room. There may be some other stuff as well, although I'd think he'd want to travel reasonably light. He may be intending to stash some stuff somewhere and come back for it later.'

'Can't we get a line on him through his business activities?'

'That may take some time. Milton seems to have done quite a bit of shredding before he left. There were two computers. Both had been smashed, presumably in an attempt to destroy the hard drives, but our boffins are pretty good at reconstructing that sort of thing — they're having a go at that now. There were probably some laptops as well but they could have taken those with them.'

'And you've no idea where they might have gone?'

'No, sir. We're checking all Milton's

holdings and his company properties as well as anything else in the name that was used to buy the bolt-hole, but no joy so far.'

Mornington's expression suggested that he thought joy was likely to be in short supply for a while.

'There's little doubt he'll be trying to leave the country,' Mariner went on, 'so we've alerted ports and airports, but there are ways and means of getting round that, of course.'

'Hmm.' The superintendent looked up sharply. 'What about DS Cooper and your friend Tanner? Milton could well be blaming them for all this. He might have another go at them before he leaves. You'd better warn them that he's in the wind and probably pretty volatile.'

'I've tried, sir.' Mariner's voice suddenly sounded very tired. 'There's no reply from either flat, they haven't arrived at the agency and their mobiles are switched off.'

The two men stared at each other for a moment. It was left to Mornington to articulate both their thoughts.

'Bugger.'

★   ★   ★

A few hours before Mariner's uncomfortable interview, Harry Milton had awoken from a brief sleep in the back of his car. He had a headache and a pain in his back. He got out and stretched, yawning. Pace was already up and leaning against the side of the van.

'Morning, Harry.'

'How long would it take you to reach the flats where Julie Cooper lives?' Milton asked, rubbing at the small of his back.

Pace frowned thoughtfully.

'At this time in the morning? Not much more than an hour. It'll take longer later when the traffic builds up, of course.'

Milton consulted his watch. It wasn't yet six o'clock.

'I won't be able to start making the arrangements for us to leave until after nine and we won't actually get away until midday.' He looked across at the other man with an expression as warm as a penguin's flipper. 'Do you fancy another crack at Cooper and Tanner?'

Pace's face split in a wolfish grin.

'It would be a pleasure.'

'You and Reggie can drive my car to Cooper's flat. If Cooper and Tanner appear before ten, pick them up. Take the anaesthetic dart gun and try to get the drop on them and bring them back here alive. If you don't see them by ten o'clock, give it up. You should easily get back here by twelve. I'll ring you on your mobile if there's a change of plan.'

'What happens if we can't get Tanner and Copper to come quietly?'

'Kill them there and then if you have to.' Milton's mouth stretched humourlessly. 'I'd rather see them die myself though — if you bring them here alive we can make it last.' He looked at Pace with flat-faced consideration. 'I'm sure you'll manage. After all, you've already worked out a way to get into the apartment block's car-park.'

Pace nodded.

'Yes, I just didn't get a chance to use it.'

'Now's your opportunity.'

★   ★   ★

It had been, Alec Tanner reflected, grossly negligent to let themselves be captured and their chances of learning from their mistake seemed to be disappearing rapidly. The relief of solving the murder had made them relax their guard dangerously. With the Tillings in custody and Milton set to join them, there hadn't seemed to be any need for caution. They hadn't just taken their eyes off the ball, they had stopped playing the game completely.

They had been walking towards Julie's car in the underground car-park beneath her apartment block when he had felt a blow on his upper leg followed by a sharp sting. Looking down, he had seen a hypodermic dart jutting from his thigh. Even as he pulled the dart clear and started to move sideways, seeking the cover of the nearest car as he searched the surrounding area for the attacker, he heard Julie exclaim and clutch at her leg. Well before reaching cover, he had stumbled to his knees on the concrete floor, his vision failing as his strength washed away. He had a brief vision of Reggie Gray's grinning face before he slumped to the ground unconscious.

When he regained consciousness, Tanner could feel movement. He was sitting upright in a vehicle; his arms turned sideways and linked to someone else's. Julie's perfume drifted into his senses and he opened his eyes.

He was sitting in the back seat of a car with Julie by his side. His right arm was round Julie's left arm and each of them had their wrists handcuffed together in front. Joined together through the circles formed by their arms, they couldn't move apart. It was, he acknowledged, a very effective way of restricting their movement. Once out of the car they wouldn't be able to move very fast and they would need to co-ordinate their movements carefully to avoid pulling each other off balance. Their current position was further restricted by the fact that they were both wearing seatbelts.

Julie was already awake and she flashed him a brief grimace that reflected his own annoyance at how easily they had been caught.

'Are you OK?' he asked.

She nodded.

'Under different circumstances, this might be quite fun,' she said drily raising her cuffed wrists.

Jack Pace glanced into the rear-view mirror when he heard their voices.

'I can assure you that what you've got coming won't be fun for you,' he said.

Reggie Gray chuckled from the passenger seat.

'But it will be for us,' he added.

Both Pace and Gray were inclined — understandably, Tanner and Julie had to admit — to gloat a little. They wouldn't say where they were going, but when Tanner asked how they'd got through the carpark's security, Gray was happy to tell them.

'Security?' He looked disdainful. 'I wouldn't call it that. You need a key pad code to raise the metal grille to get in, but there's just a pressure pad to get out and the grille doesn't drop back straight away. I just waited round the corner by the entrance for one of your neighbours to drive out and nipped in under the grille before it finished going down. Then I jumped on the pressure pad to make it go up again so Jack could drive in. We parked in a vacant slot near the lift and waited for you to turn up. Over two hours we were hanging about.' He sounded aggrieved.

'If we'd known you were waiting, we'd have got ready sooner.'

Julie's comment earned her a snort from Pace.

They had passed through the centre of the city whilst Julie and Tanner were unconscious and had now reached the outlying countryside. After a while they came to a narrow bumpy road leading to a pair of decrepit metal gates that were partially closed. Pace got out and pushed the gates open with a rusty creak. A further short drive over an even bumpier road brought them out into an old deserted airfield. There were a few small buildings in various stages of dilapidation and a large hangar.

Pace drove through the open doors of the hangar and parked next to a small white van. Horace Soames, Jane Weston and Harry Milton had been sitting in the front of the van and they got out as the car drew to a halt.

'Any problems?' Milton asked as Pace got out of the car.

'Nope, easy as anything.'

Gray opened the rear door and leant in to undo the two seatbelts. There was no room for Julie or Tanner to try anything and Gray moved back quickly.

'Out you get.'

Julie and Tanner shuffled across the seat together and got out, standing up carefully. Although Tanner's legs were a little stiff, particularly the injured one, the effect of the dart seemed to have worn off and his head was clear. Glancing at Julie, he saw her surveying their surroundings carefully and his heart lifted. At least they were both alert and ready to take advantage of any chance. The problem would be finding a chance to take advantage of.

Gray jerked his thumb to indicate that they should walk to the rear of the hangar. Pace had produced a gun, which he pointed towards them to emphasize the instruction.

Julie and Tanner glanced at each other and obeyed. There was still no obvious opening that wouldn't result in them being shot. Gray walked round to the boot of the car, opened it and produced a double barrelled shotgun. He moved over to one side, keeping the shotgun pointed towards the floor but ready to raise it if necessary.

'You have already cost me a considerable amount of money and caused immense inconvenience.' Milton spoke like a judge passing sentence. 'Now, because of you, I have to leave the country and my organization and start afresh again. I owe you for that and I've decided to settle the debt before I go.'

He stared at them with satisfaction.

'I want you to die slowly and in as much agony as possible.' Milton tapped his watch. 'Our plane will be landing here just before twelve. That gives us plenty of time. Jack will shoot you both in the knees and the stomach and we will be able to enjoy watching you writhing around in agony until the plane arrives. Jack will put you out of your misery just before we leave — I want to make absolutely sure that you're dead before we go.'

Milton turned towards Pace and nodded.

Pace moved forwards, aiming his gun.

There was one slim chance of trying something and Tanner hoped Julie was on the same wavelength.

'Before you shoot us there's something you need to know.'

Tanner was looking at Milton as he spoke and took a step forward. He was relying on the psychological inclination to wait for someone to stop speaking before responding. As he took the step that brought him into range, Tanner kicked upwards with all the concentrated force of a rugby player trying to score a penalty from the halfway line. The toe of his shoe buried itself in Pace's crotch and a jolt of pain shot through Tanner's injured leg.

Pace screamed and dropped the gun, clutching at his groin as he buckled over. This was the point where the co-ordination was essential. Tanner needn't have worried, as he bent towards the fallen gun, he felt Julie move with him. They would have a millisecond of advantage before Gray reacted and aimed his shotgun.

Even as Tanner started to crouch down for the gun, he saw Pace fall on top of it and dismay washed over him. Precious moments would be lost in moving Pace to get at the weapon. The next moment, his concern over the hitch to their last chance was swept away by a new problem as, with a howl of rage, Jane Weston lunged towards them at speed, her hands clawing towards Tanner's face.

If she had reached him, Tanner would have been lucky not to be blinded, but as the outstretched arms grew close he felt Julie move smoothly up from her semi crouch, pulling his arms with her. Pressing her hands on his shoulder for support, she launched a fierce roundhouse kick.

The toe of Julie's boot, travelling from right to left, connected with Jane Weston's solar plexus moving in the opposite direction. Air exploded from the attacker's lungs and her eyes seemed to cross and glaze over at the same time as she collapsed across the legs of her lover, making the gun even more inaccessible.

'Kill them!' Milton screamed, his voice as livid as his face. 'Forget about anything fancy, just blast them.'

Tanner felt his tiny flicker of hope flutter and die. It would take far too long to retrieve Pace's gun and there was fifteen yards of clear space between them and Gray. He could try to get in front of Julie and protect her from the first shot, although some of the blast would probably go right through him and there was no way she could escape the second barrel with no cover.

For a frozen moment, Tanner was sharply aware of two things. The look of sadistic glee on Reggie Gray's face as he raised the shotgun, temporarily lowered when Jane Weston had got into his line of fire, was coupled with the awareness of Julie's presence at his side and the aching sadness that they were about to lose each other so soon after finding . . .

The shots boomed round the hangar, making him wince, but there was no impact and no pain. Instead it was Gray who jerked like a puppet with ague, his shotgun swinging upwards and discharging harmlessly into the air as he toppled backwards on to the cracked floor, twitched once and lay still.

Slowly, Tanner's brain started to function again. The shouted warning that had preceded the shot filtered into his consciousness. He registered Julie's face, mirroring his own astonishment. Slowly he turned his head to see Milton staring at the entrance to the hangar in open-mouthed horror. His gaze moved on to Horace Soames, arms stretched upwards as if he was trying to grasp the sky, and then to the dark-blue uniformed figures, most of them armed, who were moving purposefully across the floor. Amongst them was a familiar lean figure, wearing a Kevlar vest somewhat incongruously over his old raincoat.

The anxiety around Mariner's eyes eased as he focused on Julie and Tanner, both still standing and both still breathing. He gave them a brief nod of acknowledgement before turning his attention elsewhere.

'Harry Milton, I am arresting you . . . '

Tanner turned towards Julie. His mouth felt parched and his jaw ached. He must have had it clenched for some reason. He licked his dry lips and managed the ghost of a grin as he spoke in a croaky voice.

'If it was physically possible, I'd give you the biggest hug you've ever had in your life.'

'I feel the same way.' Julie looked down at their wrists. 'I hope they've brought a key that fits.'

'I've got the next best thing.'

A police officer appeared at their side holding a small but efficient-looking pair of bolt cutters and moments later they could move apart.

'There's a gun under there somewhere,' Julie pointed towards Pace and Weston.

'Leave it to me.' The policeman signalled to a colleague and they began to sort out the still moaning bodies with clinical efficiency.

It was clear that they were not required to help with the tidying up. Tanner gently took hold of Julie's shoulders and carried out his promise.

A quiet cough separated them a short while later. Mariner eyed them with amusement.

'I take it you're both OK?'

'Thanks to you,' Tanner acknowledged. 'You certainly picked your moment, Ancient, how on earth did you manage it?'

'It was actually quite simple,' Mariner admitted. 'I was in the middle of an interesting meeting with Superintendent Mornington discussing how I'd managed to let Milton slip through my fingers when I got a message to say that Archie Tilling had decided to come completely clean and was making a full statement about the murder. He admitted to meeting his hired killers at a deserted airfield after the murder where he'd killed them before disposing of their bodies a few miles away. When I asked how he'd picked the airfield he told me that Harry Milton had suggested it. I knew Milton would be trying to flee the country and a direct connection between Milton and an old airfield seemed like a clue. I thought it was worth a look, so I got an armed response team together, turned on the lights and the sirens, and here we are.'

He paused and looked at them with an oddly quizzical expression.

'What is it?' Julie asked.

'If Tilling hadn't talked when he did, we wouldn't have got here in time,' Mariner said. 'You could say that Archie Tilling saved your lives.'

Julie's face pulled into a tired smile.

'We must remember to thank him some-time.'

17

The evening after their showdown with Milton, Julie and Tanner were seated at a table in the swankiest restaurant he could find — and afford. Tanner, whose normal restaurant of choice gave away toys with the food, thought the place was so posh that even the knives and forks looked like they should have a Michelin star.

Julie looked stunning in an ice-blue sleeveless satin dress that clung to her curves and rippled as she moved, the perfect compliment to her long black hair. Tanner was even wearing a suit. Dressing up was starting to become a habit, he thought — if it carried on he might need to buy another tie.

'If you treat all your clients this well, it's a wonder you make any money at all,' Julie remarked, sipping at a glass of wine that, judging from the price, must have been made from platinum grapes.

Tanner felt a lump in his throat. After they had been driven away from the airfield, he had gone to the agency whilst Julie had gone to police headquarters and spent the afternoon with Mariner. It had emphasized the difference in their position. He was the private eye and she was the official detective who had a right to be a party to the official investigation. Tanner had gone back to his flat from the agency to change and Julie had gone to hers straight from the police station. Apart from a brief phone call to set the time and place for the meal they hadn't spoken since the police car had dropped him off at the agency.

Tanner let his gaze wander slowly over his companion, the warm glow he always felt in her presence tinged now with unease. Julie was clearly fully fit, mentally as well as physically, the last couple of days had proved that. Now the uncertainty of the future was starting to loom ever closer, his insecurity heightened by the fact that they were coming to the meal from different locations, like friendly acquaintances rather than lovers.

'What's the news from the cop shop?' He tried to keep his tone light.

Julie gave him a satisfied smile.

'Laura and Archie have been charged with Aunt Joyce's murder. Winston and Harper's bodies have been found at the old mine location where Archie said they would be, so the murder charge will shortly be tripled. Milton's been charged with conspiracy to murder, receiving stolen goods and kidnapping. There'll be more to add to that list, too, but it's enough to be going on with. Pace has been charged with two counts of attempted murder and kidnapping. Mariner's still working on what alleged crimes to charge Soames and Jane Weston with.'

Tanner raised his eyebrows.

'Alleged?'

Julie mimicked a zipper across her mouth.

'Milton and his gang have all refused to say anything since their arrest,' she said.

'Don't tell me they've lawyered up?'

Julie gave him an amused glance.

'It sounds like you've been watching too many late night repeats of 'NYPD Blue'.'

'You can't watch too many repeats of 'NYPD Blue'.'

'True.' She nodded solemnly. 'Anyway, the police are going through the books of the antique shop now and they've got enough evidence to get access to Milton's business accounts. Mind you, if Soames is as good as Mariner suspects he is, a lot of the evidence is going to be very well hidden.'

'And Archie is an accountant too.'

'Yep. It's not about crime, it's about number crunching.' She took another sip of wine.

The waiter brought their first course — a

species of large mushroom wrapped in something else and with an accompanying small piece of salad. They both thought it tasted delicious.

'Even if some of Milton's business activities can't be used against him, he and Pace will go down for attempted murder and kidnapping and for helping Archie Tilling with his murder spree,' Julie said, after swallowing her last piece of mushroom.

Tanner watched her face carefully.

'There's no doubt about the evidence against the Tillings,' he said, 'so you've caught your aunt's killers. And you know now that she wasn't killed because of you.'

Julie nodded, her eyes warm with relief.

'Yes, I feel I can live properly again now.'

'And go back to work?' Tanner eyed her tentatively.

He was sure that if Julie went back to London they could make their relationship work long distance — others had done it successfully before them — but it wouldn't be the same. Seeing Julie every day for the past week had been something really special.

Julie seemed to catch Tanner's mood. She reached across and covered his hand with hers.

'I've been thinking about the future,' she said. 'I had a long talk with Ancient this afternoon and not just about the case. I value his judgement and advice. As a result, I have a proposal.'

'Indecent?' As always when nervous, Tanner tried to make light of it.

'Practical.' She met his gaze with a gentle smile. 'I'm quite a wealthy woman now, you know. I have the freedom to make some new choices.'

'Such as?' Tanner struggled to control the eagerness and hope that was straining to take over his voice.

'Well,' she said slowly, tapping the corner of her mouth with her finger, 'I suppose I could resign from the police — providing, of course, that some alternative job was offered. I wouldn't want to sit around all day doing nothing.'

'What sort of job did you have in mind?'

Julie shrugged.

'Retired police officers often go into private security, or something like that, don't they? For example, if there was a vacancy in a detective agency I might be interested.' She toyed idly with the stem of her wine glass.

Tanner couldn't stop the wide grin threatening to dislocate his jaw.

'It so happens, there's a vacancy in mine at the moment.'

'Really? Now there's a coincidence.' She

gave him a deadpan look. 'What time's the interview?'

'You've just had it.'

'Did I get the job?'

'What do you think?'

She gave him a wicked little grin.

'In that case, about that indecent pro-posal . . . '

We do hope that you have enjoyed reading this large print book.

Did you know that all of our titles are available for purchase?

We publish a wide range of high quality large print books including:
Romances, Mysteries, Classics
General Fiction
Non Fiction and Westerns

Special interest titles available in large print are:
The Little Oxford Dictionary
Music Book
Song Book
Hymn Book
Service Book

Also available from us courtesy of Oxford University Press:
Young Readers' Dictionary
(large print edition)
Young Readers' Thesaurus
(large print edition)

For further information or a free brochure, please contact us at:
Ulverscroft Large Print Books Ltd.,
The Green, Bradgate Road, Anstey,
Leicester, LE7 7FU, England.
Tel: (00 44) **0116 236 4325**
Fax: (00 44) **0116 234 0205**

ANGER MAN

Roy Chester

Assistant Chief Constable David Mallory and profiler Fiona Nightingale investigate three murders with a sinister connection. They release a dark evil lurking in the depths of the Ring — a decade-old paedophile scandal that still haunts the city. Anger Man emerges from the shadows to avenge the victims of the Ring. The only person who can stop him is Mary Longsdale, a patient in a mental hospital. She was abused as a teenager, and opening up the Ring has cracked her fragile personality. Mary must betray the only person she ever cared for ... and Anger Man plans one last spectacular killing spree.

BLACK FLIES

Shannon Burke

In Harlem, in the mid-1990s, paramedic Ollie Cross is in his first year on the job, gathering enough experience to start a medical degree. But the shoot-outs, bad cops, unhinged medics, and hopeless patients mean that Ollie struggles to balance his instinct to help against the growing callousness that witnessing daily horrors seems to encourage. And when lives hang in the balance, a single job with a misdiagnosed newborn sends Cross and his long-serving partner into a life-changing struggle between good and evil.

PROMISE NOT TO TELL

Jennifer McMahon

Kate Cypher returns home to Vermont, concerned about her mother's failing health. On the night she arrives, a young girl is murdered, a horrific crime that eerily mirrors another from Kate's childhood. Three decades earlier, her misfit friend Del, derided by her classmates as 'the potato girl', was brutally slain. The killer was never found, and Del achieved immortality in local legends and ghost stories. Now Kate is drawn irresistibly into the new murder investigation. Her past and present collide in terrifying ways. Nothing is quite what it seems. And the grim spectres of her childhood are far from forgotten . . .

PICK UP

J. A. O'Brien

Jack Carver is experiencing the most horrible of all nightmares: being an innocent man who is the prime suspect in the brutal murder of two women. Forensic evidence is found at both crime scenes, which implicates Carver. And when the police request that he should come forward, he goes on the run instead. He is finally apprehended, but an incident from Carver's past shakes his absolute certainty that he is not the killer. Then he is charged with murder. Can DS Andy Lukeson prove his innocence when a chance incident prompts him to reassess the case?